Plain Roots

A NOVEL

Becki Willis

Publisher's Note: This is a work of fiction. Names, characters, places, and incidents are a product of the author's imagination. Locales and public names are sometimes used for atmospheric purposes. Any resemblance to actual people, living or dead, or to businesses, companies, events, institutions, or locales is completely coincidental.

Book Layout © 2017 BookDesignTemplates.com
Editing by SJS Editorial Services
Cover Design by dienel96
Cover Photographs by Becki Willis

Plain Roots/ Becki Willis -- 1st ed.
ISBN 978-1-947686-06-9

Dedicated to my family

Books by Becki Willis

Forgotten Boxes
Tangible Spirits
He Kills Me, He Kills Me Not
The Mirror Series
    The Girl from Her Mirror
    Mirror, Mirror on Her Wall
    Light from Her Mirror
The Sisters, Texas Mystery Series
    Chicken Scratch – Book 1
    When the Stars Fall – Book 2
    Stipulations & Complications – Book 3
    Home Again: Starting Over – Book 4
    Genny's Ballad – Book 5
    Christmas In The Sisters – Book 6
    The Lilac Code – Book 7
Spirits of Texas Cozy Mysteries
    Inn the Spirit of Legends – Book 1

CONTENTS

CHAPTER 1

To my beautiful baby girl,

I was your first mother. Please know I loved you and I loved your father, but a life for the three of us was not in God's plans. I pray for you a good life.

You are my whole heart.

Rebecca

Taryn's hand trembled as she stared down at the distinctive handwriting. The letters were neat and evenly spaced, the cursive styling precise. Time lent the paper a distinct yellow cast and curled its edges inward. A ripple of ink blurred one word and left the letters smudged. *From a fallen teardrop?*

She turned the letter over, searching for another clue. The empty expanse echoed the barren canvas of her heart.

Forty-five words summed up the whole of her lineage. One simple paragraph to explain who she was and where she came from. Pathetic little to explain this aching void in her soul.

Taryn always wondered what it must be like to have a forever home. Having roots that grew so deep and so strong that one could never tug them free, no matter how hard one tried.

Not, mind you, that she would try. If she were ever lucky enough to have roots, she would never try to dig her way free. This was the first hint of the family tree she so desperately craved. A message from her birth mother, as brief and ambiguous as it may be.

"I finally find a root," Taryn murmured aloud, "but it's not even planted."

❧

"So, Taryn, any idea of what you'll do now?" Molly Shaw asked over dinner.

Taryn Clark twirled a spiral of spaghetti onto her fork, fascinated by the bits of sauce clinging to the noodles. *Like I cling to the idea of finding my roots.*

"Earth to Taryn. Come in, Taryn. Are you there?"

"What? Oh, sorry." Dropping her fork, she tucked her hand beneath the table to keep from playing with her food.

"Are you all right, girlfriend? I thought you were okay with this new phase in your life."

"I am," Taryn hastily assured her best friend. "And stop looking at me like that, because I am. Seriously. They gave me a nice severance package when the firm closed, so I'm not in a financial crunch. And they offered letters of recommendation, even though I'm not ready to look for something new just yet. Seriously, having some extended time off is just what I need right now."

"Then what's that all about?" Molly indicated Taryn's plate, with its series of spaghetti towers twirled in a row.

Taryn shoved the offending plate away with a troubled sigh. "You know how I said this was the perfect time to clean house and go through all my junk?"

"Sure. Everybody says that. But nobody means it," her friend assured her. "Don't beat yourself up over it," she advised.

"The thing is, I did do it. And I found something. Something I'd never seen before."

"What?" Molly smirked. "The floor in your closet?"

"That, too," Taryn admitted with a grimace. She leaned forward to continue. "There was a box up on the top shelf, filled with the few childhood possessions that made it through the round of foster homes." Her sigh bore the weight of a heavy heart. "Needless to say, it wasn't a very large box."

Molly's face lost all trace of humor. "I'm sorry," she said in earnest.

Taryn brushed away her friend's sympathy. "Water under the bridge," she insisted, because there was little else to say.

Teresa and Paul Clark never made secret of that fact Taryn was adopted. Momma even referred to her as their special gift. As a child, Taryn took the words in a literal sense and fantasized about that fated first meeting.

The scene played out like a movie in her young mind. *A gaily wrapped box arrives on their doorstep, covered in pretty pa-*

per and a huge pink bow. Momma stoops over and lifts off the lid, only to discover the smiling little baby inside, swaddled in pink blankets. Tiny arms reach out and slip around her mother's neck. It's love at first sight.

"Look, Paul!" her mother cries in delight, lifting the baby from the box and holding her close. "Look what someone has given us!"

"Why, it's a baby girl," her father says, his own voice filled with wonder. He comes to stand behind them, sweeping them both into his arms. The heavens smile down upon them, showering the happy little family with balloons and curling ribbons, and magical, sparkling stardust.

It was a sweet fantasy, spun by the mind of a four-year-old. It brought her comfort in the years to come, as the stardust faded. Without the sparkle, it was merely dust. The ribbons lost their curl. The balloons deflated. The magic surrounding their happy little family evaporated, taking the *happy* away.

The fantasy was all she had left when her parents divorced and when, just six months later, her mother was killed. Taryn often escaped into that fantasy of a gift-wrapped life as she moved from one foster family to another. By the time she turned eighteen, even the gift box in her dream world had become frayed and worn.

Shaking the memories from her mind, Taryn steered her attention back to reality. "There were a few small trinkets and an old doll inside, along with my mother's jewelry box. I remember how she sometimes let me play with it. It was shiny red lacquer with a castle scene etched onto it, and I used to imagine that the castle was my home, and that I was the princess who lived there." She laughed at her own foolish notions.

"Did you find a long-lost gem inside?" Molly asked, her eyes twinkling with interest as she sat up straighter in her chair. "Is that why you're not worried about finding a job just yet?"

"Nothing like that. Costume jewelry, at best. There was also a single gold earring without a mate and what might be a diamond pendant in the tiniest sense of the word. But I did discover a hidden compartment."

"And *that's* where the gem was hidden!"

Taryn rolled her eyes. "There was no gem, Molly. No diamond. No hidden coins. Just a letter and a receipt." She reached into her purse and pulled both documents from within, sliding them across the table for her friend's inspection.

"What is this?" Molly murmured as she examined the receipt. "It looks like a hospital bill from a *Lancaster Memorial Hospital* in Lancaster County."

"That's exactly what it is."

"Oh, wow, would you look at that!" Molly let out a low whistle. "It cost me four times that much to deliver my children! When was this from, anyway?" She perused the document until her eyes landed on the date. "Why, this is from January 1, 1980. Hey, that's your birthday, isn't it?"

"That's right."

"So this is from when *you* were born?"

"Don't be like Noah," Taryn warned, referring to Molly's oldest son. "He would make some wise crack like 'you mean they had pen and paper back then, not chisel and stone?'"

His mother grimaced. "I'm hoping he'll outgrow the obnoxious stage soon."

"Obnoxious or not, he's a great kid. All three of yours are," Taryn said with true affection. Having never had children of her own, she loved the trio almost as much as if she had given birth to them herself.

"They have their moments," Molly said, but her eyes lit with pride. She jiggled the paper in her hand. "Is this where you were born? *Lancaster Memorial*?"

"I suppose so. Why else would my mother have kept a receipt for labor and delivery on the very day I was born?"

Molly squinted her eyes, trying to make out the blurred print at the top of the page. "I can't see who the bill was addressed to. So, what's this other piece of paper?"

"My one and only connection to the past. Forty-five words of nothing."

Molly scanned the document. "I'd hardly call this *nothing*, Taryn," Molly softly chided her friend. "Your mother obviously loved you."

Taryn picked up her fork and began playing with her food again. "I suppose so."

"I know so! Listen to the heartache in this line— 'a life for the three of us was not in God's plans.' She obviously wanted what she thought was best for you. She wanted you to have a good life, just as she says here."

"And I couldn't have had a good life with her?" she wondered aloud.

"Maybe not. We have no idea what your birth mother's circumstances were."

Intellectually, Taryn could think of dozens of reasons her mother may have felt compelled to offer her up for adoption.

Twenty years before the turn of the twenty-first century, having a child out of wedlock still carried a social stigma; a sense of shame and embarrassment may have contributed to those reasons. Money, or lack thereof, no doubt played a large role in the decision-making process. Even though her mother claimed to have loved her father, perhaps the sentiment was not reciprocated. Perhaps he was married to another woman. Perhaps her grandparents forbade her mother to have the child. Perhaps, Taryn reasoned, her mother chose to first give her baby life, and then to give her baby away, rather than to have an abortion.

Intellectually, any of those reasons—and more—made sense.

Emotionally, the thought of being given to strangers still stung.

Blinking away the sentiments gathering in her eyes, Taryn cleared her throat and sat taller in her seat. "At any rate, both women must have intended for me to one day see the letter. That's why Rebecca wrote it, and why Teresa kept it. No doubt she would have given it to me when I was older, had she lived that long." Her violet eyes grew dewy, but no teardrops fell. Over the years, Taryn had become a master at controlling her tears.

"What a lovely gift they both have given you," Molly said softly. "To be loved by two mothers is quite special."

Taryn made no comment. Her friend's sunny disposition normally brought her comfort. Molly had a knack for finding the silver lining behind every dark cloud. There were times, however, when Taryn embraced the clouds. Times when she wanted the world to be as dim and dismal as her mood.

This was one of those times.

Molly refolded the papers and slid them back across the table before taking up her fork and continuing with her meal. Sensing her friend's mood, she chattered lightly about nothing. When the waitress came back to check on them, Molly ordered Taryn's favorite dessert.

"There's not much that warm bread pudding can't cure," she predicted.

A few bites into the delectable creation, Taryn was apt to agree.

"I've made a decision," she announced abruptly.

"About a job?"

"About my life."

"And?"

"I'm going to Lancaster County."

Molly stared at her in surprise. "Whatever for?"

"To find my roots."

"But... how? How will you do it? Where will you start?"

"I'm not sure," Taryn admitted, feeling the tiniest bit of doubt creeping in. "But I'm going to trace my roots." She took a deep breath and her face set with determination.

"Even," she added, "if it means digging in the mud to do so."

CHAPTER 2

It was an impromptu decision, but the idea took hold. Driving home from the restaurant, Taryn's mind spun with possibilities.

She finally had her first clues about her birth. She could spare a few days, she decided, to explore her past. Perhaps go to the county courthouse and search birth records bearing the name Rebecca. Check out the hospital and see if they had a legible copy of the blurry bill. Ask a few questions. Surely, someone somewhere would remember her birth mother.

The more she thought about it, the more Taryn fancied the idea of digging for her roots. By morning, her mind was set.

Despite living a scant two hours from Lancaster County, she had been there but once. Almost a dozen years ago, she attended a law seminar in Harrisburg. She and a co-worker lingered for a long weekend, touring the hallowed grounds of the Gettysburg Battlegrounds and touring the famed chocolate town of Hershey. Charmed by the area, she intended to return long before now, but something always kept her tethered to the city.

Most often, that *something* was her job. Look where that dedication had gotten her. Thirteen years with *Carver, Harris, and Harrison Law Firm* and suddenly, Taryn's career was over. Carver passed away unexpectedly, Harris was in the latter stages of lung cancer, and Harrison in the midst of a nasty divorce settlement. The entire firm went down faster than a hot-air balloon sporting a jagged rip.

Little Miss Molly Sunshine would point out there was a plus side to obsessive work habits and essentially having no life of her own: Taryn had developed a nice nest egg over the years.

And it was true. She led a comfortable but modest life. She owned a two-bedroom townhouse and a late-model, fuel-efficient car. After attending college on an academic scholarship, Taryn settled into the workforce, soon landing the coveted job with the prestigious law firm. She deftly worked her way up the ladder, earning the title of Senior Legal Administrative Assistant. Long before the firm shuttered its doors a week ago, she had her own office and her own assistant.

In all that time, Taryn had taken only one true vacation and an occasional weekend trip here and there. Even her honeymoon condensed into a weekend getaway in the Poconos, a full two months after the wedding. Three years later, she took another weekend trip to attend her ex-husband's second wedding.

Her gift-giving list was short: Molly's family of five, her next-door neighbors Josie and Stan, and, at Christmastime, whosever name she drew from the office pool.

With little else to spend her earnings on, between her hoarded funds and the firm's generous severance package—proffered, no doubt, by a guilty conscience—Taryn had the luxury of taking her time while looking for employment.

There was no reason, she decided, not to make a vacation of her Amish-country quest. While digging for her roots, she might as well dig through a few quaint shops and farmers' markets. See what all the hoopla was about, especially when it came to quilts and apple butter, and those whoopie pies her friends raved about.

Taryn tugged her virgin suitcase from beneath the bed. A gift from Molly two Christmases ago, it still wore the original plastic wrap from the factory. She felt a stir of anticipation as she peeled away the protective layer and opened the suitcase.

Despite a lifetime of disappointments and fractured dreams, she was surprised to find she still had the capacity to hope.

What if she was successful?

What if she found her birth mother?

What if—she dared to imagine—*she had a family?*

With *what ifs* dancing in her head, Taryn hurried to her closet, where she immediately faced her first obstacle.

What if she had nothing to wear? Most of her wardrobe was best suited for the office. Somehow, she doubted that tailored jackets and heels were standard attire for Lancaster County, Pennsylvania.

Eventually, Taryn found enough outfits to place into her suitcase. The rest, she decided, she could buy. A few last-minute details, and she was all set. Josie would gather her mail and Molly would water plants on Friday. With no pet and no boss to answer to, there was little else to worry about. It was depressingly easy to walk away from her life for a few days.

Long before she reached the city of Lancaster, Taryn punched the address from the hospital receipt into her GPS. The hospital name didn't come up on her screen, but the guidance system offered step-by-step directions to the exact street location.

She wondered if a larger corporation had bought out the regional medical facility and changed the name. The law firm often handled such cases. With medical costs out of control, the smaller clinics had difficulty keeping afloat in a weakened economy. If *Lancaster Memorial* had caved to a larger entity, she hoped they had kept their records in place. She didn't relish the thought of chasing them down.

Taryn's heart pounded in anticipation as she turned onto Milner Avenue. This was it. The next clue to her past. All she had to do was find a place to park, walk up to the hospital, and ask for the records department.

She nibbled her lip as she pulled into a parking space.

Now to find the hospital.

The structure before her was quite a bit smaller than she expected. Truth be told, it looked more like an office building. *But that's good*, she assured herself, as she got out and locked the car. A small hospital meant fewer records to search through.

Fewer records meant fewer patients. How many women, she speculated, could have given birth on that particular day? In a facility this small, Taryn was certain she could count them on one hand. Spurred by optimism, she quickened her pace.

As she stepped onto the sidewalk, a ribbon of worry wormed through her. As hospitals went, this one was tiny. Plus, it looked practically new. They had obviously renovated within recent years. Perhaps they were still in the process, she reasoned, because she didn't even see their name above the doors.

But why, then, did it call itself *The Grayson Group*? Feeling increasingly nervous, Taryn hurried up the sidewalk.

She stepped into a stylish reception area filled with soft music and a floor-to-ceiling aquarium. A middle-aged woman looked up with a friendly smile.

"May I help you?" she asked. With her fifties-era beehive stack of lacquered hair, she looked out of place behind the sleek, low-profile desk.

Taryn tucked a strand of her own honeyed-brown hair behind her ear and stumbled into a greeting. "Uhm, is—is this 1724 Milner Avenue?"

"Yes, that's right."

Taryn looked around in confusion. No nurses milled about in the background. No overhead intercom called for a doctor to report to a particular station, stat. No buzz of activity as patients and technicians scurried back and forth through wide, swinging doors. In fact, she didn't see a single thing that looked related to the medical field. The over-sized wall art boasted images of houses and buildings and green, rolling pastures.

Dread settled like a lead weight in the pit of her stomach. She knew the answer, even before she asked the question.

"Is—Is this still a hospital?" she faltered.

The woman shook her head. A heavy coat of Aqua Net kept each hair in place.

"You must be referring to *Lancaster Memorial*. It closed its doors in the early to mid-eighties. Why, that old building stood empty for a dozen years or so, before they finally condemned it and tore it down. This is a real estate company now."

"Oh." There was a world of disappointment in that one simple word.

She had been so busy dreaming of a happy outcome, she forgot to imagine another *what if*.

What if she were unsuccessful?

One look at Taryn's stricken expression, and the woman's voice took on a sympathetic note. "Are you looking for someone, dear?"

"Myself," Taryn whispered the word.

The receptionist had no reply to the raw admission. "Are you all right?" she asked kindly. "Would you like to have a seat?"

Without waiting for an answer, she stood and came from around the desk. Like a marionette, Taryn allowed the woman to guide her to a small settee across from the aquarium. Her movements felt as disjointed as any wooden puppet. A touch to the right elbow lifted her right foot. A motion toward the settee guided her left foot. An encouraging smile kept the momentum going, one foot in front of the other.

"Here, this will make you feel better," the woman promised, pressing a cold bottle of water into Taryn's hands. "I've worked here for five years, and I must say, you're the first person to come in looking for the old hospital."

"Leave it to me," Taryn murmured. She realized she still wore her sunshades. Pushing the tortoise-shell frames up to rest atop her head, she offered her companion a wavering smile.

A strange look crossed the woman's face, and her hand floated to her chest. If she tried to contain the tiny gasp that escaped her lips, she failed.

"Your eyes," she murmured in a faint whisper.

Taryn was accustomed to comments about her eyes. Without a doubt, they were her best feature. Long, curly lashes framed her widely spaced peepers, giving her an instant look of sincerity. But it was their unique color—violet—that made them so intriguing.

Most people did a double take when seeing her eyes for the first time, but few reacted quite like this woman.

Quick to recover from her shock, the woman thrust out her hand. Her words came in a rush. "I'm Betty, by the way. And you are...?"

"Taryn."

"Oh, what a lovely name!" she practically gushed.

Taryn murmured a polite thank you, wondering at the woman's sudden discomfort.

"I take it you're not from here?" Betty asked. The casual tone didn't match the keen expression in her eyes.

"Not really. Not anymore."

"Oh. Oh, I see. You used to live here." The beehive bobbed as she nodded, as if it all suddenly made sense. The odd lilt in her voice sounded almost like relief.

"Not really," Taryn faltered, unsure of how much to reveal. But she had come here to find the truth, and Betty's face was kind, if not curious. Taryn knew that if she wanted to find her roots, she had to ask questions. She had to dig.

"I was born here. At *Lancaster Memorial,*" she clarified, motioning to the ground beneath her. "I'm looking for my birth records."

"Oh, no worries there," Betty chirped, waving her fingers in reassurance. "I'm sure they have your records over at the county offices." Her hands were restless in her lap. If Taryn didn't know better, she would think she made the poor woman nervous.

"I'm hoping to find more than just my birth certificate," she confided.

"Well, like I said, they demolished the building around the millennium. I don't know what they did with all their old records. Stored them, I suppose, or eventually disposed of them."

The thought was devastating. "But...!"

Betty with the beehive was quick to offer a suggestion, "Perhaps your mother has a copy of the records?"

"My mother... you see, I'm adopted," Taryn confessed. "I have no idea who my birth mother is, and my adoptive mother passed away. I came here looking for answers."

A strange look crossed Betty's face. Her eyes were drawn once again to Taryn's and their unique color. She looked as if she wanted to say something, but she bit her tongue. Literally. The pink tip peeked between her teeth as she contemplated Taryn's dejected posture. When the chipper older woman spoke again, her tone was gentle, like one would use with a skittish colt. "How did you wind up here, if you don't mind my asking?"

"I found a bill from the day I was born. The name was smudged, but I hoped the original would be legible." Taryn looked around, seeing *new* where she had hoped to see old. Just like the walls of the defunct *Lancaster Memorial*, her dreams of finding the truth had crumbled around her.

"And the year?"

"1980."

Betty nodded the beehive, which still never budged. Taryn swore she saw the numbers calculating as they rolled through Betty's mind. Her announcement was abrupt. "I have a friend." Before Taryn could respond, Betty continued, "She worked here during that time. I could call her."

Thinking it was hopeless, Taryn nodded nonetheless. The woman was only trying to be kind. It wasn't Betty's fault she had been foolish enough to brush off her old dream and breathe life into it again. It wasn't Betty's fault she had been so naive, thinking this one stop could change her life. Nothing in her life had ever been that easy. Why had she thought this time would be different?

The telephone rang, and Betty jumped to her feet. "I must get that, but I'll be right back. You stay right here. I'll just be a minute."

As if she had the energy to move! It took effort to shift her eyes toward the aquarium.

Fish darted every which way, some seemingly on a mission, others floating at leisure. A long-ago memory splashed mist into her eyes. Her mother used to read to her, something about big fish and little fish, red fish and yellow fish. These were of all sizes and all species, a colorful collection with little in common, other than the water they shared. Taryn felt like one of them, all alone in a huge and overcrowded fishbowl. She felt the weight of the water around her, swirling in from all directions, tugging and pulling. It took everything she had to keep afloat, to keep the stronger current from sucking her under.

After a lifetime of disappointment, she couldn't believe how naive she had been, thinking she could find her past so easily. Had the frayed ribbons of her dreams taught her nothing?

She was unaware of the other woman's return, until she spoke from beside her.

"I'm sorry about the interruption," Betty apologized. She babbled on about something, but Taryn wasn't listening. Not until Betty nudged her gently and put something into her hand.

The contact startled her, pulling her from the drowning emotions. "What's this?" she asked, looking down at the paper with a frown. Lost in self-pity, she hadn't heard a word the receptionist said.

"It's the address to the place I was telling you about."

She blinked to clear her head. "The county courthouse?"

"No, to the coffee shop."

Taryn stared down at the paper. She was unable to connect the name and address to anything she remembered hearing Betty say. "I'm sorry," she mumbled. She blinked her eyes in hopes of clearing her mind. "What is this, again?"

With a generous display of patience, Betty repeated herself, "My friend Helen used to work here at the hospital. She may be able to help you."

"Really? She knows where the old records are?"

"I really think you should talk to Helen."

Taryn had the sensation of sleeping through class and waking in time to hear the tail end of the assignment. It had happened to her more than once, when class was the safest place to let down her guard and catch a few winks. Not all foster homes were created equal. Not all were safe, especially at night.

She attempted to focus. "And where is this?"

"About thirty minutes east, to the coffee shop she owns. Be sure and order the lemon sponge pie. An Amish woman makes it from fresh milk every morning, with a dollop of hand-churned whipped cream. It's to die for." A serene expression crossed Betty's face as she placed her hands upon her chest.

Wondering what she had to lose, Taryn agreed to meet Betty's friend. As she stuffed the paper into her purse, Betty maneuvered the marionette strings again. Before she quite knew how it happened, Taryn was at the door, thanking the receptionist for her help.

"Good luck, Taryn. I hope you find the answers you're looking for."

Her smile was too fragile to be mistaken as hopeful. "So do I."

Taryn stepped back into the sunshine and pulled the shades down over her eyes. She huffed out a sigh. "So do I."

CHAPTER 3

The town of New Holland was a great deal smaller than the city of Lancaster. Both were tiny, compared to Philadelphia.

The borough sprawled along a busy state highway, its main claim to fame the huge tractor manufacturer bearing its name. There was no denying its economic stamp on the city. Taryn drove past the factory with the monster-sized tractor on its lawn to reach *Kaffi Korner*. The coffee shop was dwarfed by the surrounding warehouses and shipping facilities that sat in its back pocket.

Taryn swore she gained five pounds when she walked through the door. Notes of cinnamon, cloves, and yeast floated on the air, carried by the sweetness of honey and brown sugar. Her stomach gave a loud rumble, reminding her that she had skipped breakfast in lieu of finding her past.

Now here she was, still without roots, and hungry, to boot.

"Hullo!" a voice greeted from behind the counter. Taryn couldn't immediately identify its source, until she spotted the woman behind a mile-high meringue pie. "What can we get for you?"

After scanning the board with its decadent offerings, she made her selection. She took Betty's advice and ordered the lemon sponge pie with a cup of their boldest brew. Wise choice or not with these nerves, the sugar and caffeine would at least give her energy.

"Is Helen here, by chance?" she ventured to ask.

A woman spoke from a table out front. Against the glare from the plate-glass window, it was difficult to see the small table tucked into an unobtrusive corner. "I'm Helen. What can I do for you?"

It wasn't something she could very well blurt out over the café, even if the other tables were all but empty. Two women chatted at a front booth and an older gentleman tapped on his laptop at another. The only other person in sight started her coffee order.

"Come on over and have a seat," Helen invited with a wave of her hand. "Katie will bring your order."

Weaving her way to the corner, Taryn took the seat Helen indicated. If the half-eaten sandwich on her plate was any indication, she was on her lunch break.

"I'm sorry to disturb you. A friend of yours named Betty suggested I stop by. My name is Taryn Clark." She extended her hand for a proper hello. She hoped it wasn't rude to keep on her shades, but being such a pale color, her eyes were sensitive to the glare.

"Betty Lawrence?" she spoke the name with affection. "How do you know Betty?"

"I'm afraid I don't know her last name. I met her just now in Lancaster, at a real estate office on Milner Avenue. Where the old hospital once stood," Taryn clarified.

A guarded expression slipped into Helen's eyes, but her facial expression never changed. "That's her. Are you looking for property in the area?"

"What? Oh, no, not at all," she said hastily. It was a reasonable assumption to make. "Quite frankly, I was looking for *Lancaster Memorial.*"

"But that closed down years ago!"

Taryn murmured her thanks as Katie delivered her coffee and a generous slice of pie. She left both untouched as she concentrated on Helen. "Betty thought you may know where the hospital records were moved to."

"Why would I know something like that?" Her voice was almost sharp.

"She said you used to work there. Were you in accounting? Records?"

"Nothing like that. I was a nurse."

"A nurse?" Taryn wasn't sure why the news took her by surprise, but it did. She assumed Helen had worked in the office, where she might have a connection to the old files. Why else would Betty send her here for help?

"Yes. Labor and delivery, for over fifteen years." There was an unmistakable ring of pride in the older woman's voice. "I helped birth half of Lancaster County. Those not born at home, anyway."

Something buzzed inside of Taryn's head. She cautioned herself to stay calm. "What—What years did you work there?"

"From the summer of 1963 until the spring of '80." A shadow crossed her face. Sadness slipped into her voice as she confided, "I gave up nursing altogether after that."

Taryn sensed there was more to the story, but she didn't pry. They were strangers, she and Helen, and strangers didn't poke into other people's heartache.

"But you were there during the first part of 1980?" she confirmed.

"I was." It was there again, the cautious look in her eyes. This time it stiffened her voice.

Taryn leaned forward eagerly. Her heart pounded in her chest as she dared press for more. "Were you by chance on duty New Year's Day? Do you remember if you delivered any babies that day?"

Helen didn't immediately answer. When her eyes took on a faraway memory, Taryn realized the woman must be somewhere in her mid-seventies. "It's okay," she was quick to reassure her. "It's been so long, and you must have delivered hundreds of babies over the years. I understand if you don't remem—"

"I delivered three that day," Helen answered quietly, her tone certain.

"You did? You remember that?"

"It would be impossible to forget." From the sound of her voice, she had tried. Like it or not, some things were ingrained into the memory.

Taryn knew it was a long shot. It was unlikely Helen remembered the *details* of any of the births. Still, hope blossomed in her chest. She tried schooling her voice, so it didn't come out sounding as excited as she felt. "Oh? Why is that?"

"We had a tradition at the hospital," Helen explained. "Fanfare for the first baby born in the new year. Free medical care for the first year, diapers and formula and a whole slew of new outfits, and a big write-up in the paper. So you can imagine what the first baby of a new *decade* would get. There were rumors of all kinds of crazy stunts, women trying to throw themselves into labor, just to win." The ghost of a smile echoed on her face.

Taryn tried to recall what time of day she had seen on her birth record, wondering if she missed the grand prize by minutes, or by hours. Would it have made a difference to her own mother if she had won? Would Rebecca have kept her baby, instead of giving it away for adoption?

It was useless to speculate. "There could be only one lucky winner," she murmured with reason.

A weary sigh accompanied Helen's reply. "You would think. But that wasn't the case."

Taryn cocked her head to one side. "Twins?" she guessed. "Or strangers, sharing the same moment of birth?"

"Neither. We had a clear winner. Over a five-minute cushion of time."

To be so forthcoming earlier, Helen lapsed into a thoughtful silence now. Taryn squirmed on the seat. It suddenly felt like it was made of pins and needles. A full moment ticked by without another word.

She could contain herself no longer. "What happened?" Taryn blurted.

"The mother flat-out refused the gifts. We explained it wasn't just bragging rights. There was a hefty monetary value, as well. The local junior college offered free tuition when the child graduated high school. One of the banks put up a thousand-dollar savings bond. Stores and businesses offered generous benefits for both the mother and the child. It was worth a small fortune."

"And the father agreed?"

"There was no father. The poor little thing was widowed, and practically no more than a child herself." Helen clicked her tongue. "It could have made such a difference for a single mother, having all those benefits."

She had been thinking the same thing earlier, about her own mother.

"I agree that's odd, but I'm sure she had her reasons."

"I don't know..." Helen's voice trailed off, sounding decidedly doubtful. She stared out the window, caught up in an old memory. "If you could have seen that look in her eyes. She looked... haunted."

"Perhaps she was simply heartbroken," Taryn offered. "Grief does strange things to people."

"The girl was scared to death." This time, Helen's voice was matter-of-fact.

"I would be, too," Taryn admitted, "facing the prospect of raising a child alone."

Helen all but pounced on the opening, her face whipping back around toward Taryn. From the fire still burning in her eyes, Taryn knew without a doubt that Helen had been an excellent nurse. She truly cared about her patients. "Exactly!" she said. "All the more reason to accept the gifts. They could have changed that poor girl's life, and her baby's, too."

"You couldn't persuade her." It was a statement, not a question.

When Helen shook her head, she seemed to age a dozen years. Sorrow had a way of doing that to a person, seeping into one's pores and stealing what was left of one's youth and vitality. "Lord knows I tried. But she flat-out refused. She was so desperate, almost in a panic. I was afraid she was a flight risk. In her fragile state, both mentally and physically, I feared for her, and for her sweet baby."

She was no longer talking to Taryn. She was talking to herself, reliving a past that still held her in its grip. Her voice dropped an octave. "I convinced the doctor we had to protect her, for her own good. He wanted no part in the deception, but he agreed to go along with it."

Caught up in the sorrow in Helen's voice, Taryn forgot her personal quest. Fully vested in the story of the young widow, she had to know why it wrought Helen such pain. "What happened?" she all but whispered.

"When the reporters came, I told a direct lie."
It was there in her face, the guilt she still carried after all these years.

"They came before we had time to formulate a plan. We couldn't force her to accept the gifts, but the first baby of the decade was big news. Back then, there was no such thing as HIPAA or patient privacy. There was no reason not to share the happy news. Before the staff could make a statement, I blurted out another name. I gave them the story they came for, but in my haste, I made a mistake. I told them about the baby born at 1:07, not the baby born at 1:01."

"Oh, dear."

"You can't imagine. The 1:01 parents were furious. They didn't even know, until they saw it on the evening news. They threatened the hospital with a lawsuit, which I knew would call attention to the true first birth of the year, at 12:56."

Having worked for a law firm, Taryn could imagine the litigation involved. Her mind ticked off possible scenarios, but it was easier to simply ask. "So what happened? How did it get resolved?"

Helen's eyes drifted back to the window, her mind adrift in the past. "It was a huge mess. The bank agreed to put up another savings bond, and a generous donor stepped up and paid for a second scholarship. A few of the other sponsors pitched in, as well, but it really wasn't their fault." Her voice quietened. "I, alone, bore that responsibility."

"It was an honest mistake."

"There wasn't a single thing honest about it," Helen said mournfully. "I lied. And then I did a terrible thing, even worse than the first."

If she once hid secrets, Helen was no longer guilty of the fact. There was no reason for her to lay her soul bare to Taryn. They were strangers, and Taryn had only asked a simple question. Yet nothing about this past deed was simple, and Helen saw no reason to run from the truth. She made her confession, the pain in her eyes honest and raw.

"I changed the time stamp on that first birth. I erased the 'one,' making it read 2:56. I willingly committed fraud to hide the truth."

She couldn't explain it, but Taryn felt a strong connection with the nurse and her plight. She felt the need to defend her, even to Helen's own self-imposed censure. "You were protecting your patient."

"Doesn't matter. As with any lie, it all came out in the end. Of course, the first reports were skewed. The 1:01 parents stirred a ruckus, trying to say the 1:07 parents paid me off, but that's simply not true. They were as innocent as those poor babies, all of them caught in the middle of my sorry mess."

She shook her head resolutely as she continued, "No. No one was to blame but me, and I paid for it with my career. The hospital came short of pressing charges, but only because I stepped down and agreed to never practice nursing again."

"That seems rather harsh," Taryn murmured, even though she was fully aware of the criminal ramifications of falsifying legal documents. She toyed with her coffee cup, her heart heavy for this dedicated and compassionate woman. "Did the first mother, the young widow," she wondered aloud, "ever thank you for your sacrifice? After all, you did all that to protect her identity."

Another layer of sadness dug into Helen's furrowed brow. "I did it to keep her safe. I'm not sure if I was protecting her from past demons or from herself, but the fear in that girl's face was real. And I was right. She was a flight risk. She snuck out of the hospital that night. I never saw her again."

Taryn couldn't help but gasp. "So she never knew?"

Helen shook her head, but she seemed less certain. "She had to have seen it. It was in all the papers, and in all the news."

"I have no doubt you were a wonderful nurse. Few nurses would go to such lengths for one of their patients."

Helen disagreed. "The ones worth their salt would." She took a deep breath and visibly pulled her tattered soul together. "But enough about me. I'm just a foolish old woman, one who gets lost stumbling around down memory lane." She peered at Taryn with curious eyes. "I still get occasional reporters now and then, trying to revive an old horse that's been ridden hard and put out to pasture."

"I'm no reporter," Taryn was quick to assure her.

"Just as well. There's no story here. Nothing left for me to hide; you can read all the sordid details in the archives."

"I'm looking for my own birth records. I had no idea about... all this." She made a gesture with her hand.

"I can't imagine why Betty thought I would know where the records went. The hospital didn't close for another four years after I retired. And after all that happened, I would be the last person privy to such information, don't you think?"

"Do you remember anything else about the babies that were born that day?" A thought occurred to her and her voice rose with excitement. "Wait. If it was in all the papers, their names will be there, too, right?"

Helen's smile was wry. "Remember? No HIPAA."

"So even without the official records, I may be able to find my mother," Taryn murmured the words to herself. Not but a half hour ago, she ridiculed herself for being so foolish, for still believing in dreams. One whiff of a clue, and here she was, her heart dancing with fanciful hopes and her mind reeling with possibilities. She leaned in closer and confided in the other woman.

"The truth is, I'm here looking for my birth records. I have reason to believe I may have been one of those New Year's babies. My birth date is January 1, 1980, and I think I was born at *Lancaster Memorial.*"

Helen's eyes filled with suspicion. "I told you, the first mother wanted nothing to do with the promotion. She ran away, to keep from claiming the prizes. And the fame."

Taryn shook her head, trying to make Helen understand. "I'm not talking about the first mother." It didn't make sense that a heart-broken young widow would give her baby away, not when the child was her only link to her recently deceased husband. "I think I may have been baby 1:01 or 1:07."

"Impossible," Helen said with complete certainty. "Baby 1:01 was a male. Baby 1:07 was black. You couldn't possibly be either."

Practically growling in frustration, Taryn grasped at straws. "Then tell me about the widow's baby." She pushed her sunglasses onto her crown and adjusted her blouse, turning up her sleeves. It was time to get down to business. She settled in to get comfortable, while Helen took to looking out the window once more.

"She was a lovely little baby girl, with the cutest bow of a mouth." Helen touched her own lips, recalling the perfection of that long-ago miracle of birth. "She had a healthy cry and eyes that were already stunning. Most babies are born with blue eyes, still cloudy from birth. But this baby's eyes were clear from the start, and just as lovely as her mother's."

Helen turned back to Taryn, the smile lingering in her words. "They were such a unique color, exactly like her m—" She stopped mid-sentence, her words swept away by an audible gasp.

She recovered with a sputtered exclamation. "Ex—Exactly like *yours*!"

CHAPTER 4

Taryn stared at the nurse in disbelief. "What are you saying?" Her whispered words were faint, but they strengthened, fueled by something akin to hysteria. This didn't fit the fantasy already weaving its way through her heart. She was so close to learning the whereabouts of her birth mother... to finding out whether she had siblings... to finding her *roots*. This didn't sound at all like roots.

"Are you saying I was the 12:56 baby? That... That my mother was the widow who ran?" Her voice hitched another notch. "Why would she do that? It makes no sense!"

Helen's voice was more than weary. It was defeated. "You're asking the wrong person. Nothing about that fateful day made sense."

She gathered her sweater around her, girding herself with its armor. The thin weave offered little defense to the chill seeping into her soul.

"I knew something was wrong, right from the start," she admitted. "That young mother was scared out of her wits. She came in all alone. Said there was no one to call. She said her husband had recently died, but at one point..." Helen broke off, shaking her head. "I'm just not sure. Something she said didn't quite make sense, but there was no time for chitchat. She was in hard labor when she arrived, and she delivered not two hours later."

"What? What did she say?"

"I—I don't remember, not exactly. Called a man's name a time or two when the pains came hard and fast, wishing he were there with her. Then the pain would subside, and she was only slightly more coherent. She begged us not to tell. I don't think she was talking about the same person, but she never said *who* couldn't know she was there. Just that whatever we did, we couldn't let him in."

"That doesn't make sense." Frustrated, Taryn ran her hands through her hair, knocking her sunglasses askew. They fell unnoticed into her pie. "What name did she call?"

Helen shook her head in apology. "It's been almost forty years. I don't recall the name. But I swear. I'll never forget the look in that poor girl's eyes. She was running from something. Some*one*."

"What about her name? Was her name Rebecca?"

"That doesn't sound quite right. But again, I'm terrible with names, and it's been so long..." Her voice trailed off in uncertainty.

Taryn pulled the old hospital bill from her purse. "Maybe you can decipher what this says. Maybe it will help jog your memory."

Helen patted her sweater pocket. "I don't have my glasses on me," she mumbled. She turned to call to the woman behind the counter. "Katie? Would you be a dear and fetch my glasses? They may be by the register. And bring more coffee." Twisting back around, she added under her breath, "We're going to need it."

"This is the only connection I have to my past," Taryn explained. "A smudged hospital receipt and a brief note from my birth mother. She signed it 'Rebecca.' No last name, no nothing." She knew her voice sounded pathetic, even as she admitted, "This is all I have."

Helen's eyes were sympathetic, but she clearly had her doubts as to whether she could help. "I wish there was more I could do."

"Tell me anything you remember. Anything at all."

"Well, let me see." It was a slow process, but a few details gradually emerged. "It was cold out, and I remember she had a dark, heavy coat. Nothing fancy. It looked almost like a man's coat, and her belly was so swollen, it didn't come all the way together. At first, I thought she had lost all the buttons, until I realized it had hooks and eyes. I remember she said she was still cold, so I laid the coat over her, atop all the covers to keep her teeth from chattering."

"Was it snowing?" Not that it mattered in the least. It was just another detail, one of the many missing in her life story.

Molly loved to tell of her first son's birth. It was raining so hard she and her husband were both drenched by the time they got into the car. The streets were flooded, and the windshield wipers didn't work. Unable to see, her husband missed the turn to the hospital. They had planned to name the baby Kevin, but after the flooded drive, they chose the name Noah, instead. Molly laughed about it now, but it was terrifying at the time.

Knowing whether it snowed on the morning she was born was a nice touch for the story Taryn would someday tell about her own birth.

"Yes. I remember the 1:07 father coming in, his hat covered in snow and dripping on the floor. He almost didn't make it in time to see their baby born."

Taryn couldn't help but feel sad. At least that mother had someone with her, unlike her own. Poor Rebecca went through the experience with no one by her side, except for this kind nurse. No wonder she was terrified.

"Isn't there anything else you can tell me?"

Katie arrived with the eyeglasses and fresh cups of coffee. Taryn gulped hers down, welcoming the burn. She needed the distraction as Helen took her own sweet time in reading the bill. The older woman cleaned her glasses before slipping them on but wasn't happy with a smudge she left. Taryn gritted her teeth while Helen repeated the process with great care. Once the glasses were back in place, she had to settle in her chair again and find a comfortable distance to hold the paper. She studied it for what seemed to be forever.

"I can't quite make it out," she fretted. "Is that an A?" She brought it closer, but then held it at arm's length. "It looks like—" She pulled it in again. "Oh, yes, that was it! Jane! Her name was Jane."

"Jane?" Taryn was clearly surprised. "Not Rebecca?"

"No, I remember now. That was part of the hullabaloo. She said her name was Jane Hirsch."

"I don't understand. Why did that cause trouble?"

"Because Hirsch is German for deer. Or," she explained, taking off her readers and setting them aside, "as we most often say, Jane Doe."

Something occurred to her. "How did my parents get this bill?"

"I have no idea. The girl left without paying and the address she gave, like the name, wasn't real."

"And later? When she snuck out?"

Helen shrugged. "I wasn't on duty that night. And it's just as well, because my nerves were shot. By then, the news had aired and the 1:01 parents demanded answers. The hospital kept calling me at home. When the reporters started calling, I took my phone off the hook."

"No one saw her leave?"

"Security cameras showed her using the back exit in the wee hours of the night."

Katie appeared at the table once again. "I'm sorry to interrupt, but they shorted us on delivery again. The driver's waiting to talk to you."

Helen sighed and told Katie she would be right there. She apologized to Taryn, handing back the fragile link to her past.

"I'm sorry, but I must attend to this. I thought opening a coffee shop would be less stressful than nursing, but most days I wonder about that."

"There's nothing else you can tell me?"

She must have seen the desperation in Taryn's violet eyes. "If I think of anything else, I'll contact you," she offered. "Are you staying in the area?"

"I don't have a hotel yet, but probably so." How could she leave now, with things still so unsettled?

"We have several nice ones to choose from. And don't forget all the bed and breakfasts in the area, and the guest cottages. I'm sure you'll find something." She struggled to her feet, and Taryn saw that the years had taken a toll on her body. Her back was hunched, and her legs were less than steady. It took her several moments to get her balance and stand upright. Taryn had plenty of time to dig in her purse to find a business card.

"Here's my cell number. Please, call me if you think of anything else you can tell me."

"I'm sorry I couldn't tell you more."

Taryn tried to be positive. "You gave me more than I had, so that's something."

"Well, good luck to you."

With that, her one link to the past shuffled away.

⁂

Helen moved as quickly as her swollen feet allowed, but her efforts were slow. She carried more than a body ravaged by time and disease. No matter what she said about having no more secrets, she carried one now, and it made her conscience heavy and burdensome.

She hadn't been completely honest with that young woman out there. She withheld the truth in an effort to spare her, just as she had done with her mother all those years ago. And there was no doubt about her being Jane Doe's baby. They had the same unique eye color.

Those eyes had looked so hopeful just now, staring at her there across from the table. The woman was simply searching for a link to her past, something that offered the connection she so desperately craved. Helen couldn't bring herself to reveal everything she remembered from that night. She couldn't be so cruel.

What did it matter now? The hopeful woman—Tara, was it? Or Terri? She was terrible with names— didn't need to know that her mother had held her but once. Helen had placed the baby in her arms and watched as the girl hugged the bundle to her. She remembered Jane staring down at her newborn for a long moment, as if remembering every line of that sweet face. She had cried big, silent tears, and one splashed onto the baby's cheek, startling her into a cry. The young mother panicked and held the baby away from her, but Helen remembered her calling her back at the last moment.

"Let me kiss her goodbye."

After a soft kiss on the forehead, the girl turned away, before the baby even left for the nursery. She never asked for the normal statistics, like weight and inches. She pretended to sleep, but Helen remembered the way she cried quietly into sheets pulled high upon her face.

Taryn didn't need to know it was the only time her mother ever saw her. She didn't need to know that when her mother snuck out in the middle of the night, she left her baby behind.

Taryn already knew she was adopted.

She didn't need to know she had been abandoned, as well.

CHAPTER 5

Pushing her shades back on, sticky pie and all, Taryn left the coffee shop.

It was déjà vu all over again. Another brick wall. Taryn knew little more now than she had before.

She assembled the scant facts in her mind.

Dressed in a drab winter coat, her mother arrived at the hospital on a snowy winter night and used a false name to give birth without anyone there to hold her hand. Not only had she refused a lucrative gift package, she skipped out in the middle of the night without paying her bill.

The other bits and pieces made no more sense than the first. Somewhere along the way, Rebecca left a note to her daughter that wound up in the hands of Teresa and Paul, who also had a hospital bill marked paid in full. Had they been the ones to pay for the delivery? With *Lancaster Memorial* closed for good and the files God knows where, she would probably never know.

Did it even matter? Taryn pulled out onto the busy roadway, unsure of where she headed. Perhaps she should just go back to Philly. She already knew the most pertinent facts. Her birth mother gave her up for adoption. Did she really want to know more about a woman who gave her away so easily?

But what if it *hadn't* been so easy?

Why had her birth mother been so frightened?

Why had she used a false name?

The *whys* rode alongside Taryn as she drove, buzzing around in her head like a pesky fly. When the car in front of her turned left, so did she. It was the ultimate family vehicle: a sturdy navy-blue SUV, complete with stickers. Window decals depicted a stick-figure father, mother, four children in staggered heights, two dogs, and one cat. One bumper sticker boasted the American flag and the slogan *I Voted for America*, while two others bragged about parenting an honor student at Leola Elementary. A car like that had to know its way around in life. If a solid family car wasn't sure of its destination, how could there be any hope for a wandering soul such as her?

She dutifully followed the stick figures down Horseshoe Road, the *whys* and the flies still abuzz in her head. The car turned right onto Old Philadelphia Pike. Taryn trailed behind, wondering if her birth mother's car boasted a similar stick-figure family. Did she have siblings? *Oh, how she wished!* The flesh and blood kind, not the decal sort. The kind that gathered at holidays and threw birthday parties and called at random moments because they missed the sound of her voice.

Traffic grew heavier as the SUV merged onto US Highway 30. A green sedan and a white panel van slipped in behind it, separating Taryn from her lead car. Losing sight of the stick-figure family, panic set in. Where was she? Where was she even headed?

She had no choice but to merge into the westbound traffic. The SUV was far ahead, moving across lanes and zipping on down the highway, leaving Taryn to fend for herself.

She saw the road sign just in time. The next exit would take her back into Lancaster. Maybe the county courthouse had the answers she looked for. Sealed or not, maybe the courthouse had her original birth certificate.

Taryn knew a recent state law allowed for adoptees to request their birth certificates, but she had chosen not to take advantage of the new benefit. It was a cowardly attitude, she knew, but she feared the truth would only lead to more heartache.

It still could. Still *would*, most likely. But she couldn't ignore Helen's story of her birth. Taryn felt as if she no longer had a choice. She *had* to know the truth now. She had to open her sealed records.

There was a process, of course. The man at the courthouse walked her through the steps. She could apply on-line, pay the twenty-dollar filing fee, and wait for her records to arrive in about forty-five days.

Forty-five days! The same number of tear-streaked words had led her on this journey in the first place. The number seemed so insignificant written in a note yet loomed long and endless on the calendar.

What was she to do in the meantime? Stay here? Return to Philly? Hang in limbo for six long weeks? Feeling the need to do *something*, Taryn combed through old records, first at the courthouse, then at the library.

It was a long shot, of course. The courthouse was a bust, as she knew it would be. Her birth records were sealed by the adoption process. The library had all the newspaper articles of the day, the story exactly as Helen told it. The first local baby of the decade, born at *Lancaster Memorial*! The front-page headlines told it all.

Taryn poured through each and every article. The names were there, just as Helen said, but only of the one o'clock babies. There was no mention of any other births that day. The headlines grew smaller over time, the stories buried further into the gazette. Only an occasional story made it back to the front, and none above the fold. The last headline came several months later, when Helen Fremont, RN, resigned from a stellar nursing career amid scandal and speculation. The article hashed out the sordid details one more time, lest readers had forgotten the previous heartache.

Two hours later, Taryn had little to show for her efforts. An aching back from hunching over the computer, hours at a time. An aching heart from reading it all in print. The story seemed colder when told in black and white. The words told only the facts. They told nothing of Helen's obvious devotion to her patient, none of her determination to keep a frightened and desperate woman safe. Nothing of the guilt she still carried with her to this day.

The paper offered only one surprise, and it was irrelevant. Helen had mentioned a generous donor had come forward to offer a second scholarship for the slighted 1:01 baby, and as it turned out, Taryn actually knew the benefactor. The philanthropist was a client of *Carver, Harris, and Harrison*. Taryn was a bit surprised to learn he had connections to Lancaster County, but she supposed she shouldn't be. The Philadelphia businessman had his eye on the gubernatorial seat. It made sense that a man as deliberate and calculating as Thomas Baxter would have started building his name and good will long ago.

That good will was one of the front-page headlines, complete with picture. Naturally, he was much younger in the grainy black and white photograph, but Taryn recognized the same smug smile around his lips, the same superior gleam in his eyes. Those eyes gave her the creeps, following her the way they did each time he came to the office. Didn't the man know he was much too old for her? Taryn avoided him as much as possible, but inevitably, his file would end up on her desk, forcing her to endure his leering gaze. The man was filthy rich and wanted everyone to know it, but what struck Taryn the most was the *filthy* part.

At least this time, his money had gone to a worthy cause.

So now, she had strained eyes and an aching back to go along with her forty-five days of limbo, and she still had to decide her next step. Stay here, or go home? The wind had picked up and thunderclouds gathered overhead, muddying the previously sunny sky.

She headed east, just in case. US 30 would take her back to Philadelphia.

Yet even as she contemplated getting home before dark, the car seemed to have a mind of its own, taking the next exit off the highway. It found its own way back to Horseshoe Road.

I can still go home this way, she told herself. *Highway 30 was a straighter shot, but really, what else is there? Short of hiring a PI, I'm at a loss for what to do. I'll go home, regroup, and decide what's next.*

Decision made, Taryn had every intention of winding back to New Holland and taking Route 23 straight over to the expressway. She could still be home by dark, if the storm held off. Besides, what did *she* know about hiring a private investigator? She hadn't the first clue.

Before she reached Leola, the *what ifs* caught up with her again, tagging along for this leg of the journey. What if she did a quick internet search for private eyes in the area? Lancaster wasn't a huge city, but surely, it was large enough for a decent investigator. What if she checked it out, purely for informational purposes? What if she kept that option open, just in case she decided to pursue it at some point down the road?

She made it all the way back to New Holland. She traveled a full six miles, before the *what ifs* forced her to pull into a parking lot and take out her phone. She did a quick search for investigation services in the greater Lancaster area.

Keystone Secure Investigations was the top pick, with a five-star rating. The blurb touted over twenty years of experience in security. It mentioned a career in the Navy, a handful of years on the police department, and five years plus in the private sector. Taryn scanned the first of fifty-something reviews, noting that most left glowing accounts of fast, efficient service. She gave a cursory glance to the few other companies listed, but she knew her decision was made. *Keystone* just had a good, solid ring to it.

She dialed the number via her car's Bluetooth feature and waited for the line to pick up.

A man's voice answered, brisk and direct, *"Keystone Secure Investigations."*

Ignoring the butterflies taking flight in her belly, she summoned her best senior administrative assistant voice and matched her tone to his. "Yes. May I please speak to Bryce Elliott?"

There was only a slight pause on the other end. "This is Bryce Elliott. How may I help you?"

A butterfly made its way up to her vocal chords, giving her voice the smallest of quivers. "I'd like to make an appointment for a consultation, please."

Another slight pause, amid the sounds of papers shuffling. "What about next Friday?"

"Actually, I'd prefer to meet with you as quickly as possible."

"Unless you're available this afternoon, I'll be out of the office until next Wednesday."

She pounced on the opportunity. "I'm free this afternoon. I can be there in—" She glanced down at her phone's search screen and hit the 'get directions' button. "Oh. Three minutes, apparently."

Oddly enough, the man sounded somewhat irritated. Perhaps he had hopes of closing early for the day. "Very well. I'll see you in three minutes."

A single, fat raindrop hit her windshield. "Let's make that five."

She whipped out of the parking lot, sensing that Bryce Elliott wasn't a man to tolerate tardiness. All those years in the military, no doubt. It was a short drive, but the address was on the opposite side of the road, and rain threatened. Finding a place to turn around to park nearer the door would kill precious time. She stopped across the street, glaring up at the bloated thunderhead and daring it to dump its contents when she had no umbrella for protection. If it would give her two minutes, she could be across the street and safely inside. Then the sky could rage to its dark heart's content.

She made it halfway into the road before the heavens unleashed their fury. She yelped in surprise, startled by the loud boom of thunder. The noise seemed to rattle the rain from the sky, prompting the dark clouds to roll over and spill their weight upon her head.

By the time she reached the sidewalk, Taryn was drenched.

CHAPTER 6

From his stance behind the window, Bryce Elliott watched the busy road out front. Cars zipped along the wet pavement, heedless of the rain that fell by the bucketful. After sunny skies all morning, the storm blew in unannounced.

A hapless woman scurried across the thoroughfare, her hair and clothes already plastered to her body. Adding insult to injury, a car zoomed along, splashing a pothole dry as it passed. The woman barely gave the car a second glance. Keeping her eyes on the far sidewalk as if it were a lifeline, she bustled out of the road, wove her way through vehicles parked along the street, and almost collided with a parking meter.

Bryce turned back to straighten his desk, in anticipation of his impromptu client. Not a single item needed his attention, but he was a stickler for a neat, orderly work environment. As he glanced at the grandfather clock that came with the house, the front door chimed out an arrival.

The impromptu was here, in exactly four minutes.

Bryce knew the entryway of the old Victorian house offered the perfect buffer for his clients, particularly the first timers. Seeking the help of a private investigator seemed an ominous task for most people. A last resort, of sorts. The elegant foyer made a nice transition area for clients to collect their thoughts and calm their nerves before stepping into his office. There was something oddly relaxing about the ageless beauty of parquet oak flooring, genuine wainscot, and hand-stenciled wall coverings. The craftsmanship spoke of a gentler, more tranquil time, before life became complicated with modern nuances. If only for a moment, clients could inhale a deep breath and imagine themselves a part of that tranquility.

When he purchased the stately old house five years ago, Bryce had every intention of following the local trend, slicing and dicing the aging residence along Route 23 into multiple office spaces. But when it came down to swinging the sledgehammer, he couldn't do it. He couldn't tear down a single wall. It would be practically sacrilegious to alter the beauty and dignity of the old girl. Bryce, a man who prided himself on having a steady head and a hardened heart, found himself getting sentimental over a pile of sticks and stones.

But, oh, what a pile it was! Dark-red brick, made right here in Pennsylvania, well over a hundred years ago, fashioned into a three-story dwelling, plus basement. Tall and trim, with graceful white columns along the porch, black shudders on all the windows, and dormers and turrets for interest. Inside, the mahogany trim was intricately carved, the floors were original, and all six fireplaces were in working order. What few changes Bryce made were executed with meticulous care and integrity.

While his client lingered in the foyer, Bryce straightened his shirt and ran a quick hand over his head, soothing his hair into place. Both actions were more from habit than necessity. Barely longer than a buzz, his closely clipped dark hair shouted of a military background. The sentiment echoed in the sharp creases of his shirt collar.

"Hello?" a tentative voice called from the entryway.

A flash of irritation surged through him. The foyer boasted doorways on all sides. The paneled double doors on the left were closed. A large potted plant effectively blocked the hallway that flowed from the center of the foyer. How difficult was it to understand that the only option was to turn through the opened doors on the right, leading straight into his office?

Not for the first time, Bryce wished he could ignore the protocol of politeness drilled into him by the military. Sometimes, being an officer and a gentleman did not suit his cranky nature.

Regardless, Bryce forced a note of civility into his voice as he strode toward the doorway. His voice preceded him. "Please, do come in. To your right."

To his surprise, it was the woman from the street. She wasn't more than five feet four at most, but every inch of her now dripped water onto his floor. A damp circle already seeped into the antique Oriental carpet. He suspected that, before the rain and the car that splashed her, her khaki trousers had been clean and neat. In their current state, he would never know for sure. They were hopelessly streaked with mud.

That, too, dripped onto the carpet.

"I'm a mess," she realized, looking down at herself with disgust. "And I'm destroying your carpet."

Bryce looked around for a solution. "Give me a second," he said. He turned and disappeared from the room, returning moments later with a full-size bath towel. "Here." He thrust the towel toward her. "Dry yourself off a bit. You won't hurt the leather chair." He motioned toward the wingback chairs stationed around his desk.

To Taryn's relief, he turned his back and strode toward his desk, offering her a bit of privacy as she rubbed the towel over her wet clothes.

Embarrassed, she realized the rain had plastered her once-crisp white blouse against her, turning it practically translucent. She didn't mind revealing her bra's lacy trim as much as she minded revealing the dimples along her waist. She could stand to lose a few pounds.

Tugging the offensive fabric away from her skin, Taryn fanned it to create airflow. She peeled the khaki away from her thighs with a deep sigh, knowing there was little hope for her mud-streaked pants. The entire outfit was practically brand new. She had doubts any of it would ever be the same.

Hurrying to the chair in hopes of minimizing damage to the carpet, Taryn knew she made a less-than-stellar first impression. So much for professionalism. The best she could hope for now was competent.

Toweling her hair dry with one hand, Taryn reached the desk and thrust her other hand forward, hoping to gain lost ground. The man's demeanor was a bit intimidating, particularly when she knew she resembled a drenched rat.

"I apologize for my soggy entrance. That storm took me by surprise. An hour ago, the sun was shining." Her handshake was firm. "Taryn Clark."

"Bryce Elliott. Please, have a seat. And don't worry about being wet. These things can't be helped," he said generously. They both knew an umbrella would have made a difference.

He wasted no time in addressing business. "You have an issue to discuss with me?"

"Yes."

She said the word quickly enough, but she was slow to elaborate. Bryce's dark brows spiked upward in anticipation.

Taryn drew a deep breath and forged ahead, determined not to falter. "I'm adopted. I need your help in finding my birth mother."

Bryce kept his expression neutral, but inside, he flinched. He had conducted two such investigations before, and neither turned out well.

In the first case, the mother had given her newborn away after being raped. Right or wrong, she hated the child upon sight. Twenty-two years had not changed that fact. His client had gone away heartbroken and disillusioned.

The second case had a more noble beginning, but a disastrous end. As difficult as it was to give up her child, the fourteen-year-old mother had known she was in no position, financially or otherwise, to care for an infant. Twenty-five

years of drug and alcohol abuse dimmed the mother's selfless-
ness. When her well-established son came looking for his birth
mother, she had been more than willing to welcome him—and
his bank account—with welcome arms. Even before the case
made the headlines, Bryce regretted his role in reuniting the
two. Within a year, her former pimp murdered both the mother and son. He told himself that was the last time he would
take on such a case.

Before he could explain that to the soggy woman dripping
onto his hardwood floors, she pulled out an envelope and
passed it across the antique desk.

"My adoptive parents are both deceased," she explained,
"so I have little to go on. I found this inside a hidden compartment in my mother's jewelry box."

He peered down at the fading ink. "This looks like a hospital bill from a *Lancaster Memorial Hospital* in Lancaster
County."

"Yes. And it's dated January 1, 1980. The day I was born."

"Is this where you were born? *Lancaster Memorial*?"

"Yes, I have reason to believe it is. Like most adopted children of the time, I have an amended birth certificate and the
original is sealed. I've applied to have the documents released,
but the process takes up to forty-five days."

"How long has it been since you applied?"

She couldn't help the flush that crawled up her neck.
"About two hours. I just left the county courthouse, where I
found absolutely nothing helpful." Seeing his frown, she was
quick to add, "But I did meet a nurse, and after talking with

her, I'm positive that I was born at *Lancaster Memorial* and that you're holding the bill from my birth."

Bryce studied the paper with care, murmuring his first impressions aloud. "It appears this was done on a typewriter, rather than a computer... A typewriter that needed a new ribbon, at that... Some of the words are hard to make out, particularly the billing name and address." He looked up, his gaze intense. "Of course, that could have been intentional."

Taryn cocked her head to one side. Her shoulder-length hair left a wet pattern on her right shoulder. "How so?"

"To protect the identity of one or both of the parties involved."

Her brow knitted in confusion. "I understand my birth mother's need for secrecy, but why would my adoptive parents want to protect their identity?"

His hesitation was slight. "I'm guessing they paid for the delivery. Some people," he added slowly, "might interpret that as the equivalent of buying a baby."

Taryn sucked in a sharp breath. The thought had never occurred to her. She took a moment to compose herself, before stating quietly, "It doesn't matter that you can't read them. She not only used a false name, but a false address, as well."

"Is this all you have?" he asked with a frown.

"That, and this letter." Still soggy, Taryn pushed another piece of paper his way.

As Bryce scanned the handwritten note, his frown deepened. Even between the two sheets of paper, they were still scant little to go on. Without her birth certificate, it would be doubly hard to uncover her past.

He raised his head, taking his first hard look at Taryn Clark. Late thirties, according to the paper in his hand, but she could pass as five years younger. The lighter strands weaving throughout her brown hair could be the first signs of gray, he decided. A youthful spatter of freckles marched across the bridge of her nose, but there were just enough lines in her face to offer character.

She was truly quite pretty, Bryce realized with a start. He hadn't noticed before. Nor had he noticed her eyes. She had the most amazing eyes. Spaced wide apart, and such a startling shade of violet.

"Ms. Clark, I'm not sure what you think I can do for you. Unless you have more than this, I'm afraid I don't have enough information to start an investigation."

Taryn ignored the dismissal. "Did I mention I spoke to the nurse who delivered me? She told me my mother was frightened of something. Of some*one*, she said. Terrified, actually. So much so, she refused to be acknowledged for having the first baby of the new decade. She gave up a very lucrative package in order to hide her identity."

"As curious as that may be—"

"Don't you see?" Taryn broke into his objections. "This isn't simply about finding my birth mother. There was something very odd going on, and I intend to find out what it was. There had to be a reason my mother was so frightened. Why she used a false name to check into the hospital. And why she snuck out that same night, when no one was watching the back entrance."

"There could be dozens of explanations. She may have been afraid of how her parents would react to her having a baby out of wedlock, for instance. She may have been involved with a married man. Perhaps her baby's father, or perhaps even her own, held a public position and she wanted to spare him any negative repercussions. One or the other could have been a man of the cloth, or a politician."

At mention of a politician, the photo of Thomas Baxter flashed through her mind. Taryn shook it impatiently aside. "The nurse said my mother was widowed."

"How did she know that? And how did she know this woman was even your mother? According to what you've said, she was admitted under a bogus name."

"Yes, that's true. But Helen—the nurse—recognized my eyes." Taryn batted them now, for emphasis. "Not many people have eyes this color, but she distinctly remembers Jane Doe and her baby having violet eyes."

"I must admit, you do have memorable eyes."

Even when made by men as attractive as Bryce Elliott, compliments about her eyes normally did not faze her. Too often, the words were a cheap come-on line. Sometimes they hinted to an unhealthy fascination. Or worse, to a 'your eyes are so freaky, I can't stop staring' obsession. But something about the way Bryce said them, burbled in his deep, no-nonsense voice, gave the words significance.

A butterfly flitted about in her stomach again, this time for an entirely different reason.

With his next words, a net fell over the enigma, stilling its wings.

"If your mother lied about her name, she could just as easily have lied about her marital status."

Taryn forgot about her wet clothes and the dribble of water tracking her every movement. She stood and paced impatiently on the rug, too restless to sit for another moment. "You should talk to Helen. When you hear her tell the story, see the way her eyes are still haunted with the memory of that day, you'll understand. You'll feel the same urgency I do, even after all these years. There's so much more to this story than we know."

Bryce might feel an urgency to save his expensive rug, but he doubted he would feel it over a case from 1980. He did admit, however, she had piqued his interest. Not on a physical level—at least, not solely—but on a curiosity level. Some of what she said did seem rather peculiar.

He was making no promises, but he ventured to ask, "And where would I find this Helen, if I were so inclined?"

Taryn whirled around, hope flashing in her violet eyes. "Right here in New Holland. She owns *Kaffi Korner*."

"Helen Fremont?" he asked in surprise. Before Taryn could ask the question, he answered, "I have coffee there most mornings."

"That's perfect! Tomorrow morning, you can ask her all about it!"

"Tomorrow morning, I'll be on a flight to Florida."

Taryn was crestfallen. "You're going on vacation?"

It was irrational, she knew, to feel so devastated. The man had a right to go on vacation. Just because she had little use for them, didn't mean that other people—*most* people, in fact—felt the same way. He was probably taking a nice getaway with his wife and family, even though he didn't wear a ring. Not that she had particularly looked, after his comment about her eyes. His long, tapered fingers were easily visible, and she didn't see a ring. The man had the right not to wear a ring, just like he had the right to a vacation. Neither should be so upsetting.

He quickly quelled her speculations. "Not a vacation. I'm working on a case."

It took long enough, but Taryn realized she tracked water upon his carpet. She returned to her chair with a sheepish apology.

"But you'll take my case?" she asked, perching there on the edge.

The investigator studied her for a long moment. Trapped beneath his dark, thoughtful gaze, she squirmed uncomfortably. "I'll consider it," he finally relented. "Let me do some digging around, see if there's anything there. I'll let you know if I find enough to pursue."

Taryn hopped to her feet, feeling exceedingly hopeful. "Yes! Yes, that will be fine."

Too little too late, particularly given her soggy clothes and bedraggled appearance, she tried to temper her enthusiastic response. She ran a hand over her wrinkled blouse and attempted a professional reply. "Excellent."

"Why don't you give me your contact information while I make copies of these?" Bryce suggested. Though within easy distance of his rolling chair, he stood and carried the papers to a nearby copy machine. "Are you staying in the area?"

This time, there was no doubt to her answer. "Yes. Absolutely. So if you have any questions, just give me a call. I can come right over." She dug in her purse for another business card.

They exchanged cards and the investigator promised to be in touch. As he showed her to the door, she apologized once again for her waterlogged entrance.

"Not a problem." This time, the words sounded sincere. A ghost of a smile hovered over his taut mouth as he nodded to the sky beyond. "And look. The sun is trying to come back out."

For the first time that day, she thought she felt some of the sun's warmth enveloping her.

Or perhaps it was the feeling of renewed hope.

CHAPTER 7

Taryn pulled into the first hotel she came to. She didn't bother to check for price or availability on her phone. She was still high on possibilities.

"I'm sorry," the girl at the desk apologized. "We don't have anything available for tonight. I could check with our other location, just over in Bird-in-Hand. Would that be okay?"

"Where is that? In the area?"

"Oh, yes. Over on Route 340, about twenty minutes from here."

She had just been on Route 340, also known as Old Philadelphia Pike.

"That's fine."

The girl punched a number into the phone and waited for it to connect. "You have lovely eyes," she said as she waited.

Taryn offered one of her standard replies. "Thank you. They are rather unusual."

The girl shrugged. "Not really. I know an entire family with eyes that color." She delivered the shocking news with easy aplomb, missing Taryn's startled reaction as the line engaged and she spoke to the person on the other end.

"Wait, wait, wait," Taryn interrupted. "You know someone else with eyes like mine?"

The receptionist frowned, torn between the two conversations. Given that Taryn looked like she might come across the counter at any moment, the girl asked the person on the phone to wait. She covered the mouthpiece and practically hissed, "Yes, that's right. Now if you'll excuse me, I'm trying to find you a bed for the night."

"What I really want to find is my family!"

After a brief pause, the girl spoke into the phone. "Lew? Never mind. Thanks, anyway." She reached for a piece of paper and wrote something down.

"You know what? The family I'm talking about has a little guest cottage they rent. I'll give you their address, and you can see if it's still available. I live just down the road from them. I know it was empty a day or so ago. With any luck, it may still be."

Taryn's knees felt oddly weak. "Really? Oh, wow."

"Don't tell my boss." The girl grinned, sliding the paper across the counter.

"Not a word," Taryn said, whisking it away before it vanished.

If she was finally catching a break, she wasn't about to let it float away.

❦

The GPS led her off the highway and into the rich farm-lands of Lancaster County. Narrow blacktop roads crisscrossed the countryside, slicing across fields lush with crops. Freshly bathed from the impromptu rain, the leafy plants glistened in the late afternoon sun. The neat rows mesmerized Taryn as they darted straight and true through the fertile soil, cutting perfect stripes through the sea of green.

Her foot eased off the gas pedal as she made a deep curve and came upon a slow-moving vehicle: a buggy, of all things, pulled by a prancing black horse and driven by a woman wearing a white head covering. Two young children rode in the back, twisted to face the road behind them. One munched on a banana and stared at Taryn with big, solemn eyes, while his brother pretended to cast a fishing rod and catch the shiny emblem on her car's hood.

Taryn had heard, of course, about the Amish people and their outdated mode of transportation, but she hadn't known, really *known*, it was true. Not until now, as she witnessed it with her own eyes.

Unsure of protocol where buggies were concerned, Taryn slowed to a crawl. A caution sign graced the back of the black buggy, but it offered no instruction on how to follow. She nibbled on her lip, uncertain of what to do.

After two cars came from behind and zoomed past both her and the buggy, Taryn eased into the adjacent lane. Her wave was almost apologetic as she left the horse-drawn vehicle behind.

How long, she wondered, *did it take to travel that way?* Did they leave the house at the crack of dawn, just to make it to the grocery store by noon? Did they even shop at the grocery store, or did they grow everything they needed, right here on the farm?

Taryn mulled it over as she followed the black ribbon of road through fields and small farms. Great barns and huge, rambling houses dotted either side of the road. As if the original houses weren't large enough already, almost all had an extension—some with two or more—added on. Some included a windmill nearby, and several had clotheslines that stretched high into the sky, operated, no doubt, by a pulley system.

The assortment of laundry amused her. Dark, somber colors ruled. Even the colorful patchwork quilts she saw were, for the most part, made of dark, solid squares. Lighter colors appeared in the bed linens and the towels, and, to her amusement, on one pair of colorful men's pajama bottoms. Smiley faces waved in the sky across two high-flying legs.

The GPS instructed her to turn right, onto another simple blacktop road. Without the guidance system, surely these roads were a maze! Another sharp curve, this one in a dip, and a small valley sprawled before her.

"Your destination is on the left."

The announcement took Taryn by surprise. She saw nothing that resembled a cottage for rent. Just another of the staggered, over-sized farmhouses and twin barns twice as large, positioned *just so* at the crest of the hill.

She dutifully turned down the lane, edged on either side by a white wooden fence. Even as she wondered if this were right, she noticed the modest sign that read 'Zook Farms.' Beneath it were smaller signs scattered about, claiming 'Fresh Butter,' 'Farm Fresh Eggs,' 'Woodworks,' and 'Quilts.'

"Seems they're selling everything but the children," she quipped, before grimacing at her own bad joke.

White rock crunched beneath the tires as she rolled her way up the lane, still wondering why she was here and what she hoped to accomplish. There was no reason to believe these people were related to her. All she knew was that they, too, had violet-colored eyes. Realistically, it didn't mean a thing. And from the looks of things, these people appeared to be Amish. Wasn't that like a completely different race? At any rate, she didn't belong in this ethnicity group.

Did she?

The thought made her distinctly uncomfortable. It also made her uncomfortable to know she had taken the advice of a complete stranger, and now here she was, in the middle of nowhere.

To be clear, it was a beautiful nowhere. The lane widened and spilled into a large yard, its grass lush and green, its beds overflowing with flowers in every color imaginable. Dual rope swings hung from the outstretched limbs of a towering tree, beckoning to her inner child. Its adult counterpart rested beneath a nearby tree, the intricate iron styling softened with over-stuffed floral cushions. A sparkling pond, complete with gazebo, contributed to the idyllic scene.

A word whispered through Taryn's heart, its flutter as gentle as butterfly wings. *Home.*

Funny, how this quaint country setting evoked such an unexpected sentiment. Home, to her, had always been the split-level house she lived in as a toddler, back when their little family was still a family. Back before divorce and death, and the deluge of foster homes that paraded through her life. Not even the apartment with Collin or the upscale duplex in Chestnut Hill filled that emotional placeholder in her soul. But one glimpse, and this unlikely farmhouse tugged at her heartstrings.

The house, itself, was large and rambling. Her best guess was that the original home stood more or less in the center of the sprawled structure, the weathered white boards testament to its age and years of service. The two-story brick addition on the right was obviously newer. She suspected the one on the left came sometime in between.

Taryn pulled into the garage's driveway. Situated near the newest addition, the garage appeared to be the newest build of all. Instead of the customary cars one normally saw in a garage, a buggy occupied all three bays. They ranged in size and style, from the deluxe family model to the flatbed utility rig. Overhead, a large space sprawled the distance, accessed by an external staircase.

Suddenly nervous, Taryn stepped from the car, sunglasses firmly in place. The still-sticky pie goo made certain of that.

"*Hullo!*"

The greeting came from somewhere behind the house. Taryn whirled around, until she spotted a woman in the garden, leaning on her rake. "May I help you?" the woman called.

Sure. I heard you had violet eyes and I came to ask. Are you my mother?

It was a ridiculous introduction, of course. Taryn quickly thought of another excuse.

"I heard you have a cottage for rent."

Please don't say it's the little red shack behind you. Please, oh, please.

"Yes. Absolutely." The woman brushed her hands against the black apron she wore. The dress beneath it was solid green and reached almost to her feet. As she stepped over the tops of plants heavy with green tomatoes and a few just turning red, Taryn noticed the woman was barefoot. She also noticed the small child who clung shyly to her mother's skirts. "I'll be right there."

"Take your time," Taryn called back.

Definitely, take your time. I need to work up my courage.

What would she say? Taryn still hadn't decided when the woman walked into the yard, carrying a wicker basket full of vegetables.

"So you're here about the room?" The woman smiled.

At closer range, Taryn saw that the woman was older than she first thought. Her body was slim and lithe, giving her a youthful appearance, but generous strands of gray intertwined with the hair peeking from beneath her white cap. Free of makeup, the lines in her face led Taryn to speculate she was close to fifty. Small, round-rimmed glasses hid her eyes. The darkened lenses were either light adaptive or made strictly for sun. Either way, Taryn had no clue as to her eye color.

Realizing the woman waited for her answer, Taryn forced herself forward. "Yes, that's right. Is it still available?" Her eyes inadvertently darted to the little building out back.

"Absolutely. How long are you staying?"

The question caught her by surprise. She wanted to say, 'as long as it takes.' Or forty-five days, whichever came first.

"I'm not sure," she answered instead. "A week?"

The woman nodded. "Good, good. It's empty for most of the month." She said something to the child still twisted up in her skirt. Taryn couldn't hear them well, but the words sounded foreign. With a nod, the little girl took the basket from her mother's hands and scampered off toward the house. "Emiline will get the key," the woman explained.

She came forward and extended her hand. "I'm Lillian. Welcome."

Not Rebecca. Taryn bit back the sting of disappointment, reminding herself it couldn't be so easy.

"Thank you. I'm Taryn Clark."

"Where are you from, Taryn Clark?"

"Philadelphia."

"I went there once," the woman said with a smile. "Such tall buildings! And so many people. I was so nervous, the full time we were there."

"It can be a bit nerve wracking," Taryn admitted.

"Let me show you the room."

She turned toward the exposed staircase next to the garage. Taryn followed her up, noticing how dirty the bottoms of her feet were. Once on the landing, Taryn saw the wide deck running almost the full length of the building's backside, overlooking the barns and the fields beyond. The wall along the deck consisted almost completely of windows, allowing plenty of light and ventilation.

Taryn belatedly remembered the Amish used no electricity.

"You're free to use this deck as often as you like," Lillian offered. "It's quite peaceful out here, and the sun rises over that hill yonder."

Before Taryn could stop the tour—she didn't require a fancy room, but power and running water were musts—they had reached the door at the end of the deck. Lillian twisted the knob and it fell open, no key required.

"The key is for your peace of mind," she explained. "This way, please." She wiped her muddy feet on a rag rug before crossing the threshold.

With a flick of a switch, electric lights came on overhead. Seeing Taryn's surprise, her hostess smiled. "Solar panels."

The room was quite spacious, although rather sparse. The floors were gleaming hardwood, covered at random with colorful hand-looped rugs. The kitchen had all the necessities: small refrigerator, microwave oven, sink, cabinets, and a round table with seating for four.

Beyond that was a sitting area, with a flowered couch and an easy chair. None of the furniture quite matched, but it all looked comfortable and gently worn. A four-poster queen-sized bed was on the far side of the room, dressed in a colorful quilt in a complicated patchwork pattern. Lacy white curtains were pulled back to overlook the pond and gazebo out front.

"It's very large," Taryn murmured.

"Is it only you, or will your family be joining you?"

"Only me." The words seemed to burn her throat.

"Then no need to tell you that the couch folds out into a bed. You'll find extra linens in the trunk yonder, and the bathroom is fully stocked with towels and paper and what-not." She motioned toward the door on the left, about halfway into the long room.

The little girl ran into the room, dropped the keys onto the table with a clatter, and was off again.

"That's Emiline, my youngest. What a bundle of energy she is!"

Her lenses had lightened a bit, but Taryn still couldn't see the color of her eyes. And she kept her own sunglasses on, even though they made the room unnecessarily dark.

"We'll set a basket outside your door each morning with breakfast. Is seven o'clock too early?" Before Taryn could respond, her hostess added, "Keep in mind, the rooster will crow long before that."

"Seven is fine."

"Good. Anything else you need to know?"

"A price would be nice."

"Of course. Eighty dollars a night."

"For this room?" Taryn asked in surprise.

"It comes with breakfast," Lillian reminded her hastily.

"You misunderstand. I would expect to pay twice that amount for a room this large."

"Oh. Very good, then." Lillian looked immensely relieved. She nodded with a smile. "Eighty dollars a night."

"Do I need to come down to sign the paperwork?"

"You're taking the room, ain't so?"

"Yes."

"I'll leave it in the basket in the morning. You pay when you leave."

"But... don't you need a deposit of some kind?"

"You just said you were staying. I have your word. Why do I need a deposit?"

Such open trust was foreign to Taryn. She wondered how often the woman had discovered that not everyone deserved blind faith. For Lillian's sake, she hoped such disappointment was few and far between.

"There's a list of local restaurants and shops there on the counter. We have a telephone shed down by the road that we share with our neighbor, if you've a mind to use it. We also have decent cell phone service."

Taryn was still digesting the part about the telephone shed, and almost missed the last few things Lillian pointed out.

"If you need anything else, just come to the house and knock," Lillian said as she made her way to the door. "Do you need help with your luggage?"

"Thank you, but I can manage. Do I need to move my car?"

"*Nee.*" She shook her head in the negative. "If we need the carriage, we'll say so."

"Thank you," she thought to call after her hostess.

"It is a pleasure to have you, Taryn Clark. *Willkumm.*"

CHAPTER 8

By the time Taryn unloaded her car and unpacked a few necessities, her stomach was growling. She hadn't eaten since the barely touched pie at Helen's *Kaffi Korner*, and even that had been hours ago. If she hoped to quieten the monster within and get any sleep at all tonight, she had to feed it.

She looked over the list on the counter, double-checking the restaurants' ratings on her phone. Finding several that looked promising, Taryn opted for the one nearest her current location. The last thing she wanted was to get lost in the dark, especially on her first night here! Her best choice was to grab a quick bite nearby and be back before nightfall.

After a delicious dinner, she ran in a convenience store, grabbed bottled water and a few snacks, and followed the GPS back to Zook Farms.

Dusk followed close on her heels, smudging the horizon with a feathery touch. With the laundry pulled in for the day, the smiley faces no longer waved high in the sky as she passed. Metal-wheeled tractors and farming implements sat idle near the great barns. Cows huddled into their stalls, content after the evening milking.

She slowed as she saw something in the road ahead. Another buggy, she wondered as she approached. No, this was another new and strange sight. A procession of cows, their udders heavy and swinging, moseyed across the pavement, moving from an open field to the barn on the other side of the road. Two farmers, one with a beard and the other still in his teens, walked on either side of the cattle, carrying long sticks to act as a guide. Both men wore the traditional black pants and suspenders of the Amish, their heads topped by flat-crowned straw hats.

Taryn waited patiently as they passed, marveling at how such a scene was still even possible. She tried to imagine the good people of Philadelphia presented with a similar scenario. Horns would blare. Tempers would rage. People would be out of their cars, screaming at the gentle bovine to move. They had places to go, people to meet. There would be no time for a farmer and his cattle. No patience for this idyllic scene on a backcountry road.

Despite the lengthening shadows of day, Taryn proceeded slowly after the cows passed. There was something so peaceful in her surroundings, softened even more so by the weakened rays of the setting sun. She rolled down her car windows and inhaled the country air. It smelled of fresh-cut grass and pungent earth. She caught a whiff of sweetness as she passed a stand of columbine. Wrinkled her nose as she passed another barn and its distinct odor. Choked on the stench wafting up from a pigpen. She sped up as she passed the muddy mess but slowed again as she neared the fertile rows of a large vegetable garden. Several members of an Amish family moved among the plants, picking the ripe bearings.

Tears stung her eyes as she imagined what it must be like to work together in tandem with family. She imagined what the conversations must be like. A father teasing his young son for missing a ripened tomato. A young girl, skipping along the rows singing a song, making a game of snagging the dangling peas. Two sisters sharing daydreams and bits of gossip as they dug for potatoes. An impish youngster, begging his mother to make his favorite dish for dinner, knowing fully well the crop was meant for market. And a mother, humming a peaceful song, pleased to turn daily chores into family time.

Caught up in her imaginings, Taryn passed up the lane to the guesthouse. She went to the next farm and turned around, admiring the horses in the field. Against the light of the dying sun, they made a stunning silhouette. She snapped several pictures on her cell phone before pulling back onto the pavement and retracing her path.

By the time Taryn climbed the steps beside the garage, shadows edged inward. A new worry struck her. Did the solar-powered lights dim with the sun? If so, she was in for a long evening.

Even so, she took her time crossing the long deck, her attention snagged on the scene below. A little boy ran among a flock of chickens, urging them toward a screened-in patch of earth and a slope-roofed coop. The fowl squawked in protest.

Some veered off, refusing to go into their pen. Hearing the lad fuss at them, Taryn was certain the words weren't English. She didn't have to understand their meaning, however, to understand their sentiment. The young boy was clearly exasperated and to the point of begging. He was obviously relieved when his sister joined him and shooed the birds along, her long arms swinging with each swish.

Beyond the chicken coop, an older boy unhitched a team of mules from a plow and offered each a bucket of grain in reward. Another young man moved toward one of two massive barns, carrying an armful of hoes and rakes.

A dinner bell clanged, startling Taryn so badly she missed a step. She snickered at her own clumsiness. But when she saw how the bell threw the scene below into overdrive, she laughed aloud. The promise of dinner was a catalyst for motion. The chickens were suddenly ushered into their cage in a no-nonsense manner. The mules could finish their feed or go hungry. The tools were stowed quickly away.

Before the dinner bell rang a second time, Taryn counted no less than seven people pouring toward the house, coming in from every direction. One girl spotted Taryn there by the railing and raised her arm in greeting. A teenage boy followed close on her heels, his expression more guarded.

None were close enough for her to see the color of their eyes.

Taryn waved her own greeting and moved along to unlock her door. Relief flooded through her when the lights seemed as bright and powerful as ever.

She hadn't relished an evening alone in the dark, just her and her thoughts.

⚘

The rooster roused her from her sleep. An odd, strangling sound broke into her dreams, clucking and snorting right through a gorgeous field of violets.

Caught somewhere between dreamland and reality, the soundtrack didn't fit the movie playing out in her mind. In her sleep world, an Amish family waded knee-deep through a field of violets, singing a happy song. They plucked the petals with care, collecting them into expertly arranged bouquets that magically appeared in their hands. (Did dreams ever really make perfect sense?) As sounds of the morning penetrated her senses, the Amish family slowly morphed into chickens. One feathered foul flew into the clothesline and scattered the day's laundry. A fat, colorful rooster ran amuck through the garden, parting plants and sending an assortment of vegetables flying through the air.

The last image playing through her mind's eye was of a crookneck squash and a red, juicy tomato landing smack in the middle of an elaborate violet bouquet.

Taryn woke with a start, just as the rooster warmed up and released a loud, perfectly executed "cock-a-doodle-doo." It sounded so good, he repeated it again. And again.

She couldn't help but smile. Lillian warned her this would happen.

Taryn stumbled through her morning ritual and stepped onto the deck with her first cup of coffee. Aside from the rooster, it would be a quiet, peaceful start to her day. Perfect for easing into the morning, one sleepy step at a time.

Nothing, she soon discovered, could be further from the truth. Morning on a farm was a busy time.

The sun wasn't even fully up and awake yet. Still crawling from its bed beyond the horizon, it lingered there in the cover of early dawn. The sun stretched its golden arms with tentative strokes, testing intensity of early morning light, in no particular hurry to claim its spot in the lightening sky.

The sun, it seemed, shared none of the urgency playing out on the busy farm below. It struck Taryn that this was a re-wind of the scene from last night.

There was the same young girl again, the one with the swinging arms. She carried a basket with her into the chicken coop, while the same little boy scattered feed around the barren patch of dirt. The gate swung free and chickens flocked out in a flurry of flapping wings and noisy clucks. While the hens squawked and fussed over the scattered grains, the rooster perched above them on a fencepost and continued his early morning roll call.

The same pair of mules hitched to the same plow. Another horse hitched to a wagon, and already, both rigs were heading out into the fields.

The whir of an engine came from one of the barns, a steady pump and hiss, intermingled with the sound of cattle bawling. Taryn suspected it was the morning milking.

She hadn't noticed them so much last night, but assorted outbuildings and livestock pens fanned out from the barns, a maze of organized disarray. Between the great barns stood a huge silo. This morning, a bearded man assembled his work tools near the base of the round vessel as he worked on a nearby pen. A younger man came from one of the sheds, carrying an armload of boards and a long, two-handled saw. Taryn had seen one before in a museum, but she had never seen one in action. This should be enlightening.

It was also exhausting, simply observing the buzz of activity.

She never heard the footsteps or the swish of skirts as they climbed the stairs and crossed the deck. She jumped when she heard the soft voice behind her.

"Here's your breakfast, miss."

"Oh!" Taryn clutched her hand to her chest, a belated attempt to catch the breath that escaped her. Her eyes closed to steady her senses, even as she laughed at her own foolishness.

She snapped her eyes open and found herself staring at a young woman with long, honey-colored hair, twisted neatly into a bun and covered with a proper white prayer cap. The girl wore a simple dress and black apron, but even the unimaginative cut could not disguise the lush figure beneath it. She appeared to be in her late teens, edging toward twenty.

The young woman stared back at her, her shocked expression a duplicate to Taryn's. Looking into each other's eyes was like looking into a mirror. The color was almost an exact match.

"I—I'm Susannah," the girl said hesitantly. She thrust the basket between them. "I brought breakfast."

"Thank you, Susannah." It was amazing that her voice came out sounding so normal, when her heart rattled as if she ran a footrace. "I'm Taryn."

"*Mamm* says you're from Philadelphia." She stretched the syllables out, pronouncing each one distinctly.

"Yes, that's right." Taryn smiled politely, all the time wondering how *this* girl had *her* eyes. Surely, it was no coincidence!

Her mind raced with possibilities. Was this girl her sister? Her niece? Did they share blood, as well as eye color? How did she even begin to ask?

"I've always wanted to see the city." There was a wistful note in the girl's voice. "*Mamm* says I can go, but *Daedd* doesn't want me to."

Taryn didn't want to talk about the city. She wanted to talk about the one percent of the population known to have violet eyes. She wanted to talk about the chances of them both having the rare eye color and not being related.

"Philadelphia's an awfully big city," she finally offered.

"That's why I wish to go. I wish to see the big, tall buildings and the statues made of marble. I wish to visit the museums and see the history of our nation. I think it would be *wunnderbaar gut*."

"Then you would love Independence Hall and the Liberty Bell." Taryn smiled.

"Oh!" When she clasped her hands together in delight, Taryn thought the girl might be younger than she originally guessed. Susannah's face lit with pleasure and her eyes, those so uniquely violet and so like Taryn's, danced with excitement.

"Oh, I would love to go there! Please, tell me all your favorite places in the city."

The girl's enthusiasm was contagious. Taryn set aside her own questions to answer the ones volleyed at her, one after another. Susannah helped herself to one of the chairs. She even took it upon herself to unpack the breakfast basket and lay the offerings out before her guest.

"Let me," she said, waving away Taryn's attempt to help. She set out an assortment of breads, with jellies and jams and freshly churned butter. After peeling the plastic wrap away from a bowl of fruit, she unveiled a plate filled with scrambled eggs, thick slices of ham, and an oblong chunk of something dark and not particularly attractive. "This," she said, pointing with an accusing finger, "is scrapple. It has a rather strong and unique taste. Most *Englisch* must acquire a taste for it."

Susannah arranged the silverware and poured fresh milk from a small thermos. "The same can be said for our *milch*."

Taryn tilted her head to inquire, "*Englisch*?"

"What we call those whose first language is English," she explained. "We speak Pennsylvania Deutsch. Plain children don't learn your language until they start school."

That explained the strange words Taryn had overheard.

"Plain?" she questioned.

"We are a plain, simple people. We hold ourselves apart from others. We are Plain by choice. But, please," Susannah begged. "Keep telling me about your city. I hear it is home to America's oldest farmers' market!"

"I suppose. I went there once, with a friend."

That friend was actually her ex-husband Collin, but she didn't need to explain that to this sweet girl.

In truth, Taryn didn't like thinking of herself as divorced. The word divorce held such negative connotations. In her mind, she and Collin hadn't failed at marriage. They had succeeded in sharing a piece of their lives together and had parted as friends.

Susannah was still imagining what the farmers' market must be like. She spoke about it the way most children spoke of Christmas. "Only once? I would go so often they would think I lived there! It would be a *wunnderbaar gut* place for my *rumspringa*, don't you think?'

Taryn had heard of the strange tradition, when Amish teenagers were allowed to indulge in worldly influences. Some, she heard, ventured from their farms, and moved to the city to immerse themselves in modern pleasures. It was meant to be a time of reflection and experimentation, giving young people time to decide if they could commit their lives to the Amish faith. At the end of *rumspringa*, they had only two choices. Leave their roots behind and join life in the mainstream or commit to their family and their faith. If they chose the latter, baptism—and most often marriage—followed.

"Well, I —"

Before she could comment, Susannah rushed on in excitement. "Maybe you could be my sponsor!" She hesitated slightly, searching for the right word. "Perhaps not sponsor. More like my guide."

Taryn was already shaking her head. "Oh, I really don't—"

"Surely *Mamm un Daedd* would agree, since you are family!"

It was the opening she had hoped for, but it snuck upon her without warning and rendered her speechless. Susannah had no such infliction. She kept talking, spinning daydreams about Philadelphia, and having Taryn as her personal tour guide. She never noticed the way Taryn's mouth had frozen into a perfect 'O.'

"Susannah!" Lillian's voice floated up to the deck. "Are you still up there? Susannah, are you bothering our guest?"

The girl jumped to her feet, appalled by her own manners, or lack thereof. Shame moved through her. "*Ach!*" she cried, hands against her face. "I—I'm so sorry! I intruded on your breakfast. I barged in and started talking, and I didn't even think! *Mamm* says I am too forward. That I engage my mouth before I engage my mind. She says I must learn humility. I—"

Taryn reached out and touched the girl's arm. "Please, don't apologize. I've had a wonderful time visiting with you."

"But the way I carried on!"

"I love your enthusiasm. And for your sake, I hope you get to visit Philadelphia, one day very soon."

"Could you—could you put in a good word for me?" she dared to asked. She stopped herself with a wail of exasperation. "Oh, listen to me! There I go again! Just ignore me!"

Lillian's voice revealed a pinch of impatience on the second call. "Susannah!"

"Coming, *Mamm!*"

She started for the stairs, remembered her original mission, and whirled back toward Taryn. "Can I get you anything else?"

Answers. She wanted answers. She let the perfect opportunity slip by earlier, and now the moment was lost. Taryn managed a smile. "Not right now. Thank you, Susannah. Please come back and visit with me again."

"If *Mamm* lets me. Have a *gut* day." She had a charming way of mixing her Pennsylvania Deutsch words in with her English. Taryn returned her wave as she disappeared down the steps.

Long before Susannah reached her mother, Taryn heard the girl chattering about the new friend she had made.

CHAPTER 9

Taryn spent most of the morning fretting over how she would broach the subject of family with her hostess.

She had no proof they were related, not really. They had the same uniquely colored eyes, but so did a few hundred other people in the world. At one time, the estimate was around six hundred. Six *hundred*, out of the billions of people worldwide. Yet even that small number didn't mean she and this Amish family shared the same blood.

Scientists were at odds over the origin of violet eyes. Most said it was impossible to be born with eyes that color. The most common explanation for such a phenomenon was albinism. Or, defect. Sometimes, disease or severe sun damage could change the color of the iris. Mutation offered another explanation. If a mother carried a genetic mutation, it was likely her children would have it, as well. Other scientists insisted the eyes were, in fact, deep blue and only *appeared* purple under light.

Taryn didn't know about science, or genetics, or the reflective qualities of light. She only knew her eyes fascinated people, and she had never met another soul who shared that same color. Until today. And if the girl at the hotel was right, Susannah wasn't the only one in this family with violet eyes.

It wasn't definitive proof they were related. Nor was the fact she was born in the same county, only twenty or less miles away. But did such rare coincidences truly exist? Taryn didn't believe so.

Her mind heavy, her spirit dragging so low it all but scraped the soles of her feet, Taryn wandered out to the pond. It was a gorgeous day, spun of sunshine and soft breezes. Despite the sounds of a working farm and a busy blacktop road out front, it was peaceful there alongside the pond. Taryn welcomed the serenity as she stepped into the gazebo.

Suspended over the pond, the gazebo offered the perfect spot for quiet reflection. Even the creak of the porch swing hummed a relaxing melody. Bit by bit, the burden in her heart lightened. Ever so slowly, Taryn felt her troubles drift away, carried on the ripples of sky overhead and water underfoot.

Her pale eyes protected by the ever-present shades, she watched the horses in the neighboring pasture, the ones she spotted the night before. They were magnificent animals, sleek and muscled. She became fascinated with them, mesmerized by their movements. They ran with abandon, tossing their manes into the air, their powerful bodies cutting through the wind with ease. They moved with such grace and confidence.

Taryn found it difficult to pull her eyes away from the horses, even as she heard footsteps behind her.

On her approach, Lillian noticed how the horses captured the English woman's attention. Her own voice held a quiet sense of reverence. "They are magnificent, ain't so?"

"Indeed," Taryn murmured in agreement.

She was slow in turning toward the other woman. Something in the air changed with Lillian's presence. A new tension rode on the breeze, thickening the atmosphere of the open-air gazebo. As inexplicable as it was, Taryn experienced a mild sense of claustrophobia.

"My father's farm produces the finest horses in Lancaster County." Lillian's tone was matter-of-fact, devoid of pride or praise. She simply spoke the truth.

Taryn turned to her in surprise. "Those belong to your father?"

"*Jah.* That's his farm yonder, and his horses."

"They're beautiful."

Small talk exhausted, Lillian motioned toward the swing. "May I sit?"

Taryn scooted over, even though there was plenty of room for them both. The swing could easily accommodate three or more people. "Of course."

A long moment of silence yawned between them. Taryn turned her head as if to watch the horses once more, but she had difficulty concentrating. Only moments before, she saw their race along the fence as spirited and free. Now their movements struck her as restless.

Lillian was the first to speak. "Why did you come here, Taryn Clark?" The words were too quietly spoken to interpret as rude. "I do not advertise. Few folks know of our spare room."

"Your neighbor. The—The girl at the hotel. She told me you had a cottage for rent." Even she could hear the flimsy excuse in her sputtered answer.

"Again. Why did you come *here*, Taryn Clark?"

Lillian always spoke her full name. Strange, that Taryn should notice it now. Now, when there were so many more important things to focus on.

Those things came out slowly, daring to test the light of day. The words had been tucked away for so long, buried deep inside her soul. Hidden in the dark crevices of her heart, and all but forgotten in that secret spot, in her heart of hearts, where her most sacred dreams still lived.

"Roots," she dared to whisper aloud. "I'm trying to find my roots."

"You have... reason to believe they're here?" Lillian's voice came out higher, tighter, than it had before. Stretched taut like a bowstring.

Her face still averted, Taryn saw no reason to be anything but truthful. She was here to find answers.

"I've always known I was adopted. My parents made no secret of it, but they offered no details. All they ever said was that they had *chosen* me as their child. To search for my birth parents seemed an insult." A sigh escaped her, along with an admission. "Besides, my birth certificate was amended, and the original records sealed. Even if I wanted to search, I had nothing to go on, so I never even tried, even after my adopted mother passed away."

"But now?"

"I finally have a clue. I know I was born not far from here, at *Lancaster Memorial*. In Lancaster."

She heard her companion's tiny hitch of breath, but Lillian spoke not a word.

"The hospital closed down years ago," Taryn continued, "and no one knows for certain where the records are. I was able to speak with a nurse who worked there. In fact, she was working on the day I was born."

"Which was?" The words rode high and tight, as squeaky as any violin's highest note.

Taryn turned toward her hostess, watching her expression as she answered. "January 1, 1980."

Once again hidden behind darkened lenses, Lillian's eyes didn't reveal her thoughts. But Taryn heard that little hitch of breath again. She felt the woman on the other end of the swing stiffen, and saw the color drain from her face.

"The nurse remembered the day I was born. She remembered how frightened my mother was when she came in, so young, and all alone."

With each bit of information, Lillian seemed to shrink there on the seat. Her shoulders dipped inward, until her spine was crooked and her body was little more than a ball. Taryn pushed on, determined to finish.

"She checked in under a false name and sneaked out in the dead of night. The nurse said she was afraid of something. Or of someone."

A single sob broke from Lillian's hunched form.

"Please," Taryn begged, her voice now breathless. "Tell me the truth." She laid her hand onto Lillian's arm, drawing her full attention. Taryn slipped off her shades and looked directly into the Amish woman's face. "Are you my mother?"

She hadn't meant to be so blunt, but the question burst from her, burning in its intensity to be free.

The words were a shock to the other woman, even more so than seeing Taryn's eye color revealed. But to Taryn's grave dismay, Lillian shook her head.

"No, Taryn Clark, I am not your mother." She spoke the words with great sadness. She saw the tears that sprang to Taryn's violet eyes, saw the raw pain that turned them a dark, stormy purple. Lillian laid her hand atop Taryn's, which still lingered on her own arm. "I think I may be your aunt."

Taryn stared at her in surprise. Beneath the crushing disappointment, a tiny ray of hope pushed through the rubble of her heart and dared to squeeze free. "My aunt?" she sniffed.

Lillian answered haltingly, "I—I... I had a sister."

Taryn didn't notice the past tense. Didn't hear the sadness in her voice. She only heard the possibilities. She grasped at them with both hands. "Is her name Rebecca?"

The look on Lillian's face turned leery. "How did you know?"

"I found a note. From her. From Rebecca, my birth mother."

Lillian turned her face toward the horse pasture. "*Jah.* My sister's name was Rebecca."

It was so much more than she had hoped for. Even when she blurted out the question, asking if Lillian were her mother, she hadn't expected an answer. Not really. Not so easily.

"Really?" she whispered in awe.

Her hands came to cover her mouth. There was no hope for the clamoring in her chest. Her heart raced wildly, a staccato so fast and erratic she might hyperventilate at any moment. But it was worth it. She had located her birth mother!

"Where is she? Can you take me to her? Can I meet her?" Taryn asked, already half off the swing. Her mind raced in a hundred directions. "Does she live nearby? Does this mean I'm Amish?"

"Sit."

The single word, uttered without preamble, without apology, stopped her in her tracks.

Taryn sank back onto the porch swing, dreading whatever words she was about to hear.

"It's true," Lillian confirmed. Her back was straight once again, her shoulders squared. She held herself stiffly in the swing as she gazed toward the neighboring field of horses. "*Die Schweschder* was named Rebecca. She was older than me by five years, and I adored her. She called me *der Schadde*. Her shadow. Once upon a time, we did everything together." A ghost of a smile cracked the veneer of her face, before falling away. "It broke my heart when I lost her."

"She... moved away?" Taryn asked, hoping against hope that was all it was.

Her mind was already spinning explanations. Rebecca hadn't come home after *rumspringa*. Deciding to adopt the

'English' way of life, she was shunned by her family. Wouldn't that be the equivalent of losing her? No other explanation was acceptable. Not now, not when she was so close to finding her roots. So close to finding a home.

With Lillian's next words, her house of cards imploded. "She disappeared. Poof! Just like that. Here one day and gone the next."

Taryn stared at her, slow to comprehend. "She ran away?"

Did Amish kids even *do* that?

"Call it what you may. Ran away. Forced to leave. The end was the same. I never saw my sister again."

"Wait. Forced to leave? Are you—Are you saying she was *kidnapped*?"

"I never said that."

"Then what? How could she be forced to leave?"

Lillian never said a word, but her eyes strayed toward the neighboring fields. Her face was set like stone.

Taryn gasped. "Are you suggesting your father sent her away?" Her voice dropped, hushed with a note of shock. "Was it because she was *pregnant*?"

Lillian shook her head. "*Nee*, I don't believe she carried a babe when she left. Rebecca was too disciplined for that. She took her faith seriously."

"Then why? Why would your father send her away? And if he didn't, why would she leave?"

"That question has haunted me, all these years."

"Did you look for her? Call the police?"

"Yes and no. We searched for her among our Amish friends and neighbors. Districts far and wide pitched in, helping with the search. My father refused to call the police."

Taryn stared at her in horror. "How could he not call the police? What if someone hurt her? Kidnapped her? Forced her into a car against her will?" Her voice grew shriller with each scenario.

"The People prefer to handle matters in our own way. We don't favor calling the police. Few *Englisch* understand our customs, thinking them too harsh. The police would have said Rebecca was a typical teenager, running away from home." Resignation moved into Lillian's sigh. "It's happened before."

Taryn still sputtered her outrage. "I can't believe no one reported her missing! Why didn't you just do it yourself?"

"I was a child. The elders made a decision, and it wasn't my place to question them."

Her reply was so calm, so matter-of-fact. Taryn couldn't imagine herself ever being so complacent, even as a child.

"When was this? How old was she?"

"That's the other thing. She was seventeen. Old enough to leave, if she so wished."

"But you don't think she wanted to. I hear it in your voice. You don't believe she left of her own free will."

Lillian worded her answer carefully, "I don't believe she *wanted* to leave."

Taryn put a hand to her spinning head. For one glorious moment, she thought she had found her mother. She had found her roots. Now her mother was gone, and those roots, still so fragile, were snatched away from her.

She took a deep breath and tried to make sense of it all. "When did this happen?"

"She disappeared on the fifth day of March, 1979."

"And you never heard from her again?"

Lillian squirmed on the seat but remained silent. Taryn noticed immediately.

"Lillian. I thought you said you never heard from her after that day."

The older woman hesitated for a long moment. The indecision was there upon her face, whether to speak up or to remain silent. It played across her features like a tug-of-war.

"Please," Taryn pleaded softly. "If Rebecca was my mother—and I truly believe she was—I have a right to know what happened to her. If you know something, anything at all, please, please, tell me."

Another moment of debate, before Lillian spoke. "I never saw my sister after that day, but I did hear from her. She wrote to me. She never told me what happened, never explained why she left without saying a word, but she wrote to tell me she was safe."

"Where was she?"

"She wouldn't say. She refused to tell me. The letters were postmarked from different places." Lillian's apron twisted beneath nervous hands, mimicking her mouth, twisted now with old memories. "One letter revealed she had married. Even though she missed her family, she was happy, and in love. She was expecting a *bobbli*."

Lillian turned toward Taryn on the swing. "It was due just after the new year." Her voice softened as she said, "I believe that child was you. I believe you are Rebecca's baby. You have her facial features. Her strong chin, and the slight curl of her hair."

She reached up to take off her eyeglasses, revealing eyes the same unique shade as Susannah's, and as Taryn's. "And you have the King eyes," Lillian stated.

CHAPTER 10

If her heart hammered earlier, it was nothing compared to now. For one long, tentative moment, it stuttered, stalling there in her chest as if its maestro had forgotten how to play. When it kicked back into rhythm, the beat was wild and erratic. Too fast, and too intense, to resemble any tune. Its maestro was as confused and disoriented as she was.

This was what she had come for. The answers she sought. These were the words she had wanted, the news she had always longed to hear. She had a name for her birth mother. She had family. Roots.

Why, then, did it feel so different from what she had imagined it would?

Her senses were numb. The only thing Taryn could feel was the blood draining from her face. For all she knew, it pooled there at her feet, leaving her lifeless and spent.

"Taryn Clark? Are you all right?" Lillian asked in concern.

Taryn attempted to speak, but the words would not come. She gave a slight shake of her head. When Lillian's concern deepened, Taryn attempted a nod, hoping to convince at least one of them. She ended up with a deep, sorrow-filled sigh, strangled by a sob.

She finally found her voice. After a couple of false starts, she managed to speak, "I have more questions now, than ever."

"So do I, Taryn Clark."

It was illogical, but it was the first question out of her mouth. "Why do you always call me by my first and last name? Is that an Amish custom?"

"No. Although with so many of our friends and family having traditional names, the clarification does help," Lillian admitted with a slight smile. It did little to dim the sad light in her eyes. "But the truth is, I heard the name from Rebecca. It means innocence. I call you by your full name, because I, too, named my first child Taren, spelled with an 'e.'"

The news stunned her guest. "But—But Susannah never said a word!"

The sadness deepened. "She wouldn't, now would she? My innocent Taren never drew her first breath."

"Oh, Lillian. I'm so sorry," Taryn breathed the whisper-soft words, at a loss for what else to say.

"Who am I to question God's plan?"

After a long moment of reflection, other questions penetrated Taryn's numbed brain.

"My mother's letters never said why she left?"

"Her letters spoke of other things. Her new husband, and the tiny apartment where they lived. She never mentioned the

city it was in, but she told me all about her new home. Described each room, and the wondrous English inventions she
had discovered. She spoke of the plans they had for the future."

"Who was my father, Lillian?" she asked softly.

"A handsome young man named Ahndray Lamont. He
came here, to work on my father's farm."

"Was he Amish?"

Lillian actually laughed. "Oh, no. He was French. Your
mother was immediately smitten with his dark eyes and his
exotic accent."

"Was that unusual? To hire someone who wasn't Amish, I
mean?"

Lillian took pause, cocking her head to one side as she considered the question. "*Daedd* had to get the bishop's
permission, of course, but he knew so much about horses. And
Daedd was eager to improve the quality of his herd."

Confused, Taryn tried to sort it in her own mind. "The
bishop? Of France?"

"*Nee*. Of our district. Amish communities are divided into
districts," she explained. "Each district consists of about twenty-five to thirty families. They are our church family. We're
guided by a bishop, a deacon, our elders, and our preachers. If
there is anything we question, we go to our bishop. Some bish-
ops are more progressive than others. Some are more
traditional. We trust his guidance to be in accordance with the
Lord."

Taryn couldn't help the grooves forming between her drawn brows. "You must have permission to hire workers on your farm?"

"Normally, no. But *Daedd* was concerned about bringing in someone so different from us. He was worried about, I think you call it, owed influence?"

"I think you mean undue influence."

Lillian looked a bit confused but nodded in agreement. "*Jah*. And you can see, his concern was justified. Rebecca fell in love with the foreigner."

"They ran away together?" Taryn guessed.

"Not exactly. But *jah*, in the end, they were together."

"Is my father... Do you have any idea what became of him?"

"He was forced to leave your mother. He was forced back to France."

The surprises just kept coming. "He wasn't a legal citizen?"

"I think not. I think the men came for him and forced him to go."

Taryn's heart ached for her birth mother. No wonder she was so frightened. Forced to go through labor without her husband, it was, no doubt, easier to say she was a widow, than to explain deportation laws.

"Why didn't she just come home?" Taryn wondered aloud. Her eyes drifted to the adjacent horse farm. Her voice fell as she softly asked, "Would she have been welcomed?"

Lillian took a long moment to answer. "I want to think so," she finally chose to say. "But I'm not certain."

Taryn stared into the distance, wondering about the people who lived there. Her grandparents, so it seemed, but she felt no connection to them. What kind of parents wouldn't welcome their daughter home at a time like that?

"I've heard of shunning," she said, her voice still low. "Did they shun her?"

For this, Lillian shook her head. "*Nee.* Your mother was never baptized. Shunning is only for members who turn their back on the Church and the People."

"But she left the farm. She left her family, and their way of life."

"We do not force our faith upon our children. They must choose it for themselves. That is what our *rumspringa* is about. It allows each young person to choose for him or herself. Once baptized, they make a pact with God. A solemn oath to abide by the ways of the Church. Rebecca never made such a pact. She... left, so young. Before she was baptized." A sigh escaped, and her next admission sounded troubled. "That doesn't mean she would have been welcomed home with open arms, but she wasn't shunned."

"I must admit, I don't understand some of the Amish ways."

Lillian's smile was bittersweet. "And we don't understand all the ways of the *Englisch.*"

Taryn still had many questions, but one troubled her more than any other. Her voice came out raw.

"Tell me the truth, Lillian." She gathered her courage around her like a shield and asked the most difficult question of all. It was a question she had avoided asking. Taryn wasn't certain she wanted to know the answer.

Still, she had to ask. Had to say the words. Had to know the answer.

"Is my mother still alive?"

For the longest moment, Taryn thought she would not answer. The other woman stared into the pond, her violet eyes staring vacantly into the rippling water. There was pure heartache in her voice when she finally spoke. The words came slowly.

"My mind wants to believe she is. That she finally found peace, and happiness. Sometimes I think she may have made her way to France, to be with her beloved Ahndray. But my heart. My heart knows otherwise. Rebecca would never have forsaken her family in such a way. There can be only one explanation. *Die Schweschder*, my best friend and my confidante, my partner in mischief and fun, my dearest Rebecca..." Her voice hitched, but she soldiered on. "Your mother. In my heart, I know she lives in Heaven now."

When Taryn offered her hand, Lillian clutched it within her grasp. They sat in silence, tears rolling down both their faces.

After a long moment, Taryn confided in the woman beside her. This stranger, who was also her aunt. "I came here, searching for my roots," she admitted. "I've always felt so ungrounded. So adrift. Can you—Can you tell me a bit about my mother? What she was like?"

Lillian leaned toward her, a conspiratorial tone in her voice. To Taryn's surprise, she wore a smile. "I can do better than that. I can introduce you to her."

"What? How can that be?" In spite of her best intentions, Taryn pulled back just a bit. Was this woman deranged?

"Wait here. I won't be but a few minutes."

"But—"

"Wait here, Taryn Clark." Lillian stood from the swing and adjusted her long skirts and apron. Just before slipping her eyeglasses back on, a shy smile stole over her face. "My niece."

Taryn's mind was full. Her brain actually hurt from the overload of unending questions, unexpected answers, and the enormity of them all. When her head became too heavy to hold upright, she propped it against the swing's chain for support. Too overwhelmed to process the information, she rested her eyes and concentrated on calming her still-clamoring heart.

That was how Lillian found her, ten minutes later.

"Are you asleep?" she asked softly, fearful of disturbing her.

Without opening her eyes, Taryn replied, "My mind is too busy to sleep. In fact, I may never sleep again."

"Then I bring you reading material for those sleepless nights." There was almost a playful lilt in her voice, which snapped Taryn's eyes instantly open. Lillian smiled, holding a cloth-covered book toward her.

"What is that?" Even to her own ears, her words sounded suspicious.

"One of your mother's prayer journals. I thought you might like to read it."

"Are you kidding me? I'd love to!" When she reached for it with eager hands, Lillian laughed aloud.

"I thought you might appreciate that. It will be almost like meeting her in person."

"Well, not really," Taryn said with a frown, even as she thumbed through the pages. She recognized the writing imme-

diately. The loose, flowing script was so precise, yet so graceful. Exactly like the letter from the jewelry box.

If she still harbored any doubts about Rebecca being her
birth mother—which she didn't—this journal dispelled them.

"Well, I have chores to do, and I suspect you have an afternoon of reading ahead of you. Do you need anything in the
cottage? Fresh towels? More linens?"

"I've barely gotten settled. Everything is perfect but thank
you."

"Very well. Again, if you need anything, knock at the
house."

When Lillian turned to go, Taryn stopped her with a heart-
felt acknowledgment. "Thank you. Thank you for giving me
this. It means the world to me." She hugged the journal to her
heart, already bonding with the young girl who wrote it.

"I hope the journals give you the answers you seek."

"Wait. Journal*s*, as in more than one? There are more?"

"*Jah.* And letters, too."

"Really? Can I read those, as well?" she asked, the excitement glowing in her violet eyes.

"All in good time. Patience, my Taryn Clark. Patience."

CHAPTER 11

From the Journal of Rebecca King

My name is Rebecca King. My teacher says the best way to learn perfect English is to immerse ourselves in it. Im-merce. I like that word. It reminds me that I am (I'm) surrounded by our Lord's great mercy. I am immersed in it.

A benefit to writing my journal in English is that my younger siblings (we learned that word today) Lillian, Rose, Abigail, and John cannot read English letters yet. I can keep my thoughts to myself. Josiah and Gilbert read, but they have no interest in the foolish ramblings of their twelve-year-old sister.

Thank you, oh great and mighty God, for our blessings. Thank you for my family and my siblings. Even the nosy ones.

❖❖❖

Today I helped my mother with baking. (It is hard to remember not to call her Mamm, but teacher says we must write entirely in English.) It will be our turn to host Church next week, so the cleaning and the baking are well underway! The men brought the bench wagon yesterday, so my brothers are busy mucking out the barn and cleaning it. Mother says it must shine! When they are done, we will line the benches up for the service, in nice, even rows. Little John is old enough now to sit with the men, and not with our mother on the women side. He missed last service because of his cough, so he is excited to be among the men next week. It is sometimes hard to be excited about a three-hour service, preached entirely in German, while sitting on a hard, backless bench. At least he has this small accomplishment to look forward to.

Thank you, oh great and merciful Lord, for all of life's small pleasures.

✣✣✣

Twenty snitz pies. Ten apple pies. Two gallons of smear cheese. Two gallons of peanut butter spread. Twenty loaves of bread. We have whipped and fluffed, beaten and kneaded, baked and cooked.

Thank you, our dear Lord, for letting it be over. Tomorrow is Church.

Further pages in...

Today is my thirteenth birthday. Mother made my favorite meal and my very own chocolate shoofly pie. My best friend Con-

stance came for dinner. She gave me a new bookmark, one she crocheted herself. Her stitches are so neat and even, unlike my own. I would much rather spend my time with the horses than with the crochet needles.

Please give me patience, dear Lord, to count neat stitches and showcase your talents and mercy through my humble hands.

✦✦✦

An English came today, to see my father's horses. He drove a silly-looking little car, no bigger than our courting carriage, and not half as tall. I wonder how he folded his long legs to fit inside the cramped space. It must feel strange, sitting so low to the ground!

He asked to buy one of Daedd's (here the word was marked through and corrected with its English translation) Father's horses. They talked for a while, and the man examined each horse with care. Before he drove away, they shook hands, so he must have purchased Sweet Sage. I will miss her.

Dear merciful Lord, please watch over the man who is buying our horse and guide him in caring for Sweet Sage. She is one of my favorites. Please help me to remain humble and ever grateful for your many blessings. Amen.

CHAPTER 12

The journal continued throughout that year and part of the next, offering snippets and insight into her mother's pre-teen life.

Lost in the pages of flowing script, Taryn had no concept of time. The shadows of the day lengthened, and still she read on. She moved from the gazebo to the deck. When darkness fell, she moved indoors to the couch. She snacked for supper, finishing the journal well before bedtime.

By the time she crawled into bed, she felt a new connection to the woman who gave her life. She still had no idea why Rebecca had given her up for adoption. Why she checked into the hospital under an assumed name, or why she was so paranoid about being discovered. Taryn still didn't know why she left the farm in the first place, or why she never returned.

But there were so many other things she knew about her mother. She knew that she favored the color red. She knew she liked to read, and that she adored horses. Rebecca spent as much time as possible in the barns, combing the horse's manes and grooming their slick, shiny coats until they shone. She gave them all names, even when their official papers registered them under more auspicious-sounding monikers. She dreamed of one day owning—or of marrying a *man* who owned—a horse farm of his own. Rebecca adored her father, but she hinted at things she would do differently, if the choice were hers.

The journals offered Taryn not only a glimpse into her mother's thoughts, but into her everyday life. Living on a farm, her childhood was vastly different from the one Taryn had known, and yet it seemed that eleven and twelve-year-old girls were much the same, no matter where they lived or what their faith. Rebecca worried about the same things Taryn had worried about at that age, had enjoyed many of the same pleasures as her, and shared similar tastes and opinions. Even though Rebecca was raised Amish and Taryn was raised with no particular faith, they still had much in common.

Her birth mother, it seemed, had a mischievous nature and a witty personality. Though often subtle, both shone through in her writings. More than once, Taryn laughed aloud at some of her musings.

And when Taryn crawled into bed that night, the most amazing thing happened.

She slept. Soundly and peacefully, with the journal tucked safely beneath her pillow.

The same scratchy sounds awoke her the next morning. The preliminary garble of the rooster nudged her from sleep, as the fowl tested his vocal chords, warming up for his big performance. By the time he unfurled the first of his perfectly enunciated wake-up calls, Taryn stood at the coffee pot.

She treated herself to another morning on the deck, where she once again watched the sun make its grand appearance as the busy farm came to life. She tried familiarizing herself with the people she saw, wondering if she would ever have the opportunity to meet them. They were her family, after all.

She was still adjusting to the thought. No matter how many times she took it out and tried it on, the reality still fit like someone else's clothes. How could something be too constricting, and too large, at the same time?

For an only child who spent over half of her childhood shuffled from foster home to foster home, and with no one to call her own, the thought of suddenly having family—and so much of it! —was overwhelming. The very thought threatened to swallow her whole. The concept was too big.

Knowing that her family was of the Amish faith manifested an entirely different emotion. They may as well have been from Mars. She couldn't imagine anyone being more different from her. These people, this family of hers, spoke a different language than she did. They wore different clothes than she. They drove buggies, when she drove a motor vehicle. They grew their own vegetables and milked their own cows, when she simply ran to the grocery store to fill her refrigerator, the one run by electricity. They depended on propane and solar panels to operate their necessities. Taryn relied on the power company to run her gadget-oriented, device-riddled luxuries. Their restrictive lifestyle, dictated by their faith but adopted entirely by choice, felt two sizes too small. The concept of Amish roots was too confining.

So where did this leave her? Completely and utterly confused, and still pondering the magnitude of it all when Susannah appeared with her breakfast basket.

At the sight of the young woman, Taryn immediately brightened. "I hoped you would come again today," she greeted with a smile.

"Hot from the griddle," Susannah confirmed, but something was missing from her smile. It lacked the vibrancy from yesterday.

"Are you feeling well today, Susannah?" Taryn asked in concern.

She dipped her head to admit, "*Mamm* says I'm not to bother you again today."

"You aren't bothering me. I enjoyed our visit yesterday." Taryn pulled out the chair next to her. "Please, have a seat. You can keep me company while I eat."

Some of the enthusiasm returned to her smile. The girl eagerly took the offered seat and pulled items from the basket. "You're in for a treat today. *Mei Grossmammi* made her special hotcakes this morning."

Taryn wasn't sure whom she referred to, but she didn't question her. She had another line of questioning in mind. "Yesterday, you asked me about my life in the city. I thought today could be my turn."

The young woman made a face as she brought out a bowl of freshly whipped butter and a decanter of syrup. "My answers won't be nearly as exciting as yours, but that seems fair."

"Tell me about your church services."

"Good choice," Susannah muttered, only half under her breath. "We'll get the most boring item out of the way first." Taryn hid her smile as she continued. "Church is a long affair. Three hours, every other Sunday, on a hard pew with no back. The preachers deliver prayers and two sermons, and the congregation sings from our *Ausbund*. Everything is in German. After service, we have lunch. We don't have church buildings, so church is held in our homes. On the off Sundays, we visit other churches or relatives. Each family in a district has a turn at hosting, so your turn comes around every year or so. Good thing, too. Preparations for your turn are quite rigged!"

"You mean rigorous?"

"If that means scrubbing and cleaning, sweeping and mopping, polishing and shining, cooking and baking, and being so tired at night, it hurts to even close your eyes, then, *jah*. Preparing for church is very rigorous."

Rebecca had shared much the same sentiment in her journal. Taryn couldn't help but smile.

"How do you fit so many people in your home? How many are even in a district?"

"That's what that room is there, yonder." Susannah pointed to the long, window-filled room behind them. "When it's not our turn to host, it is a workshop and storage. Next month, we will begin cleaning it out and getting it ready for our turn, two months from now. It's the only way to hold so many people at one time. With twenty-five or thirty families in our district, and each with so many children, it requires a large space."

"Speaking of large families, how many brothers and sisters do you have?"

"Four brothers and three sisters."

"There are eight of you?" Taryn gasped. "No wonder I see so many people milling around outside!"

The young woman misunderstood the term. She was quick to correct her friend. "Oh, we don't mill our grains. Not for food. In late summer, we harvest silage for our animals. We chop up the full cornstalk—husk, ears, and all! —for the silo, but we buy our cornmeal and flour."

Not wanting to embarrass her, Taryn rephrased her statement. "That's a lot of people for one house to hold."

"Oh, it holds more than just us. *Der Grossdaadi un die Grossmammi* live here, too. It was their house first. When my parents married and started having so many babies, *Grossdaadi un Grossmammi* moved into the back house and gave the big house to *Daedd un Mamm*. My oldest brother Samuel is married and lives in the east side."

Taryn turned to study the construction of the house. "Is that what all the roof lines and additions are about?"

"*Jah.*" Susannah pointed out the section of home occupied by each family unit.

A thought occurred to Taryn, tripping her heart into another of its crazy patterns. "Are your grandparents your father's parents, or your mother's?"

"My father's. My mother's family lives on the farm next to ours. When her eldest brother took over running my grandfather's horse farm, he and his family moved into the main house there."

Did Susannah realize the grandfather she spoke of was Taryn's, too? Her words were so casual, so off-handed, but these were Taryn's *relatives* she spoke of! Family she never knew existed. Family who, most likely, had no idea that *she* existed.

Those were pieces of a whole other suit of clothes. Taryn wasn't at all certain she was ready to try them on for size just yet.

Taryn asked a dozen more questions, most that touched upon things Rebecca referenced in her journal. She inquired about daily chores, and a few of the customs she didn't understand. The young woman was able to explain some of them, but others were beyond her grasp. She simply knew it was a tradition among her people or sanctioned by their bishop. She did not question the wisdom behind the rules. Like any good Amish girl, she simply obeyed.

"It is time for my chores," Susannah announced reluctantly.

"I'm sorry if I kept you, but I enjoyed our talk."

"As did I."

"Tomorrow, it's your turn to ask the questions," Taryn promised.

The girl grabbed up the basket and turned to go. "I will make a list!" She grinned before disappearing down the stairs.

Taryn was still smiling, long after she was gone. She was truly fond of the girl. Her enthusiasm and fun personality were a joy to be around. Given to her own bouts of depression, Taryn knew positive influence was good for her.

She kept thinking of Susannah as a girl, but in truth, she was a young woman. Their latest conversation revealed she would be seventeen on her next birthday. Her body, poorly hidden beneath the bulky dresses and uninspired aprons, revealed that fact upon first sight.

Seventeen, Taryn recalled, was the same age Rebecca had been when she disappeared from the farm. Within the year, Rebecca had been a married woman and a mother.

What came after that was anyone's guess.

Determined to find out the full story behind her mother's disappearance and subsequent death, Taryn pulled out her phone and typed in Bryce Elliott's cell number. Was he still in Florida, or back in the Keystone State? He said he wouldn't be back in the office until next week, so she guessed he was still out of state. After a moment's consideration, she composed a text.

This is Taryn Clark. I don't mean to disturb you, but I have made progress on my end. I now have a full name for my birth mother. Rebecca King. Surely, this will help.

She went back in to make another cup of coffee. On her return, she was surprised to see a reply from the private investigator.

It should. But do you have any idea how many Kings there are in Lancaster County?

She typed a quick reply.

I'm guessing quite a few.

Then, remembering the dark luster of his eyes and the way their thoughtful gaze released the butterflies in her stomach, she kept typing.

But I wouldn't begin to usurp your area of expertise. Isn't that what you PIs do? Dazzle us with statistics and facts?

She started to erase her comment, but the damage was done. She had already hit send.

Taryn bit her lip, wondering if she had overstepped her bounds. Bryce Elliott didn't seem the particularly playful sort. He might not respond. Worse, he might respond with a crisp, professional reminder that he hadn't yet taken the assignment.

The bubbles of a reply in progress appeared almost instantly. She held her breath, dreading the worse, hoping for the best.

To her relief, she could almost hear the smile in his response. Maybe Bryce wasn't such a stick in the mud, after all.

We have a large repertoire, actually. We also dance to the tune of insecure wives, suspicious business partners, and greedy family members. Occasionally, we even combat crime.

She shared the next news with a big smile plastered across her face.

Speaking of family... I have one!

Again, his reply was immediate. A stray butterfly wandered into her stomach.

You've been a busy girl. How did this come about?

The sigh came through with the text.

Long story. I've found several pieces to the puzzle, but they don't complete the picture. I need your help.

This time, there was a slight lag in his response, but the bubbles soon appeared.

I'll be back on Tuesday. We'll talk then.

She smiled again.

Thank you.

As an afterthought—and perhaps because she hated to end their connection, tentative though it was—Taryn added,

Safe travels.

He replied with,

Have a good weekend.

When he added his own afterthought just a few moments later, she cautioned herself not to read more into than it was.

Update me as needed.

CHAPTER 13

Lillian appeared at her door an hour later.

Taryn greeted her aunt with a warm smile. "Hello. Come in."

"I'm sorry, but I can't visit just now. I hate to bother you, but could you move your automobile? I must use the carriage."

"Of course. Just let me grab my keys." She noticed the anxious look on the other woman's face. "Is something wrong? You look flustered."

"Don't mind me. Just an unexpected complication to my day. I have much to do, and now I must fit in a trip to town."

"How long does that take you, by the way?"

"Travel alone takes almost two hours, each way."

Taryn hesitated only briefly before making her offer. "Would you like me to take you? It would save so much time. You're allowed to ride in automobiles, right?"

"*Jah*, we are allowed. But I can't ask you to do this for me."

"You didn't. I offered."

Indecision played upon the Amish woman's face. "I would have to ask my Peter."

"I tell you what. I'll go ahead and get ready, and if he says yes, I'll be more than glad to take you."

"That is very kind of you."

"Not a problem. Oh, and here's the journal. You have no idea how much I appreciate it. Do you have more for me to read?"

"I'll bring another when I come with my answer. And you keep that, at least for now."

The gesture touched Taryn. "Are you sure?"

"You're Rebecca's daughter. It's only fitting."

Lillian returned a half hour later, bearing a smile, a purse slung over her shoulder, and two more cloth-bound journals. As tempted as Taryn was to snatch the journals from her hand and begin reading, her offer stood. Reading would have to wait.

Once they were in the car and headed in the direction Lillian pointed, Taryn asked, "Where are we headed?"

"I have two stops, I'm afraid. I must go by the pharmacy for my mother-in-law and pick up more therm-gel at the grocer. The Lord's bounty has been good this year, and I've canned more jelly than anticipated."

"I'll be happy to take you to as many places as you'd like. The more, the better, to make the most of your time."

Lillian peered at her in surprise, her eyes once again hidden behind her light-progressive glasses. "Are you sure? You have no plans for the day?"

"None whatsoever. Although, I have wanted to do a bit of shopping in the area. Today is the perfect opportunity."

"I imagine you wish to shop for trinkets and treasures, not paper goods and canning supplies!" Lillian said with a spurt of laughter.

"It will be a new experience for me. And I'm always up for something new."

"You are like Rebecca, in that regard. Life was an adventure for my sister." Lillian peered out the window, her mood turning melancholy. "We are taught not to covet, but I envied her of that. She was so full of curiosity and enthusiasm."

It sounded like someone else they both knew. "Like Susannah?"

"*Ach*, that girl." Lillian shook her head with a smile, the affection obvious in her voice. "*Jah*, she is so much like Rebecca. Please, do not let her pester you. Tell me if she's asking too many questions."

"I've enjoyed my visits with her." Taryn drove in silence until she ventured to say, "I'd like to meet your other children, too. And your husband. Do you think that's possible?"

Instead of giving her a direct answer, Lillian said, "They will have questions, you know. When they see your eyes, they will know."

"Do they even know they had an Aunt Rebecca?" It hurt, somehow, thinking her mother may have been forgotten. Or

worse, that she had been overlooked, her memory too insignificant to acknowledge.

Lillian dispelled that worry. "They know I had a sister that I
loved and lost. They don't know... the rest."

"Neither do I, Lillian," Taryn reminded her softly. "I still
have so many questions."

Her answer was enigmatic. "In time, Taryn Clark. In time."

⁊⁊

The day was, indeed, a new experience. Taryn received a
crash course in Amish culture.

The first stop was at a CVS Pharmacy, where they picked
up the elder Mrs. Zook's prescription. Taryn didn't know what
she had expected, but it wasn't this. *This* was a mundane, everyday experience, the same as anyone else might have. They
pulled up to the drive-through window, waited for the refill,
and Lillian paid by debit card. It was completely at odds with
the image of the woman sitting beside her, with her Plain
clothes, ugly black shoes, and face devoid of makeup. If Taryn
hadn't known better, she would think her passenger was
plucked from the early part of the last century and deposited
there in her front seat.

They dropped by a hardware store, where Lillian picked up
new canning jars and a few extra cylinders of propane.

A visit to a fabric store yielded spools of thread, five yards
of dark-green material, and two packages of snaps. Taryn
learned that the Amish had little use for buttons; they relied
upon straight pins, gripper snaps, and hooks and eyes to secure

their clothing. This, she realized, explained Helen's account of Rebecca's overcoat from the morning she was born.

They stopped at a fast-food chain for lunch, where Taryn discovered her aunt's weakness for tacos and spicy salsa. As an afternoon snack, they indulged in ice cream.

Their last stop was to an Amish-owned grocery store, where there were no overhead lights and the coolers were powered by propane. Taryn had to take off her sunshades to see, but she averted her eyes when they passed other shoppers. The lighting was dim enough that her own eyes were hidden in shadow. She tried her best to be inconspicuous, but she saw the children stare at her in curiosity, intrigued by *her* strange wardrobe and hairstyle.

By silent accord, Taryn kept her sunglasses on during most of their excursion. There was no need to stir gossip among the locals. And if today was any indication, the Amish engaged in chitchat and idle speculation, the same as every other culture on earth. Taryn and Lillian were privy to some of those conversations, as her aunt stopped to visit with friends she knew and to exchange pleasantries with some she didn't.

For her part, Taryn did her best not to ogle the horse and buggies hitched to the posts out front. It was still such a new experience for her, seeing these Plainly dressed women stroll the aisles alongside *Englisch* shoppers. She did so serendipitously, but she peeked into their shopping carts, finding they purchased many of the same items she, herself, would buy. Everything from toiletries and personal hygiene products, to greeting cards and batteries, to junk food and snacks.

She was smiling by the time they drove from town, back toward the farm. The day had provided her with an excellent lesson that she would be wise to remember. Despite their differences in so many areas—religion, culture, language, dress, and customs, to name but a few—people were still basically the same, the world over. They all craved creature comforts, even when they used different parameters to define them. They all needed food and shelter, even if some of those shelters were void of electricity and most foods were grown at home. They all craved junk food, now and then. They all needed personal interaction and communication, even when it resulted in gossip and misinformation. They needed community.

"*Denki* for taking me today," Lillian said as they drove home.

"It was my pleasure. Honestly. I had a wonderful time today, seeing what your world is like."

A knowing smile played around the other woman's mouth. "And what did you think?"

Taryn laughed at her own prejudices and earlier misconceptions. "That despite appearances, your world is just like mine!"

"*Jah.* The truth is, Taryn Clark, we both share the same world. We simply see it through our own eyes, ain't so?"

"Absolutely."

After a moment of silence, Lillian turned toward her in the seat. "I have one more favor to ask of you."

"Absolutely."

"Will you have dinner with us tonight?"

A wide smile spread across Taryn's face. "That's no favor, Lillian. That will be my pleasure."

⁂

Dinner in the Zook household was a noisy, fast-paced affair. With so many people competing for the heaping platters of food set along the long trestle table, it was easiest to pass plates, pile on food, and toss hot rolls through the air. Sandwiched between Susannah on her right and Deborah, the girl from the chicken coop, on her left, Taryn was too busy listening to the various conversations and watching the antics of Lillian's brood to fully enjoy her meal.

Not that it wasn't delicious. She had no idea how Lillian had done it, particularly when they spent most of the day in town, but the woman had managed to lay out a veritable feast. There were platters of cold roast beef, bowls of stewed tomatoes, cream peas fresh from the garden, mashed potatoes, and hot yeast rolls, alongside smaller dishes of pickles, peppered cabbage, jams and jellies, freshly churned butter, and soft cheese. Dessert was an assortment of homemade pies and a large package of Oreo cookies that disappeared like mag-ic.

All through the meal, the sounds of laughter and conversation circling the table captivated Taryn. At one point, a heated discussion escalated into a screaming match between two of the teenage boys, until their father said just one word. A firm 'hush!' was all it took to settle the argument. But Taryn had loved even that, because it was the sound of *family*.

Just as quickly as the food had been passed and devoured, the table was cleared, and the dishes done. Taryn offered to help, but her hostess would hear none of it. She assigned her mother-in-law and little Emiline to give her a tour of the house while she and her daughters tidied the kitchen.

The house was a study in simplicity and function. Nothing was out of place. There was a place for everything, with little excess and no accumulated junk. The floors were so clean, Taryn was certain she could eat off them. She was surprised to find that despite the stark absence of *stuff*, the rambling farmhouse was warm and inviting. She attributed this to the generous use of color and creativity in the many quilts, runners, and hand-looped rugs displayed in every room. There were no photographs on the walls, but there were a few watercolor paintings, most depicting pastoral scenes, flowers, and animals. Framed samplers quoted Bible passages and inspirational quotes, and decorative calendars graced several walls.

By the time they returned to the sitting room, Friday game night was underway. Several tables were scattered throughout the room, the action visible by overhead gas-powered lights. A rousing game of *Sorry!* occupied one table, while another hosted a round of *Yahtzee*. The men gathered to play a game of dominoes, and in one corner, the youngest children played *Candyland*.

"What shall we play?" Susannah asked Taryn with a smile. "I favor *Pictionary*, even though I struggle with some of the words."

"Don't worry," Taryn assured her. "So do I."

"Then we'll be one team, and *Mamm*, Melanie, and Caroline will play against us. Deborah, we need you on our team. You are a good artist."

To their credit, no one mentioned the obvious relationship they had with their English guest. If five people in the room shared the unique violet eye color, no one commented on the fact. Granted, there was little time for visiting. Each table was engrossed in their game of choice.

And when Lillian announced it was bedtime, no one complained. The younger children immediately put away their games, said their good nights, and disappeared into their bedrooms. Accustomed to the wailing and fits of protest displayed by Molly's children and others Taryn had been around, the calm order of acceptance was dumbfounding. She made a note to ask Lillian her secret, so she could share it with her best friend.

"You do not have to leave," Lillian offered, even though the room had cleared out like magic.

"After that wonderful meal and all the excitement of the game, I'm more than ready for bed," she assured her hostess.

"Very well. It is rather late."

In truth, it was not late at all, but Taryn was polite enough not to mention the fact. She knew the Amish held to an early to bed, early to rise schedule. When she moved toward the door, Lillian followed.

"I want to thank you, Lillian, for inviting me into your home. You have no idea what tonight has meant to me."

"It was our pleasure."

Emotion moved into Taryn's eyes and clogged her vocal chords. "Everything was amazing. Thank you so much for including me."

"We're family, ain't so?"

By the time Taryn stumbled up the stairs to her room, happy tears streamed down her face and blinded her path.

Back in her room, it was too early to go to sleep, and too late to read. She knew if she started another journal tonight, she wouldn't have the good sense to stop. Restless in the too-quiet room—doubly so now, without the chatter and hustle of the house next door—Taryn decided to call Molly and give her an update.

When the call went to voicemail, she did the next best thing. She sent a text to Bryce.

It was odd, she reflected, how the anonymity of a simple electronic device masqueraded as a layer of protection. There was a time when letter writing was an art form and considered quite intimate. The most sensitive subjects, the most important of questions—the most magnanimous of announcements—held to the time-honored tradition of the revered letter. Receiving a letter had been *special*.

Then along came the electronic age, and all of that changed. Emails invaded the landscape, cheapening the effect of a well-executed letter. Who needed hand-written papers, sent at the mailer's expense and at the postal service's mercy, when one could send an email instantly?

And when that became too slow and bulky, along came the text. It was even faster, even more efficient. Poor grammar and non-existent punctuation were suddenly acceptable. Brief, catchy acronyms were standard. Despite the message—from hirings and firings, to marriage proposals and break-ups, to formerly taboo subjects and this new art form called sexting— texts had become so common, they were now considered mundane. Safe.

Lured now by that false safety net, Taryn sent her message. It didn't matter that in person, the man had been little more than professionally polite to her. Despite the way his gaze lingered just a second too long, despite the tiny smile that finally appeared just before she left, his attitude toward her had been almost aloof.

That was in person. Through the magical realm of the cell phone, his texts had been witty. Borderline playful. Approachable.

And he had invited her to update him.

She was merely doing as he asked, she assured herself.

It's been an enlightening day. I'm learning so much about my family. I still can't get over that word. Family.

His text came back within the minute.

I'm glad one of us had a productive day.

It seemed like the most natural thing in the world to reply with,

Tough day at the office?

The familiar 'dear' was silent, just as his chuckled reply was.

You could say that. Your day sounds more interesting. Tell me about it.

Taryn curled up on the couch and took him at his offer.

I have an aunt. Cousins. A houseful of noisy, rambunctious cousins. And I love it!

Bryce:

How did you find them?

Taryn:

The eyes.

Bryce:

Ah, yes. Those eyes.

It was crazy, how an unspoken text could *sound* so sexy. She could hear his voice in her head, as surely as if sound resonated from the screen. The sudden flight of a dozen butterflies sent a shiver scattering across her skin.

She didn't realize a full two minutes had elapsed, until she saw his text.

You still there?

Taryn:

My father was French. Ahndray Lamont. He was deported before I was born. How do I find him?

Bryce:

Let me do some digging. I'll see what I can find.

Taryn:

My aunt believes that my mother is dead. Gone, before I even found her!

She immediately followed the statement with a raw admission.

This isn't how I thought it would go.

Bryce:

It seldom is. That's why I avoid these kinds of cases.

Taryn fingered the journals awaiting her. The first journal had been endearing. Enlightening even, offering her a glimpse of her mother's personality. Would these offer something more substantial? Would these offer answers as to why her mother disappeared?

She turned back to her phone.

But you'll help me, won't you? I've found names, and some of my family. But I haven't found the answers I came for.

His answer was long in coming. Taryn knew he had read the message, but it took a while before he wrote back. She could hear the reluctance in the words.

Yes, Taryn. I will help you.

CHAPTER 14

When Susannah brought the breakfast basket the next morning, she made a rookie mistake. She squandered prime question-asking time by reliving the highlights of last night's game. Taryn laughed along with the young woman, finding the memory every bit as delightful as she did.

The girl didn't know it, but the truth was that Taryn spent much of the overnight hours, replaying every aspect of the previous evening. The memory of laughter and loud, healthy belches even saturated her dreams.

The family dinners in her past were nothing like the one in the Zook home. The only thing to come close was the meals shared with Molly and her brood, and even those were different. Try as she might, Taryn couldn't recall ever enjoying a meal—at least, not its atmosphere—as much as she had last night.

Over the years, she tried to forget the time spent in foster care. Last night, however, she had deliberately dredged up some of those memories, purely for comparison sake.

The first family she lived with was a blur in her mind. In retrospect, she realized they had been nice enough, but she was too overwhelmed with pain and sorrow to give them a chance. The older couple had given up on her before she could break through the crippling haze of grief and respond to their kindness.

Dinnertime with the second family, the McNaughtons, had been a formal affair. Children were to be seen, and not heard.

The Shannons had executed mealtime with military-like precision. All nine children in their care were lined up, trotted along the bar cafeteria-style, and issued a tasteless meal with strict caloric guidelines. The children had mess detail while the Mr. and Mrs. enjoyed their gourmet meal. Once the kitchen was clean, it was bath time and lights out. There was never such a thing as family game night.

The Goodman family had a game night, of sorts, but it never included the children. If it wasn't poker with a bunch of smelly men who reeked of cigar smoke and alcohol, or private 'couple games' when the scantily clad Mrs. Goodman seduced her husband without regard to privacy, the couple went out on the town, leaving the younger children under the care of eleven-year-old Taryn and their thirteen-year-old son Donnie.

Donnie, on the other hand, had plenty of suggestions for games. He tried to teach her a game he called 'Hide the Weenie.' One night, the boy, stronger than her, caught her off guard and insisted she play. Her savior turned out to be one of the smelly poker men. He dropped by unexpected, found the children unattended, and one of them about to be raped. Taryn was removed from the Goodman household that night.

There were three more families in staccato succession after that, each worse than the one before. Taryn had no idea how much money people made for taking in foster children, but those next three were desperate for whatever cash they could rake in. There must have been a shortage in the system, because no decent social worker would have given children to those people, unless there was no choice. At two of the homes, they were lucky to be fed dinner. At the other, it was usually junk food eaten in the car, on the way to conduct a 'business deal.' It didn't take a genius to know they were selling drugs, but it took over a month for the cops to catch on.

Her time with the Sternenbergs stretched miserably long. Dinner with their clan was noisy, but the atmosphere was never happy. Stan Sternenberg was the most miserable human being Taryn ever had the displeasure of knowing. He made it his life mission to assure that those around him were every bit as miserable. Dinnertime was prime fodder for yelling and ridicule. God forbid someone spill a single drop, even of something as innocuous as water, on Mrs. Sternenberg's pristine white tablecloth. It meant laundry detail for the week, corporal punishment, and solitary meals in the kitchen.

More than once, Taryn deliberately spilled her water glass. Sitting through a meal with Stan Sternenberg was by far the greater punishment.

The only mealtimes Taryn remembered even remotely comparing to last night's happy, noisy affair were at the Michelin household. Over the years, she had been sloughed-off on so many families, she could no longer remember all their names and faces, even when she wanted to. The Michelins were the only ones she ever felt an attachment to. Her first year there was promising. She had hopes of living out her foster time there, staying until she graduated high school and left the system. She liked her school, made good grades, and had friends. When their busy schedules allowed, the family sat down for dinner together and occasionally had movie night, complete with popcorn and candy.

Then Bob moved in. Bob was Jennifer Michelin's brother, and from the very beginning, his presence there put a strain on the family. Homer Michelin didn't like his brother-in-law, and he made no efforts to pretend otherwise. Taryn overheard the couple arguing one day, quite by accident. Homer didn't want the man in his house, not after 'what he's done,' but Jennifer begged him to give her brother one more chance. It was all a big misunderstanding, she claimed. Poor Bob, always the underdog, was innocent of the charges.

That was only the beginning of countless arguments. The couple quarreled all the time after that, too consumed with their own bickering to notice the way Bob began leering at Taryn. Dinnertime was a tense affair, when Bob eyed the teenager as if she were dessert. Taryn stayed out of the house as much as possible, testing the limits of her curfew and skipping what few movie nights remained.

When she awoke and found Bob in her room one night, staring down at her, she never said a word. He claimed he was half-asleep and turned into the wrong room, so she chose not to make a big deal of it. The Michelins fought so much, as it was. Why add to their stress? She worried they would end up getting divorced, and where would that leave her?

But it happened a second time, and then a third. He never laid a hand on her, but even in the dark, Taryn could see where his hands were. Whether his sister wanted to acknowledge it or not, Bob was a sick man.

It was the beginning of the end. Taryn lay awake at night, too afraid to close her eyes. At school the next day, she was too exhausted to keep her eyes open. Her grades took a direct hit. Word filtered back to the Michelins, which caused a new round of arguments. Before Taryn found the courage to speak up and tell her foster parents what was happening, eleven-year-old Kailey woke them all up screaming one night. Uncle Bob had visited her room, too, and he hadn't been disciplined enough to keep his hands on himself.

It all came out after that. Bob had a more sordid past than his sister realized. He was a repeated sex offender, and his being there cost them not only their foster care license, but also their family's innocence, and, so Taryn later heard, their marriage.

By then, she was shuffled off to a new family. She couldn't remember their name.

The countless parade of so-called 'homes'—with their dysfunctional families and their dysfunctional mealtimes—left Taryn scarred and cynical. Last night's dinner with the Zook family was a special treat for her. It showed her what life could be like, surrounded by a true, loving family.

By the time Susannah launched into her volley of questions, Taryn was through eating. The young woman was halfway through her list (yes, she actually made one) when her father called her name.

"Susannah! You need to help *die Mamm!*" Peter called from below.

She made an exaggerated face. "*Ach!*" she wailed, but on-ly loud enough for her companion to hear. "I've barely started."

"Rookie mistake." Taryn grinned at her.

"Susannah!"

"Coming, *Daedd!*" She quickly grabbed up the empty dishes and stuffed them into the basket. "*Mamm* is making pickles this morning, and I must help."

Their lively talk and reminiscing of the game left Taryn in a playful mood. Violet eyes twinkling, she made the girl a deal. "I'll grant you two questions in the morning. But only if you promise to bring me a piece of pie from last night."

Susannah perked up, her own eyes revealing the same violet sparkle. "Deal! What kind?"

"Pie is pie, right?"

Pushing in her chair, she warned, "Snitz pie may be an ac-quired taste. I'll bring peach or strawberry."

"Sounds delicious. Have fun canning."

With her morning companion gone, Taryn eagerly pulled out the journals. She found the one sequential to the first one

she had read and settled in for a day of reading, but her playful
mood soon soured.

She found that the tone of the journals had changed.

From the Journal of Rebecca King

*The man with the funny little car came again. This time, he
came with a truck and trailer, and he left with three of our horses.
He pulled out the largest stack of money I have ever seen, and he
handed several of the bills—dozens! —to Father.*

*Dear and generous Lord, please bless the man and keep him
safe, so that he might return and share more of his wealth with
our family.*

His generosity brings this thought to mind:

The joy you give to others is the joy that comes back to you.

♦♦♦

*Little John continues to cough. The sound echoes in his lungs
and rattles his small chest and turns his face purple. He has not
grown as he should. He's four now, and still wearing clothes
meant for the cradle.*

*Please, sweet Jesus, heal my little brother and make him whole.
In your precious name I pray, amen.*

♦♦♦

*I heard my parents whispering again tonight, after the house
was dark and quiet. Their voices sounded sad. When Little John
began his nightly cough, I heard my mother crying. Please, Lord,
lay your hand upon this child and make him well.*

✦✦✦

We have tried everything we know for Little John's cough. My parents have finally taken him to a doctor in the city. I know my father is worried how he will pay for it, so I will say a special prayer that the English man returns, even though I don't think I like him much. Forgive me, Lord, for my uncharitable thoughts. Please send the man back for more horses.

✦✦✦

One of the horses is sick. I asked Father what is wrong with her, but he did not answer. The mare had a strange look in her eyes. They looked glassy and wild, as if she had a fever. I hope it is not contagious. With Little John still so very sick, the horses are the one bright spot in my day. It's been so long now, over a year, and still my little brother coughs and cries, and grows weaker each day.

Sometimes, I see that same glassy look in his eyes, and it frightens me.

✦✦✦

I think I made a mistake. I prayed for the man to return, and he did. But I heard him arguing with my father. Father never raises his voice, but he did today. I will no longer pray for the man to return. I will pray for someone new to buy our horses. Someone who is kinder and gentler. I do not like the way this man touches the horses, or the way he forces them to run. I do not like the way he speaks to my father, no matter how many bills he pulls from his pocket.

I try to keep charitable and positive thoughts in my mind while the man is here, like this one:

Live in such a way that if anyone should speak badly of you, no one will believe it.

***

The mare has that look again, and this time, she truly went mad. She crashed through the fence and trampled the hay field. She tangled herself in the clothesline and destroyed a day's worth of laundry. Her cuts are deep, and her eyes are still glassy.

The saddest sound in the world has to be the echo of Father's gun, echoing through the hills as he put the mare out of her misery.

***

I was wrong. I heard the absolute saddest sound in the world tonight. I shall never forget it.

Little John's cough was worse than ever. I heard my father pacing the floor, and my mother sobbing. The sounds of his cough reached a frightful peak, and then gradually grew weaker.

And then, there was no sound at all.

***

Today is my fourteenth birthday, but we are not celebrating. Today, we are turning our dear, sweet Little John over to God's eternal care. Lord, please bring peace and healing to our family, and to my mother, whose heart is most surely broken.

CHAPTER 15

The journal ended there. After reading the heart-wrenching entries, Taryn had to get out for a while. She took a drive into town, but the roads were busy on a Saturday afternoon. Tourists clogged the otherwise sleepy backroads and crowded into the quaint shops and businesses.

Still seeking an outlet for her dark mood, Taryn visited one of the malls in the area. After the rainstorm the other day, she was short one pair of pants, and she had few to spare. She could do a little shopping and hopefully shake the gloom that settled upon her shoulders like a heavy cloak.

An hour or so later, Taryn exited the stores.

Although normally not one to believe in retail therapy, she had to admit that even with two bags dangling from her arms, her shoulders felt lighter already. Maybe there was something to the phenomenon, after all.

A cluster of people gathered outside the complex, and a television news van sat squarely in her path, blocking the way to her car. Curious as to what the commotion was about, Taryn stopped to look.

It appeared to be a ribbon cutting for a new restaurant. Now that she thought about it, she could eat. She had skipped lunch, lost in the pages of the journal, with only a slice of strawberry pie to fill her belly. Maybe she could hang around long enough to get an early table.

A dozen or so people posed for the cameras, their smiles practiced and overly bright. Two men balanced a gigantic pair of golden scissors between them. A beauty queen, or so the sash stretched taunt across her ample bosom claimed, took center stage, her smile the brightest of all.

With all the fanfare of the local dignitaries and the pretty girl, Taryn couldn't even see the name of the restaurant. She shook her head with a mild sense of amusement.

Any amusement she may have felt promptly died when she caught sight of one of the scissor bearers' faces.

"What is *that man* doing here?" she muttered between clenched teeth. He was like a bad penny, turning up where she least expected him.

Taryn ducked her head and scurried away, before Thomas Baxter saw her there in the crowd. With that man's ego, he would surely think she was there for him, following him around like some political groupie!

No doubt, this all tied into his upcoming bid for public office. It never hurt, being seen with beauty queens and small-town officials, particularly while welcoming new businesses to

the area. He would probably be kissing babies next, and helping little old ladies across the street, whether they wanted to
cross, or not.

Feeling her dark mood returning, Taryn decided to treat
herself to dinner, at a restaurant far, far away.

Or, at least, one town over.

☙❧

Back in her room, Taryn tried on the clothes she had just
purchased. She had nothing better to do, and the ego boost
might keep her spirits buoyed. An excellent meal, followed by
an even more excellent glass of wine, had gone a long way in
doing its part to lift them. Trying on the figure-flattering outfits might push her cheerful meter right over the top.

Taryn studied herself in the full-length mirror. So maybe
without the specialized lighting—and after that delicious but
fattening meal—the outfits didn't look quite the same now, as
they had earlier. But they still looked fairly good, and she
needed the additions to her closet.

Yes, she decided, they would just have to do. She peeled
the blouse from her body and snipped off the tags, before she
could change her mind. Her phone dinged as she padded
across the room in only her underwear.

Her cheerful meter pegged out when she saw Bryce's name
on the screen.

Any new relatives today?

A smile touched her face. Today, he was the first to reach
out. That had to account for something.

Not yet, but the night's still young.

Bryce:

Really? Feels late.

She plopped down onto the couch and typed a reply.

Another hard day?

Bryce:

Taking depositions. Always long and tedious. Headed down to the pool to relax. How was your day?

Reluctant to tell the truth, she went with an amended version.

Ended well. Did some clothes shopping and discovered an amazing restaurant.

She could all but hear his chuckle.

I didn't think those pants would survive.

Taryn laughed at the reminder, knowing she must have looked a fright that day.

They're goners. Bought a nice, mud-proof gray.

There was a brief lag in response. So much for scintillating conversation. She was an idiot, discussing her sad little wardrobe with the man.

Her phone finally binged.

Looks hot.

Taryn's breath caught in her throat. She threw a hand over her scantily covered chest, clad only in a lacy bra. Her fingers flew frantically across the screen.

You can't actually SEE me, can you?

Bryce:

No.

Then,

What are you wearing?

She gasped. Even she knew the sound was only part outrage. The other part, she had to admit, was just the tiniest bit
of thrill. Was he *sexting* her?

Okay, a fourth bit thrill.

Half, tops.

When the screen remained blank on her end, he wrote
again.

It was a joke. A bad one, at that.

And a typo before that. Should say pool's hot.

Taryn wracked her brain for a smart comeback. She
couldn't let him know how the ill-fated joke affected her.

Too bad.

It was all she could come up. To clear up any confusion, she
inadvertently made matters worse.

About the pool. Not about the joke.

She could practically hear him laughing at her. Her cheeks
flamed in embarrassment, even though he, blessedly, could not
see her. His reply came with a built-in chuckle.

We'd better quit now, before we get ourselves in real trouble.

Was he being a gentleman, saving her from further humilia-
tion? Or was this line of conversation simply too outrageous to
continue?

Either way, she wrote back,

Agreed.

Bryce:

Say good night, Taryn.

She followed his instructions.

Good night, Taryn.

With that smart reply, she fell sideways on the couch and buried her heated face into the pillow.

CHAPTER 16

From the Journal of Rebecca King

I wonder if our world will ever return to normal. It's been almost a full year since Little John passed, and still we mourn. Mamm is not the same. There is an emptiness in her eyes. If the eyes are truly a window to the soul, it does not bode well for our family.

***

The man came again today. It has been so long since he was here, I hoped he had forgotten us, but no such fortune. I overheard him arguing again with Father. I couldn't hear the words, but I know the look. Father is not happy. The man is smug. And Mother still weeps at night when she thinks we don't hear.

***

Samuel Stoltzfus has asked me to Sunday singing with a group of friends. I am not quite fifteen and do not wish to go, but Mother says I should spend more time with people my own age, and less time with the horses. I suppose I must go, if only to make her happy.

✦✦✦

I have completed my eighth-grade studies at school and am moving on to three-hour school. Unless I'm needed at home or have a job elsewhere, the state says I must go, once a week, until I turn fifteen. I must also keep a journal, which I do. At my next birthday, I may stop my schooling, but I like getting out of the house, if only for a few hours a week.

✦✦✦

Today, Samuel stopped by for a visit, but I am not interested. He is nice enough, if he can hold his complaints to himself.

While in Samuel's presence, I often think of Father's favorite quote:

There is no sense of advertising your troubles. There's no market for them anyhow.

✦✦✦

I find that I like keeping a journal. With my education behind me, it is no longer required, but I think I shall continue.

Constance tells me that Samuel was seen last week, swooning over Beatrice Lapp. I think they make a perfect couple. Both boring as a stick, and skinny as one, to boot.

Since this is no longer a prayer journal, I do not have to ask for Gott's forgiveness for my wicked thoughts or worry about writing strictly in English. But I know my thoughts are uncharitable, so Gott, please forgive me.

✦✦✦

The man came again today. He has traded his funny little car for a long, shiny model. He thinks it makes him look important. Was there a time when I prayed for this man? This toad? He is full of hot air and self-importance, hopping around and issuing orders, expecting everyone to do his bidding. Why does Father not send him away? Why did I ever want him here to begin with? I wish he would leave, and never return, but he is my father's best buyer.

He always has money. He thinks money means power. He tries to push my father around.

Today, I was in the barn when they came in. I did not mean to hear, but they did not see me, and I did not want to disturb them.

The man said my father must do something. Whatever the something is, Father is reluctant. He said he regretted ever agreeing the first time, but the man only laughed. He said he paid my father well for the deed, whatever it was, and that my father owes him. I know Father dislikes being beholden to anyone, least of all this toad. I wish there was something I could do to help, but I am only a girl.

So I will wait, and I will listen. And I will never trust this man.

✦✦✦

Thought for the day:
Think all you speak, but speak not all you think.

Mamm says I should begin to consider my rumspringa. I will be sixteen soon, and several boys have invited me to Sunday singing, and on carriage rides. Robert Beiler has a car now and asked me to go riding with him. Samuel continues to stop by, uninvited.

Oh! Constance and Rueben are a couple now. I am happy for my friend.

Mother is steadily improving. Some days, she is almost jubilant. The mood swings are unpredictable, but they are beginning to level out. The emptiness is gone from her eyes, but I'm not certain I like its replacement. Something seems odd about it.

Father spends more and more time with the horses. Word is spreading about the fine quality of horseflesh he raises. People come from all over now to buy them and are willing to pay top dollar.

Sadly, the man still comes.

Molly returned Taryn's call on Sunday evening. The farm had been quiet all day, as the family had attended Church at a neighboring farm. It had been just Taryn and the journal, so she welcomed the interaction.

Besides, she had missed her friend.

"When are you coming home?" Molly wanted to know.

"I'm not sure. I'll be here at least the rest of the week."

"Whatever are you finding to do down there? Aren't you going out of your mind, with no television?"

"Honestly, I haven't even noticed. I've been quite busy, actually."

"Doing what? Don't tell me you've gone to milking cows!"

Taryn made a face through the phone, even though her friend could not see it. Molly knew only the basics. She knew Taryn had discovered her birth mother's name and located some of her family, but she didn't know her friend was staying with them.

"No. They use automatic milking machines for that. But I did help Deborah gather eggs this morning. It was actually rather fun," Taryn admitted with a giggle.

"Who's Deborah? The owner of the house where you're staying?"

"Her daughter. Lillian is the owner. She and her husband Peter. And there's something I didn't tell you before. Lillian is actually my aunt."

"Your aunt? Your *aunt*? You've actually met your family and you're just now telling me? Why would you do that?"

The answer was simple. Taryn had known her friend would react this way. With Molly, everything was loud and exaggerated. It was part of her sunny disposition. Taryn loved her dear friend to pieces, but sometimes Molly made things more complicated than they needed to be. Taryn was a fan of simple.

She needed simple in her life right now. With so much being thrown at her, she needed the quiet and solitude of simple, even if it meant keeping this new phase of her life from Molly.

For once in her life, at least since she was a little girl, Taryn had a family. It may have sounded selfish, but she wanted to savor it to herself for a while.

She explained things to Molly now, pausing several times for her friend to make exclamations and interject her thoughts on the subject.

"So what now? What will you do next?"

"I'm reading my mother's journals, searching for some clue as to why she disappeared. I'm also learning about the person she was." Her voice warmed with affection. "She was pretty cool, Mol. I know we would have been close, if things had been different."

"Did you ever hear back from that private eye? Is he going to help you? Or do you even need his help now? It sounds like you've learned the things you went for, without his help."

"I haven't even started. Sure, I know the names of both my parents now, but that's all I know. I don't even know for certain if my mother is dead. Lillian believes she is, but we have no proof. And I haven't even read the letters yet. I'm still working on the journals."

"What letters?"

"The ones my mother sent home to my aunt."

"This is sounding all rather complicated, Tar. Are you sure you're up to it? Do I need to come down for a couple of days?"

"Thanks, Molly. I really appreciate the offer. But this is something I need to do on my own. Well, with Bryce's help, maybe."

"Bryce? Wait, who is Bryce?"

"The private detective I contacted. In answer to your earlier question, he's agreed to help me. And yes, I definitely need it. I've only just begun to scratch the surface." Her eyes strayed to the second journal, still only partially read.

"You'll call me if there's anything I can do?"

"Of course."

Her friend still sounded doubtful. "Well, if you're sure..."

"I'm sure, Molly. But thanks, all the same."

"Taryn? You know if this doesn't work out with your new family, you still have ours. You're always welcome here."

Tears swam in her violet eyes. "Thanks, girlfriend. That means the world to me."

⚜

When Bryce texted her an hour later, Taryn was in a mellow mood. He picked up on it immediately.

Something wrong?

Her answer was evasive.

A bit overwhelmed, I think. It's starting to catch up with me.

Bryce:

Understandable. You've had a lot on your plate.

She waited a few minutes to write again.

I think I'll go to bed now. Good night.

Bryce:

Good night, then.

Instead of going to bed, Taryn picked up the journal.

CHAPTER 17

From the Journal of Rebecca King

Something is not right, but I cannot put my finger on it. Some days, Mother is fine. Happy. Then she will go off into a rage. It ends with her taking to her bed. The house will go unkept, and I must do all the cooking and washing. I don't mind, except that this is so unlike our Mamm. And then, just like that, she will be happy again. Almost giddy.

✦✦✦

I still worry about Mamm. If I did not know better, I would think she indulged in spirits. There are times when she gets down-right silly, like a giddy child. Much like Robert Beiler and Peter Sams, when they go in Robert's car to one of their parties. They come back smelling of alcohol and acting as foolish as children.

They took me once, to one of the parties, but I did not like it. I did not like the taste of beer. The music was too loud and the dancing too frenzied. I much prefer to stay and work with the horses.

***

He came again. This time, it was early in the morning. Father was not happy to see him. I heard them arguing, so I followed them into the barn. The man gave Father two small packages. He said one was for my mother, and one for the horses. Why ever would this man bring a gift to my mother? I do not trust him. And why does he bring sugar for the horses? We have cubes of our own.

He used the word 'partners,' and I thought my father might strike him. I have never seen my father so angry. He said they would never be partners and demanded that the man leave. The man laughed, but he finally left.

Father went into the house, and soon, I heard my mother laughing. I suppose she liked her gift, whatever it may have been.

***

Today, the man brought someone with him. The second man took my breath away. He was the most beautiful specimen of mankind I have ever seen! A stallion amongst stallions. A race-horse amongst plow mules. He was tall and dark and speaks with the most amazing accent. His eyes flash like black gems, his hair is as black as a raven's wing. Simply put, the man is beautiful.

This man, this dark and dashing stallion, runs circles around the silly boys who beg me to go riding. Although I wish the English man would never return, I pray that his companion does.

***

He did! He did return! He came alone this time, without the toad. His name is Ahndray Lamont, and he is from France, of all places. He has applied for work here, even though Father told him he is not looking for a hired hand. He is a true gentleman and speaks excellent English. He also speaks softly to the horses, which I adore.

I hope Father changes his mind and hires him.

***

They have returned together this time. Ahndray and the toad. The toad and my father had a long conversation, while I showed Ahndray the horses in the lower field. Father did not look happy, but there was no shouting this time.

The toad brought my mother another gift. Why does Father allow this? Is it because it seems to make my mother happy? I do not understand.

***

Father has spoken to the Bishop, and he has approved Ahndray's hiring. I am delighted to have him here each day. He will live in the room behind the barn, which I have tidied up and made presentable. He has an automobile, a shiny red car that puts Robert's car to shame, but he does not mind riding with me in the *carriage or the two-wheel cart. He is so good with the horses and has already proved a great help to Father.*

✦✦✦

The toad returned today. He spoke for a while with Ahndray, his manner as cold and aloof with him as it is with my father. He thinks he is the boss of everyone. I heard him say he needs more horses. Faster horses, and that my father must provide them. He insists that they must be ready for racing in just a few short weeks. Ahndray will barely have time to break them in or get them into shape. I did not like the way the toad insisted it be done on time.

I'm not sure, but I think he made some sort of threat to my father. I am deeply troubled over this.

✦✦✦

I am spending more and more time with Ahndray. He reads me poetry and brings me silly little presents, like a single flower or a delicately shaped leaf, or a pebble that is smooth and polished. He found one shaped like a heart, and as he pressed it into my hand, he pressed a kiss onto my lips.

I think I am in love.

✦✦✦

Robert Beiler and Samuel Stoltzfus are foolish, silly boys. They are jealous over Ahndray and have spread tales about him. I don't listen to their foolishness. I love Ahndray, and he loves me.

Even if my mother insists I attend Sunday singing with Samuel. I shared with Ahndray this old wisdom:

A wise man lays a firm foundation with bricks that others throw at him.

CHAPTER 18

Taryn read late into the night.

The stories about her father fascinated her. Some of the entries went on for pages, describing each and every detail of a day spent in Ahndray's company. Rebecca made even the most mundane activities sound romantic.

The other stories filled her with dread. She inexplicably knew she was on the verge of uncovering a deeper, darker secret than any of them had imagined.

Susannah noticed the difference in her demeanor. Taryn answered the questions she asked, but she had few of her own. The younger woman filled the mealtime with idle chatter, sharing a few stories about Church the day before. Some of them were amusing, even though Taryn knew none of the people involved.

"I'll leave you be, then," the girl offered, after collecting the dishes. Taryn had hardly touched her food. "You didn't like the baked oatmeal?"

"No, it was delicious. Honestly, it was. I'm just not very hungry this morning."

"You're feeling fine?" Susannah asked in concern.

Not wanting to tell a lie, Taryn avoided a direct answer. "I have a lot on my mind right now. I'm afraid I didn't sleep well last night."

"The bed is lumpy?"

"The bed is fine. It's just me. Honestly, Susannah, I'm good." She hoped her half-hearted smile was convincing.

"Very well. We're about to do laundry. Do you have anything you wish to wash?"

"I can do it. Would you like me to come down and help?"

Though not unkindly, Susannah laughed at the suggestion. "You have not seen *der weschmachien*! It is a wringer style, powered by gasoline, but we also have a spinner."

"On second thought, I'll use a laundromat," Taryn murmured.

"Or give it to me to do. I don't mind. In fact, I insist."

It was easier to go along with the insistent young woman than to argue with her. Before she left, Susannah stripped the bed and gathered dirty towels, carrying them along with Taryn's personal laundry.

The delay left Taryn feeling antsy. She wanted to return to her reading.

She had barely started when her phone binged, and she saw Bryce's name on the screen. So far, their texts were confined to evenings. She wondered if something was wrong, even as she opened the message.

Does your father spell his name Ahndray or Andrae?

She quickly replied, her pulse ticking up a notch.

Ahndray. Have you found him?

Bryce:

Maybe. Still looking.

Eager to share her concerns with someone, Taryn wrote back.

I may have found something, too. I have so much to tell you, and something I need to show you.

His reply was quick in coming.

Sounds a bit ominous.

Biting her lip, Taryn replied,

That's what I'm afraid of.

When no other message came through, Taryn returned to her mother's journal.

From the Journal of Rebecca King

I learned a new word today, and I do not like it. Doping.

Apparently, there are people who give drugs to their horses, to make them perform better. This is a vile practice, used only to bring riches and fame.

Many of our horses have had success at the races. Big races, not just those here in Lancaster County. Ahndray does an excellent job in training the animals, but now those silly boys have started rumors. Samuel and Robert, sometimes others, have ac-

cused my Ahndray of giving the horses something to make them run faster. *Performance drugs, they called them. Doping.*

⁕⁕⁕

I have begged my mother to see a doctor. Something is clearly wrong with her. Her hair has lost its shine. Some of the roots have lost their hold on her scalp. I saw her as she put on her prayer cap, and she is all but bald in one place! I told her I would take her to see Dr. Travis, but she refused. She said she was fine, but I see the way her hands tremble. Her movements are jerky and her skin, once so clear and soft, is now marked with sores.

Please, oh dear and gracious Gott, lay your loving hands on my mother and heal her, body and soul, so that she may become your faithful servant once again. Please save her, oh Lord.

⁕⁕⁕

Most nights, I have trouble sleeping. Between worries for my mother, and my father, and now Ahndray, my mind is troubled. It keeps me awake, spinning out of control.

The toad continues to come. I have asked my father why he must do business with this man, but he told me not to interfere. His words were harsh. My father seldom raises his voice, and never to me.

Today that changed.

⁕⁕⁕

There is a strain between my father and me. This troubles me greatly. I have always been close to him, but there is something between us now. I think of it as a wart, left by that toad.

✦✦✦

My father saw Ahndray and me today, down by the lily pond. It was only a few kisses, but my father was clearly unhappy. He asked me to stop seeing Ahndray. I asked him to stop seeing the toad. He made no comment, just turned and walked away.

✦✦✦

Mamm has been in bed all week. Perhaps I overstepped, but I went down to the telephone shed and called the doctor. I don't understand why, but when he arrived, Daedd sent him away. He said Mamm was just tired.

But of what? Lillian and I do all the cooking. Rose and I do the laundry. Abigail tends the winter garden. Mamm stays in her bed.

✦✦✦

Father asked me, once again, not to see Ahndray. He said it was time I thought about the future and committed myself to Gott and our faith. Ahndray, as he pointed out, is not Amish. Samuel, he pointed out, is.

I told him Samuel was a self-centered, ferhoodled boy. He is jealous of Ahndray. Why else would he start such cruel and vicious rumors about him? Somehow, Father had not heard. He was clearly upset when he heard the tales going round of doping. His face lost all color, before it turned a bright, angry red. He left before I could ask:

Was he angry at Samuel because he started the rumors? Or at Ahndray, because he believed them?

Samuel's pettiness brings to mind another wisdom:

Great minds discuss ideas. Average minds discuss events. Small minds discuss people.

***

Mamm took a fall last night. I have no idea what she was doing outside, and in the cold, but somehow, she came to be on the porch railing, and she fell. She cut her leg and has a banged-up knee, but she is blessed to have no serious injuries. Father gave her a special powder for the pain, and she seems to be resting peacefully.

***

Something is happening, and it makes me most anxious. The toad comes more often now, and I see him deep in conversation with Ahndray and my father. I have asked them both what they discuss, but they say it is business, and nothing to concern me. Sometimes I hear their voices rise in anger. The toad puffs out his chest and orders everyone around.

Yesterday, he saw me there in the barn, as I brushed down Midnight Royal. He told me to leave. Who is this bloated toad, to bark such orders to me? I left, but I did not go far. I heard him tell my father I shouldn't be allowed in the barn. Something about jeopardizing the project.

Ahndray came looking for me, and his dark eyes were troubled. He hinted that he might have to go away for a while, but that he will return for me. He says they have much business to do, and it is for a better future.

He has not asked me yet, but if he proposes, I will accept.

***

Thought for the day:

Being happy doesn't mean everything is perfect. It means you decide to see beyond the imperfections.

✦✦✦

Mamm sent Lillian and me to town today. She says her knee is still weak and she cannot do the shopping. We stopped to visit Constance and hear plans for her wedding. I am so happy for her and Rueben. I wish I was planning my own wedding, but Ahndray still has not asked. He seems more troubled these days.

Something frightening happened today while we were leaving town. I saw the car coming from behind, but I thought it would slow down. I did everything I was taught to do. I yielded right of way, guiding the horse as far to the right as space would allow. I had on my flashers. Still, the car came up fast and close, clipping the hub of our wheel as it passed. Old Bess bolted. If not for Lillian's help, I would have lost control of the reins and we would have been dragged into oncoming traffic. Together, we managed to stop her and get her under control.

We lost a bag of groceries and a year's worth of growth.

I do not wish to drive into town, anytime soon.

✦✦✦

Our near accident upset Father more than it should have. Of a sudden, he has become overly protective of me, saying I should stay near the house. At first, I thought it was to keep me from Ahndray, and our evening walks to the lily pond, or our occasional trips into town. But the fear in Daedd's eyes is real.

I suppose after losing Little John, he is trying to keep me safe, the only way he knows how.

CHAPTER 19

Taryn heard the whir of the washing machine's motor, even before she turned the corner and saw it there on the back porch. The women gathered around it, engrossed in the labor-intensive task of doing laundry for a family of fourteen.

Caroline, who was married to Lillian's oldest son, put garments into the spinner after pulling them from the washing cylinder. With most of the water now spun out, fourteen-year-old Melanie took the garments from the spinner and carried them to the clothesline, where she and Lillian hung them up to dry. Even little Emiline helped with the chore, sorting the laundry before it went into the water.

"Oh, *hullo*, there," Lillian smiled, seeing Taryn approach. "Come to watch, ain't so?"

She forced herself to laugh. "Only if you promise not to put me to work! You ladies seem to have this down to a science. No doubt, I would mess things up."

"We have plenty of practice."

Taryn watched for a moment, amazed at how efficiently the women worked. She couldn't imagine doing laundry this way, not when there was a host of modern machines that made the task so much easier and faster.

After a moment, she made her way to the clothesline. "I know you're busy, but I was hoping to speak with you for a moment."

Lillian glanced down at the basket, still half-filled with sheets that needed attention. "Help me hang these bed linens, and I can take a short break," she decided.

Taryn gladly offered a hand. It struck her that she must make an amusing sight, working alongside these Amish women. Their dark, solid dresses and work aprons were at direct odds to her tailored slacks and patterned blouse. Their hair was twisted and pinned into buns beneath crisp work kerchiefs, while her honey-brown tresses scattered in the breeze. More than once, she had to push the stray strands from her eyes. Perhaps there was something to the bun, after all.

"There, now, that didn't take long," Lillian said in satisfaction. "Melanie, I think I'll take a short break. I'll bring us all a glass of iced lemonade when I return."

She led Taryn through the back door, into the kitchen. She motioned for her guest to have a seat at the table while she prepared their drinks.

"I'm sorry to disturb you, but I felt it couldn't wait," Taryn apologized. "I've finished the journal." She watched Lillian's face, waiting for her reaction as she added quietly, "What was there, anyway."

Lillian's hand faltered, splashing a bit of lemonade onto the counter. Her movements were jerky as she reached for a dishcloth. She had spilled only a few drops; she mopped the counter long enough for a full gallon.

"Lillian. The last pages of the journal were missing. Torn out. Do you know what happened to them?"

When she still did not answer, Taryn stood, her fists clenched at her sides. Her voice was urgent. "Lillian. Do you know where those last pages are?"

The movement was slight, but Taryn detected a nod. Lillian reached for the glasses, steeled herself to face her niece, and slowly turned around. Her feet were heavy as she brought the lemonade to the table. Her heart was heavier.

"Have you read the journals, Lillian?" Taryn asked, her tone softer now as she sank back into the kitchen chair.

Her aunt nodded in acknowledgment.

"You took them, didn't you?" Taryn guessed. "You tore the pages out, so that no one else would see them."

Again, she nodded. Her words were barely audible. "No one could ever know."

Taryn placed her hand over her aunt's, drawing her eyes to hers. Violet to violet, even behind the lenses. "Where are they, Lillian? Do you still have them?"

"Yes." It was a whisper.

"May I read them?"

She saw the panic in her aunt's eyes, the way they rounded in horror and fear.

"It's okay, Lillian," Taryn said softly. "You don't have to hide the truth from me. I know about your mother." Seeing the pain and worry there in the lines of her aunt's plain face, Taryn squeezed her hand and continued, "I can't imagine the pain of losing a child. I know your mother was clinically depressed. She certainly wasn't the first person to turn to unprescribed drugs for help, and she'll hardly be the last. I know your father was only trying to help her."

Lillian gasped with surprise. "How—How did you know?"

Taryn envied the innocence and naivety of these sweet Amish people. "Oh, dear Lillian, the signs were all there. The mood swings, the nerves, the sores on her face. Wandering out in the middle of the night, no doubt thinking she could fly. She was addicted to cocaine. And the Toad gave it to her."

The faintest hint of a smile feathered along Lillian's mouth. "I had forgotten that name. My sister had a vivid imagination, and a sharp tongue, at times."

"Reading her journals, I feel as if I know her. Oh, how I wish I had!" Tears sprang to Taryn's eyes, burning in their intensity.

Lillian sniffed away her own tears, but when she spoke, her voice steeled against emotion. "You were wrong. The Toad did not give the drug to my mother." Her voice hardened. "My father did that."

Taryn wasn't certain she wanted to defend the man. She still had mixed opinions about her grandfather, but her mother had obviously loved him, even when she disagreed with him. While the jury was still out on whether he deserved such a gesture, Taryn nonetheless spoke on his behalf, "He thought he was helping."

"At first. But over time..." Her voice trailed off, fading into a sad silence. She sniffed again, speaking with difficulty. "I know the Bible preaches forgiveness. *Gott* does not like us to hold a grudge, or to feel bitter toward one another. This hardness I feel in my heart is a sin. But because of my father, I lost both my sister, and my mother."

Taryn came here searching for family, for roots, and so far, she had found an aunt and cousins, but no mother. It was too late to have a relationship with Rebecca. Could she bear it if her grandparents were gone, as well?

"Is—Is your mother still living, Lillian?"

The older woman played with her untouched lemonade, studying the condensation that formed on the sides. She rubbed a thumb through the moisture, her answer slow in coming. "Yes, and no. Her body lingers, but her mind... Her mind has been gone for too long. Burned away with the drugs, the doctors say. Shuttered away from the rest of the world. She doesn't speak. Doesn't respond to our touch, or to the sound of our voices. She merely exists."

"At home?"

"At a facility in Ephrata."

"I'm so sorry, Lillian. That must be so difficult for you. For your entire family."

"I tell myself she is at peace now, no longer mourning the child she lost. The *children* she lost." Her sad eyes met Taryn's. "Shortly after your mother disappeared, she took an overdose. She's not been the same since."

"What about your father? Is he still—?"

Lillian shook her head. "Complications from an accident, a year after Rebecca left."

"Such heartache," Taryn murmured.

Her tone was resigned. "We all have our burdens to bear."

Taryn reached for the hand idly playing with the glass. "I know this is difficult for you, but I need to see those torn-out pages. I have to know what happened next."

The thought obviously still troubled her, but Taryn pressed on. "Please, Lillian. I have to know."

Her aunt drew in a long, unsteady breath. Without another word, she pushed back from the table.

She was gone for a length of time, no doubt pulling the pages from their secret hiding spot. When she finally returned, she carried a small bundle of jagged-edged papers atop several tattered envelopes, bound together with a faded red ribbon.

"This was your mother's favorite ribbon," Lillian said as she handed the stack to her niece. Her hand trembled only slightly less than her voice. "I've kept it all these years, but I'd like for you to have it now."

"You really don't have to, you know," Taryn protested softly.

"I have my memories of her. You deserve this, at least."

Taryn hugged the ribbon-bound papers to her, the tears already gathering. A few slipped over her lashes and made a slow trek down her cheek. "You have no idea what this means to me. Thank you, Aunt Lillian. I can call you aunt, can't I?"

Lillian's smile was indulgent. "Nothing would please me more, niece of mine."

CHAPTER 20

From the Journal of Rebecca King

Mamm is not getting better. She begs for more medicine. I have rubbed her knee in peppermint oil and made a poultice of vinegar, comfrey leaves, and egg whites, just as I learned from her. I bring her warm milk, sweetened with honey and a sprinkle of nutmeg, just the way she likes it. Nothing helps.

Today, she knocked the cup from my hand and begged me for her 'special powders,' the ones I saw Father give her after her fall. I want to help her, I want to take her pain away and ease the torture I see there in her eyes. But I don't know how much of the powder to give her, and there is so little left. Perhaps we should save it for when the pain is worse.

I pray we won't need it.

✦✦✦

The toad came again today. He brought a small package with him. I suppose it is another gift for my mother. I should appreciate his thoughtfulness, but I do not like the thought of another man giving presents to Mamm. Even if Daedd knows about it, it seems wrong.

+++

When I went in to say good night to Mamm and bring her evening milk, I saw it. I am certain it is the package from the toad, but Mamm is calling it her special powder, and she wants me to give her some with her milk. I didn't know what to do, so I pretended to hear Daedd calling, and I quickly left the room.

+++

These days, I often remind myself:
God doesn't give us what we can't handle. God helps us handle what we are given.

+++

Ahndray and the toad had a terrible row this morning, and Ahndray says he must leave. I'm not sure I understand. He works for my father, but the toad seems to have some strange control over him. It has something to do with his own father, but the details are not clear.

He has finally asked me to marry him. How can love be so wonderful, and so terrible, all at once? I love Ahndray and want to be his wife, but I can't leave Mamm, not until she's better. Even Daedd's shoulders, once so strong and wide, have begun to shrink inward. He walks with a hunch, and he is not yet fifty. His eyes, once so much like mine, are a stormy purple now, and filled with shadows. I feel that my family needs me, even though my heart longs to be with Ahndray.

He promises he will wait for me. He has found a job in the Village of Intercourse and will save up the money for us to be wed, as soon as I feel I can leave.

I reminded him of this truth, but he says we must be practical: A man is rich according to what he is, not what he has.

❧❧❧

It has been a harsh winter, and I am so ready for spring. Without Ahndray here to brighten my days, I find other ways to keep busy. Lillian and Rose are such a blessing, taking over most of the household chores for Mamm, who shows no improvement. My brothers tease me, because I have chosen to start spring cleaning early, and I have started in the barn. I remind them, cleanliness is next to Godliness.

❧❧❧

I found the oddest thing in the barn today. A handful of syringes, tucked into a satchel and stuffed behind a board, practically buried beneath the haystack. Why would someone store medicine in such an odd place? And what sort of medicine is it? I suppose it is for the animals. I shall ask Father tomorrow. He has gone to the horse auction today, with some of our cull mares. I know it is a sin to be prideful, but even our culls far outshine the best of the horses at die Vendyu.

❧❧❧

I am so confused. And if I am truthful, I am afraid.

I asked Daedd today about the medicine. I had the syringes in my hand, showing him what I spoke of, when the toad arrived. He took one look at me and flew into a rage. Daedd told me to go, but I only pretended to leave. I tiptoed back in to hear what they were shouting about.

The toad said he had warned my father about me being underfoot all the time. He said if Daedd didn't take care of it, he would, and the result would not be pretty. He said he had handled his son, and it was time for Daedd to handle his daughter. What that meant, I do not know.

The toad stood right in my father's face and yelled at him, shaking his finger in anger. I know it is not our way to fight, or to indulge in confrontation, but it took great faith, and true inner strength, for my father not to respond in kind.

Just before the toad left, he said something very strange. I couldn't hear everything he said. Matilda chose that moment to moo out a greeting, hoping I brought a bucket of grain. I heard something about my mother, and I knew the words upset my father. And then he said something about my carriage incident. He said it would be a shame if I were seriously injured the next time, or worse.

It was the way he said that last part. 'Or worse.' I don't know why, but I think the toad just threatened my life.

✦✦✦

I'm crying so hard I can't see the lines to write upon. I suppose it does not matter that my words are crooked and sprawled across the page. This may be my last entry for a while.

I must leave. It breaks my heart to go, at a time when Mamm still needs me and Daedd is looking so frail. But Daedd says this is the only way.

He won't tell me the full story. I know there is more, but he says I only need to know that he did what he did (whatever it may be) to provide for his family. The doctor bills piled up for Little John, and he needed better care. He says he made a deal with the devil and now he has to pay for his sins. I think the devil is the toad. Father refuses to say. He says the less I know, the safer I will be. But he says he fears for me, and for my future. He hasn't said it, not in so many words, but I read between the lines. He fears for my life.

He says a good daughter and a good Christian will do as she is told, without questioning her elders, or her Gott. I have tried to be both.

So now I will go, because my father says it must be so.

He tells me not to worry. He will take care of Mamm and our family and keep them safe. He says his greatest fear is that he cannot keep me safe, as well. He would rather send me away than see me harmed. I don't understand, but I trust my father. I must honor his wish.

I'm not sure I can honor him on this: Father says I cannot trust Ahndray. He says I mustn't go to him, that he will only lead me to danger. I must pray over this. It seems prayer is now all that I have.

Daedd has given me money, a long, sorrowful hug, and his most humble apology. He begged for my forgiveness, and I gave it. How can I not?

I told Lillian I am going into town to buy Constance's wedding gift. Only Father and I know the truth. I will not be back for dinner, as I told her I would be. Not tonight, and perhaps not ever.

I don't know if I will ever return here, to my home, and to my family. I love them all so dearly.

My heart is in pieces.

⚜

Upon completing the journal, Taryn's heart was also in pieces. Shattered. Her emotions were fractured, so badly splintered she feared they might never come back together. There was a deep, aching void in her soul, and she wasn't sure it could ever be filled.

She couldn't face Lillian right now. She was too raw.

She couldn't stay cooped up in the room. It was too confining.

She couldn't drive. The tears made it too dangerous.

She set out walking.

She wandered down the lane, no destination in mind. Her feet turned left. Before she knew how it happened, she stood at the edge of the horse pasture.

Had her mother stood in this very spot? Gazed upon this very field? Were the horses grazing in the patch descendants from the same stock her mother had nurtured and cared for? Were they from the same stock her grandfather had doped?

Taryn had no doubt that was what happened. This went far deeper than young lovers running away to be together, only to be separated by immigration rules. This hinted at crime and corruption.

The Toad had loaned her grandfather money to care for his dying son, and then bribed him into doping his stock. Blackmailed him, no doubt, after getting his wife hooked on drugs. Then the Toad threatened his daughter's life when she stumbled upon the truth. Grandfather King—she didn't even know his given name, Taryn realized—did the only thing he knew to do to keep his daughter safe. He sent her away.

Had the sacrifice been worth it? There were so many unanswered questions. Taryn knew that despite her father's wishes, Rebecca found her way to Ahndray and married him. According to Lillian, he was deported before Taryn was even born, leaving Rebecca alone. Had she somehow managed to get to France and be with her true love again?

Taryn's splintered emotions were at war, teetering between hope and despair.

Was it possible? Could her mother still be alive?

Or had it all been in vain? Had the Toad somehow gotten to her?

It was almost incomprehensible, but deep inside, Taryn knew it was possible. Rebecca may have been *murdered*.

Close to hyperventilating, Taryn pulled her phone from her pocket. Her hands were unsteady as she pounded out a text to Bryce.

Have you located my father? Do you know where he is?

She preferred to go with the better theory first, before moving on to the darker—albeit more probable—scenario.

He responded as she was halfway up the lane.

Just landed. Caught an earlier flight.

Now was not the time to back off.

I really need to talk to you. I know you're tired, but can we meet tonight?

After a significant pause—she imagined him deboarding the plane and entering the concourse, unable to check his phone— he replied.

Seven. My office.

CHAPTER 21

Taryn had much too long to wait. She managed to work herself into a frenzy during that time, her mind running amok with possibilities.

She hadn't read the letters yet, but Lillian said they revealed few clues. Taryn wasn't sure her emotions could handle anything more in one day, so she chose to save those for tomorrow.

She dressed in her new gray slacks and a vibrant blue blouse that made her eyes pop. By the time she had paced the floor, impatiently thrown herself onto the couch at least five times, squirmed in the chair, and finally crawled into the car, only to sit outside his office until the clock showed straight-up seven, her blouse was unmercifully wrinkled. Her hair hadn't fared much better, tortured by her restless hands.

He opened the door just as she knocked. He had probably seen her sitting there on the curb.

"I'm sorry to barge in like this, dragging you out to your office the minute you get in, but I have to talk to you!" she said without preamble. She squeezed in under his arm, which still held the door.

Bryce looked as if he were caught in an unexpected tornado.

"I thought you were pizza," he admitted. He stuck his head out the door, his gaze sweeping the street before he followed the whirlwind into his office.

"I didn't even give you time to eat, did I?" Taryn fretted. "I know you must be exhausted."

Had she not been so focused on her mission, she might have noticed the similarities between herself and Susannah. She apologized again for intruding, even as she helped herself to one of the leather wingback chairs.

"So what couldn't wait until tomorrow?" he asked, taking his own seat behind the desk. Without the anonymity of the phone screen, he was back to that cool, aloof professionalism.

"I don't even know where to start," she admitted. "So you start. What did you find out about my father?"

He sighed and clicked a button on his desktop. Reading from the screen, he informed her of his progress. "I've found six men by the name of Ahndray Lamont that seem to fall within the presumed age range of 55-65. Does that sound about the right age to you?"

Taryn scrunched her face in thought. She assumed he was a few years older than her mother, since she compared the magnificent *man* to the *boys* she was accustomed to. If still alive, her mother would be in her mid-to-late fifties. "I suppose," she agreed.

Bryce turned back to the screen. "One is a surgeon in Brazil. One is a prison inmate in Georgia. Another is an artist in Paris. This one is a horse trainer just outside Bordeaux, France. Another is—"

"That one!" Taryn interrupted, scooting to the edge of her seat. "The horse trainer. That's him!"

He cocked a speculative brow but made no comment. After a few more clicks, he attempted to keep pace with the barrage of question she threw his way.

"This says he is the owner of *Roi Ecuries*, a world-renowned breeding and training facility for top-quality Thoroughbreds... He is the owner and trainer of *L'esprit de Rebecca*, who became one of the most famous race horses in France... He is a strong advocate for the humane treatment of animals... No mention of a wife here..."

"That's him! I know it is!" She bounced in the chair, unable to contain her excitement.

"That's all I can see, without doing a full-fledged search. Which will cost time and money." He turned his dark gaze directly upon her. "So tell me why I would want to do that, on this particular man."

"Because that's my father, I know it is. *Roi* means King, right? King was my mother's last name. And Rebecca's Spirit? How could that be a coincidence? Rebecca isn't even French."

"I suppose I see some logic in that," he granted.

Taryn pulled out her phone. "What's your printer's Wi-Fi code? I need to print some things out."

"And you struck me as such a meek little thing, that day we met," he muttered.

"I'm not always so pushy," she assured him, but there was no apology in her words. "But this is important, and there's no time for the normal pleasantries."

The doorbell rang as she accessed the printer via its wireless connection. "Is there time for pizza?" he asked, his tone just a bit sardonic. The papers were already printing as he rounded the desk.

He returned a few minutes later with a hot, steaming, aromatic pizza.

"Don't mind me," Taryn said, waving her hand in dismissal. "You go on and eat."

"Are you kidding? I can hear your stomach growling from here. When was the last time you ate?"

She collected the papers from the print tray with a vague, "I think I had breakfast."

"Follow me."

She did so, not thinking to question why. A second door led from the office and into the central hallway, well beyond the large potted plant acting as a detour. A smaller hallway led to a bright and airy kitchen, completely renovated for a modern-day cook.

"Wow, you must have some landlord!" Taryn whistled in appreciation. "We didn't even have a kitchen this nice at the law firm, and we owned the building."

"So do I," Bryce replied dryly. "This is also my home."

"Really? It's gorgeous."

"I like it."

He opened an overhead cabinet and withdrew two plates. As he gathered napkins and utensils, he nodded toward the refrigerator, "Help yourself to whatever you'd like to drink."

One look into his refrigerator dispelled any notion that he might be married.

"Let's see," she pretended to contemplate. "There's a choice of bottled water, beer, a half-empty jug of orange juice with something brown floating around on top, what looks like a very flat, fizz-less Coke, and ketchup. What shall it be?"

"I'm working. Water."

She pulled two from the cavernous space and cracked the seals. Bryce already had the pizza open and the plates laid out in the adjoining breakfast nook. Following the delicious aroma, she slid around the cozy banquette, leaving him the open space to accommodate his long legs.

"So tell me what you've discovered."

"I don't even know where to begin!"

"You can start with all these papers," Bryce suggested. He handed her a slice of pizza. "Hope you like pepperoni."

She held a hand to her face, only half-hiding the fact she spoke around a mouthful of pizza. "I'd better back up and start before that." She hadn't realized how ravenous she was, until she took her first bite of spicy goodness, smothered in cheese.

Taking a few bites of his own, Bryce waited for her to swallow.

"When I left here the other day, I went to check into the hotel down the road. They didn't have any vacancies, but the girl took one look at my eyes and said she knew an entire *family* with eyes this color!" She paused to let the words sink in.

She wasn't sure if it was for his benefit, or hers; the concept of having family was still so new to her. "Turns out, the family has a room to rent, and I took it."

He waited for her to continue, his expression expectant. Taryn took another bite of pizza, hastily chewing and swallowing. The sudden dew in her eyes could have been from gobbling down hot food, but he thought not.

"They're my family, Bryce," she said, the wonder of it softening her voice. "I have an Aunt Lillian, and at least eight cousins. Ten, if you count Caroline and the baby. I already adore them all, especially sixteen-year-old Susannah."

"Your aunt has eight children?" he asked in surprise.

"They're Amish," she said, as if that explained it. Which it did.

His eyes widened. "Wow. I didn't see that coming," he admitted.

"Neither did I." The edge taken off her hunger, Taryn settled back against the cushions to thoughtfully chew her second slice of pizza. "I know I'm rambling. I know I sound just like Susannah, bursting at the seams with enthusiasm. *Girlish* enthusiasm. The thing is, I was never like this, even as a girl." She knew he couldn't possibly understand. "Sometimes, I think I was born with an old soul," she admitted.

Bryce released a sigh and stretched out, settling his large body more comfortably into the space. "I know what you mean," he agreed. His tone said he understood better than she thought.

"This is so new to me," she continued. "I've never had a family before, and suddenly, I have a large, rambunctious family, and they're Amish, of all things! And I'm just so happy and scared and confused, all at the same time."

"I get the happy and the confused. But scared?"

Who would have thought this man would be so easy to talk to? He had the look of a seasoned military man. Everything about him screamed discipline. Formality. Protocol. But he had an intriguing voice, so deep and even, so... commanding. It spoke to her. Not just in the literal, but in the guttural sense. It stirred something in her, something sweet and low, and almost forgotten. It had been so long since she was physically attracted to a man, Taryn wasn't even certain that was what happened now. She thought it was something more meaningful than physical attraction. This man made her feel safe.

She turned toward him a bit, taking a chance on bearing her soul to him, this stranger. But they weren't quite strangers, not really. There had been a connection between them in those texts, as silly and irrational as that sounded. She chose to ignore all that and continued.

"It's what I've always wanted, what I've always dreamed of. And now I'm so close, but not really. It's like someone hands me an ice cream cone but tells me I'm not allowed to lick it. But if I don't, it will melt before my eyes."

The logic didn't quite make sense to the man watching her, but he understood her dilemma. "You're afraid of finding your family, only to lose them."

Her nod was sad. "If my mother is truly dead, I've already lost the opportunity to know her. My grandparents are gone, too. One died years ago, the other may as well have. Her body has long outlasted her mind." Taryn fingered the printed pages, still lying to the side of the pizza. "And if I'm right, I may be biting off more than I'm prepared to chew."

"Well," Bryce said, his deep voice both pragmatic and philosophical, at the same time, "you know the best way to eat an elephant."

The analogy made her blink in surprise. "No. How?"

"One bite at a time." He inclined his closely shorn head toward the papers. "Wanna tell me what those are?"

"Excerpts from my mother's journals."

"So you're pretty certain about these people being your family." It wasn't a question.

"Not a doubt in my mind."

He pushed the forgotten pizza box aside. "Why don't you show me what you have?"

"The life and times of Rebecca King, as told in her own words," Taryn explained, arranging the papers in chronological order. She had snapped pictures of the most important excerpts, at least as they pertained to the case. To her starving heart, each entry was sacred. "There's some letters I haven't read yet, but according to my aunt, they don't reveal much. Of course, she didn't realize these journals revealed as much as they did, either. She was surprised to know I could read between the lines and know that my grandmother was addicted to illegal drugs, most likely cocaine."

"Just to clarify, this was your Amish grandmother, right?"

"Long, sad, sordid story, as you'll see here. And apparently, my grandfather was caught up in a horse-doping scheme. It all started so innocently, of course, but it blew up into something huge and ugly and dangerous."

Bryce gave her a tight, sober smile. "You really know how to build up a story."

"It's more than a story, Bryce. This is my mother's legacy, the good and the bad. This is her life." She handed him the pages, not quite turning them loose. "What I hope it's *not*," she said, drawing a shaky breath, "is a blueprint to her murder."

CHAPTER 22

While Bryce read the journal excerpts, Taryn did a search on her phone for *Roi Ecuries* in Bordeaux, France. When a picture of Ahndray Lamont came up, she could understand why Rebecca had been smitten, all those years ago. Even now, he was a handsome man. Taryn thought she might have the shape of his nose.

It took a moment for her to realize Bryce had finished reading, and that he simply sat beside her, a dazed expression upon his face.

Misreading it, she hastily explained, "This is just a snapshot of the journals, to give you an overall gist of what I've found. It's by no means complete."

"It's complete enough."

Was that a good thing, or not? A bit nervously, she probed, "So, what do you think?"

Instead of answering, he had a query of his own. "One question. Is this for real, or is this an elaborate setup to make me hire you?" There was just enough of a glint in his eye to signal he was joking. It brought to mind his ill-fated joke about phone sex and what she was wearing.

"Why, are you hiring?" she quipped.

"If this is any indication of your investigative skills, maybe I should be."

She shrugged. "I'm not looking for a job, even though I happen to be freshly unemployed at the moment. And this isn't a display of any particular skill on my part. It's more like dumb luck. Or, if you believe in it, fate. Mostly, though, it's about being the one percent of the population with violet eyes."

"No matter how you came about it, it was good work. And it definitely paid off. This is some pretty heavy stuff," Bryce acknowledged.

"It's crazy, isn't it? I came looking for my roots, and I find *this*." She spread her hands to encompass the enormity of it all.

"Taryn." She heard the cautionary tone, even before she heard what he had to say. "Right now, all we have is a young woman's diary and her rendition of events, as she saw them. We have no proof. We have no way to prove this happened the way she wrote it."

She bristled immediately. "But it had to! Why else would she have been so frightened at the hospital? She was scared to death the Toad would find her! That's why she left in the middle of the night, and why she used an assumed name. You didn't read the whole journals. The heartache was real. She couldn't have made it all up!"

"Slow down, tiger," Bryce said calmly. He placed his hands over hers, as if to gentle her. "I never said she fabricated any of this. I said we have no proof. We don't even know who the Toad is. With no name, and no specifics, all we have right now is speculation."

"Then let's find it. Let's find the proof."

"And we will. But we have to go about this the right way. We can't just blow in and start asking a bunch of questions." His dark eyes probed her face. "You have to know how dangerous this could be."

Pushing her impatience aside, Taryn knew he was right. She acknowledged the wisdom of his approach with a solemn nod. "I realized that, the moment I read the journals."

"The Toad was obviously a rich and powerful man. The whole doping and horse racing scenario reeks of organized crime. He could be part of a drug syndicate. We have no idea who we're dealing with, who the Toad is, or if he's even still alive. But if we stir up too much fuss, someone's going to get wind of it."

Bryce curled his fingers over hers, forming the long, tapered digits into a perfect cocoon of warmth and protection. While the tone was gentle, she heard the ominous warning in his words. "If this man killed your mother to keep her quiet, he won't think twice about doing it again."

Her sigh was so deep, it could have been pulled from the soles of her feet. "I know."

They sat in silence for a moment, contemplating the dangers ahead.

"I suppose we should make a contract of some kind," she finally said. "I want it on paper, before you decide this is too risky and back out on me." She was only half-joking.

"I'll tell my secretary."

"Oh, you have a secretary?" she asked in surprise. She hadn't seen another desk. She wondered where she worked.

He tapped his chest. "You're looking at her."

"In that case, maybe I really will apply for a job here," Taryn teased back.

Keeping the conversation light, he eyed her in speculation. "So was your grandfather really Manuel King?"

"Honestly? I have no idea what his given name was. I didn't think to ask Lillian."

"If it is, he was known as having the best horses in the county. He built quite a legacy for himself. People still come from miles around, to buy a genuine King horse."

A frown dipped the corners of her mouth. "If his horses were so good to begin with, why the need to dope them?"

"Because for some people, people like the Toad, good is never good enough. They can't be happy unless they're pushing for more. And they'll get it any way they can."

Taryn turned to face him on the bench. "I know this may be a reach, but I'd like to run an idea by you. What if... What if my mother is still alive?"

"Taryn—"

"Just hear me out. My grandfather gave her money. He stressed how important it was for her to go away, for her own safety. What if she gave me up to keep me safe, but somehow made it to France? Maybe she's living her happily ever after with my father, away from the toad man and the dangers of knowing too much." She turned hopeful violet eyes to his. "It's possible, don't you think?"

Bryce hesitated for a long moment, before being honest with her. "Possible, I suppose. But not probable."

Her sigh bordered on defeat. "I know. But I think I would like to find out for certain, before I just assume she's dead."

To her surprise, he agreed.

"But how do we go about it? If she's in hiding, she won't be using her real name."

"We wouldn't want to put her at risk," Bryce acknowledged. "I suppose we could quietly check into Ahndray's private life. Find out if he has a wife, or a girlfriend. You don't by chance know anyone with connections to Bordeaux, do you?"

Taryn recalled a case they had handled at the law firm.

"Just one person, but I certainly wouldn't ask him."

"Same here. I know a man who has dealings there, but he's not the sort of guy I'd ask for help. He likes to have people beholden to him, so that he can use it to his advantage."

"Sounds like The Toad," Taryn smirked.

A thoughtful expression crossed Bryce's face. "I know another guy," he said. "An old Navy buddy. He has a summerhouse in the south of France, not far from Bordeaux. Maybe I could call him, get him to make a few discreet inquiries."

A wistful yearning moved into Taryn's eyes, turning their color a dark purple. "I know it's not likely, but I wish she were still alive. Even if I never have the chance to meet, I'd just like to know she lived, and that she had a good life."

Because there was no good response to her unrealistic sentimentality, Bryce simply squeezed her hand.

"Do you have family, Bryce?" she asked, titling her head a bit.

The edge of his mouth lifted ever so slightly with a tight, tiny smile. "I've been accused of being cold, but I wasn't hatched from reptile eggs, if that's what you're asking. Of course, I have family."

His manner was off-handed. Bryce wasn't a man comfortable talking about himself. "All the usual suspects. A father, mother, two brothers. All military brats. An ex-wife, if that counts as family. She didn't seem to think so."

Why, he wondered, had he told her that? It was something he rarely talked about.

"I like to think it does," Taryn replied. "Until this week, my ex and his new wife were a full one-third of the only family I had to call my own."

Bryce deftly switched the topic to smoother ground. "So, tell me about the family you discovered this week."

It was all the encouragement she needed. Taryn launched into a long story about her aunt and many cousins, and the loud, noisy, wonderful meal they had shared. She told him about Susannah's dream to see the city, and little Pete's plot to train his chickens. He planned to teach them to walk single file into their coop, and not scatter about when he tucked them in each night.

Quite some time later, Taryn arched her back, realizing how stiff she had become. "I guess I should go. I know you're beat, having just flown in."

"I'll follow you home."

"That won't be necessary," Taryn assured him. "I'll be fine."

"Call me overly cautious, but I don't want you out on the dark country roads this late at night. It's almost midnight."

"It is?" she gasped. "I had no idea!" She scooted around the opposite side of the banquette, already gathering the dirty dishes.

"Leave those. The maid will get them in the morning."

"Another one of your job descriptions?" she guessed with a smile.

"I have trouble getting her to cook, though," he admitted. "Want to join me at *Kaffi Korner* for breakfast? Eight-ish? We could talk to Helen, try to jog her memory on a few more details."

"I get a breakfast basket delivered each morning, promptly at seven. Roughly three hours after the rooster wakes me up," she exaggerated. "But I could always drink more coffee."

"Nine, then?"

"Perfect."

She almost said, 'it's a date,' but held her tongue. This wasn't a date, by no stretch of the imagination.

This was the beginning of what she feared would become a very dangerous investigation.

CHAPTER 23

Despite keeping late hours the night before, Taryn was up early. She had time to read the first of Rebecca's letters before Susannah arrived with the basket.

My dearest Lillian,

Please, do not worry on my behalf. I can't say where I am, but I'm safe. I'm sorry I had to leave. I'm most sorry that I could not say a proper goodbye, but it was too gawwerich. *In time, I hope you will forgive me. Someday, you may even understand.*

I have no right, but I have a favor to ask. There are things in my last journals that are pivvish, *and best forgotten. Silly ramblings of a lovesick girl, I think. Too ferhoodled to bother reading. Please destroy the journals. You know where I kept them.*

I do not have to ask that you look after Mamm un Daedd, for you are a good daughter. You are a good sister. I will keep you in my heart, and in my most humble prayers.

Forever your loving and devoted sister, Rebecca

Oh, one more thing. Please tell Daedd, and only Daedd, about this letter, and that I am safe.

Taryn folded the letter and returned it to its envelope, postmarked from Peabody, Massachusetts. The date was March 15, ten days after Rebecca disappeared.

Obviously, her mother had begun to worry about the journals she left behind, afraid they might put her family in danger. Just as obviously, Lillian hadn't done as requested. She not only kept the journals, but she also read them.

In her shoes, Taryn knew she would have done the same thing.

When Susannah brought her breakfast, Taryn asked about some of words she did not understand.

"What does *gawwerich* mean?" she asked her cousin.

Susannah looked amused. "And where did you learn this word?"

"I overhead it the other day," Taryn said evasively, cutting into her warm waffle with whipped cream topping and slices of strawberry.

"It is not something you would ever worry with," the young woman assured her. "It means awkward. If, for instance, I sat at an angle on the hard bench seat and my apron was mussed, *die Mamm* would caution me that I was *gawwerich*." Her eyes twinkled with mischief. "Which she often does, by the way."

"And *pivvish*? What does that mean?"

She thought for a moment, searching for the best way to describe it. "Just an exact way. Particular. When I learned to stitch my samplers, I did them in a very *pivvish* manner."

A thought occurred to her, and she clapped her hands together in excitement. "Yes! That is what we can discuss today! I shall teach you Amish words!"

❦

After her lesson, there was time for one more letter. Taryn pulled the second one from its envelope, which was marked April 12 from Tupelo, Mississippi. Rebecca had sent a single page written on pink stationary, telling her sister how happy she was. She had married the love of her life, Ahndray Lamont. This was not to be shared with anyone, especially their father. He would only worry. She could, however, tell him she was safe, and happy, and she had her very first job. She was working as a seamstress, although she was careful not to mention where. She closed with another plea for forgiveness, and a pledge of her eternal love.

Bryce was waiting for her at the coffee shop when she arrived. If the half-eaten muffin was any indication, he had started without her.

He stood when she arrived, a show of good manners instilled in him by his military background. That, incidentally, had begun when he was a toddler.

"You said you would have already eaten," he said in his own defense.

"Yes. I'm stuffed. My aunt is an excellent cook." She laid a hand to her stomach, afraid she might need larger clothes by the time she left.

"Katie will take your coffee order," he said. He looked around and caught the eye of the woman behind the counter, signaling they were ready.

"Have you had a chance to do anything this morning?" she asked eagerly, as she scooted in to the table.

"Nothing pertaining to this case."

Taryn had the grace to look apologetic. "I'm sorry. I know I'm not your only client. Please excuse my overzealous *aafratze*."

He cocked an eyebrow in amusement. "Learning Amish words, are we?"

"Susannah decided it was time I had a lesson, especially when I asked her about some words I didn't understand." She crossed her arm on the table and made a rather breathless announcement. "I started on the letters."

"Really? Learn anything new?"

His question took the wind out of her sails. Despite her grand proclamation, she really hadn't discovered a thing of importance.

Katie came to take her order, and to refill Bryce's cup.

"You, again." She smiled, recognizing Taryn upon sight. Her eyes slid knowingly between the two of them. "You didn't tell us you knew Bryce."

"We've just recently met," Taryn assured her. For some reason, she felt her face heat.

"Ahh-h." With a bit of a smirk, Katie went to make her coffee.

Ignoring the two-syllable 'ahh-h'—which only depended her flush—Taryn said, "I've read two letters so far, but they weren't helpful. Rebecca wouldn't say where she was, only that she was safe, and she hoped that one day, Lillian could forgive her. She wanted her to tell their father she was safe, but she didn't want him to know she had married my father. That was in the second letter."

"Postmarks?"

"March 15 and April 12. From Massachusetts and Mississippi. You don't suppose she was truly in those places, do you? The others were marked from all over the States."

"She probably had someone mail them for her. Truckers, most likely, from their next destination."

"That would make sense."

Her coffee was delivered, but by the hand of the owner.

"Well, well," Helen said, her smile a match to the one sprawled across Katie's face as she watched from the register. "If it's not the girl with the violet eyes. Terry, was it?"

"Close. Taryn."

Helen nudged Bryce with her elbow, her manner teasing. "That big old house getting a bit lonesome for you, huh?"

He looked nonplussed by her assumptions. "Something like that. How do you know Taryn? And please, join us." He stood and pulled a chair from the next table, pushing it in for the older woman.

"Oh, we met the other day," Helen said evasively, her gaze wandering to Taryn's. There was a question in her eyes, asking for her approval on how much to share.

"It's okay, Helen," Taryn approved quietly. "Bryce knows all about my past." She put the slightest of emphasis on the word 'my.' If Helen wanted to share her own past, that was her business, and none of Taryn's.

Judging by the twinkle in the older woman's eye, it never occurred to her that theirs could be a business relationship. She obviously thought it was of a personal nature.

Perhaps, Taryn thought, it was best to mislead her. If this proved as dangerous as she feared, the fewer people involved, the better.

Seeing the opening he needed, Bryce took the lead. "Helen, Taryn tells me you were actually the one to deliver her. That's quite a coincidence, you two meeting again after all these years."

"It is," the old nurse agreed. "Then again, I keep in touch with many of my babies. As you can imagine, quite a few live in the area."

"But the fact she was adopted and managed to find the place she was born, and the very nurse who delivered her... That's really something," he said, watching her closely as he took a long drag of coffee.

"I agree. But we have Betty Lawrence to thank for that." Helen was quick to give credit where credit was due. "She's often heard me mention those violet eyes. They've haunted me through the years. The minute she saw Tara's eyes, she knew we had to meet."

"Yes, those eyes are really something, aren't they?"

Bryce turned his gaze upon Taryn. She saw the mischief dancing in their dark depths, as he played out the charade for Helen's sake. She was tempted to place a pointed toe in his shin, but Helen's swollen and heavily veined legs were in the way.

Perhaps because her first career had been babies, the older woman was a born matchmaker. She smiled in satisfaction at the look flowing between the couple at the table.

"It wasn't just the color that haunted me," Helen continued. Her flirty voice turned serious. "It was the look in that poor girl's eyes. She was terrified, and it wasn't because she was afraid of the pain. She refused an epidural."

Taryn perked up. "You didn't tell me that."

"Said she wanted to be fully alert." Helen's tone dropped to conspiratorial. "I think she was afraid the wrong person would come in, and she wouldn't know. I'm telling you, that girl was scared to death."

"Who was she afraid of?" Bryce asked. "What did she say?"

"Like I told Tara here, I'm terrible with names. She kept calling for someone, wishing he were there. I've been trying to wrack my brain since our visit the other day, but I just can't recall. Seems like maybe it had a funny pronunciation, but the girl had a bit of an accent. *Deutsch*, I think."

"Was the name Ahndray?" Taryn suggested.

The nurse gave a helpless shake of her head. "No idea. I'm just no good with names, and it's been so long. But I do recall now that she kept talking about frogs. Poor girl seemed to have a phobia about them."

"Frogs? Or did she use the term 'toad'?" Taryn pressed.

Helen shrugged. "Same difference, isn't it? At any rate, we promised to keep them away. Kept reassuring her that no frogs were getting into our delivery room. That seemed to comfort her, until another pain hit, and she called for her man again. Wanted to know why he left her." She clipped her tongue. "Can't say I blame her. Such a shame, to be widowed at a time like that."

"Can you remember anything else about that day?" Bryce asked.

"Oh, I remember plenty," the old woman said, her words heavy with meaning. "I suppose Caryn told you the full story."

"Only as it pertained to her."

She turned to Taryn. "You can tell him, you know. I have no secrets."

Well, just the one. And it was best kept.

"That's really beside the point right now. But there's one thing I still don't understand, Helen," Taryn said.

"Just one?"

She allowed a small smile. "You're right. There are dozens of things I don't understand about my birth, but maybe you can clear up this one. How did my parents—my adoptive parents, the Clarks—come by the receipt?"

The older woman looked suddenly uncomfortable. She glanced at Bryce, whose eyes held an encouraging light. He inclined his head ever so slightly, urging her to simply say it, whatever it was.

"I—I assume they paid for your delivery," Helen answered haltingly.

"And the note from my mother? How did they get that?"

"Uh—"

Bryce sensed the retired nurse knew more than she was saying. "Please, Helen, tell us what you know."

"Your mother left it," she finally answered, her tone gentle. "Your birth mother, Jane Doe. Or Jane Hirsch, as she claimed. She left the note pinned to your blanket, when she snuck from the hospital."

At Taryn's soft gasp, Bryce placed his hand over hers and gently squeezed.

"You mean—" Taryn hesitated, finding the words difficult to say aloud. Even after all the heartache she had endured, this new revelation still cut deep. "You mean, she... abandoned me?"

Hoping to soften the impact, Helen chose a different word. "She left you behind, yes. But I'm convinced she did it for your own good."

Bryce tightened his grip as Helen added, "I'm telling you, that girl was scared out of her wits, and it wasn't just of frogs. She used a false name, a false address, and she left behind her precious baby girl. Mark my words, she was running from someone."

The unspoken question lay silently on the table between them.

Had she succeeded in escaping?

۶

"I'm sorry, Taryn, but I need to get back to the office."

Bryce apologized after Helen left them, their coffee now cold. "I came in a day early, so I can wrap up my current case and concentrate on yours."

"I understand."

He could see how distracted she was. Helen's announcement left her understandably upset.

"Are you okay?"

"I will be." She offered a wan smile. "It shouldn't be a surprise. Of course, she left me behind. How could she hide, with a newborn baby to care for? I would have slowed her down, made her more conspicuous."

"You can't really believe that she left you to save herself, can you?"

Taryn thought about it for a moment, but in the end, she shook her head. "No. After reading her journals, I feel like I know the kind of person Rebecca was. She would never have done something so selfish. If anything, she would have sacrificed herself, to keep her baby safe."

A terrible thought came to her. She sucked in her breath and clutched the fingers that still held hers. "Bryce? You don't think that's what happened, do you? You don't think she would have drawn the Toad to her, just to take attention off me, do you?" Her voice rose in panic. "You don't think she sacrificed herself for *me*, do you?" The thought was unbearable.

"Shh. Don't hyperventilate on me. Just calm down." He used his calming voice, talking her down off the ledge of hysteria. "Take a deep breath and look at me."

She did so, if unsteadily.

"It's what mothers do, Taryn. They do whatever it takes, to keep their children safe."

Taryn gave a tiny hiccup of a nod. "Fathers, too," she whispered. "I understand now. That's why my grandfather sent her away in the first place. He chose to never see his daughter again, if it meant keeping her safe."

"I just wonder if it was in vain," Bryce murmured aloud.

"I need to read the rest of the letters."

"Let's regroup this evening." He stood and threw a twenty-dollar bill on the table, making sure Katie saw the gesture. As he ushered Taryn out the door, he asked, "Where was that restaurant you found? I have a busy afternoon, but maybe we can have dinner there tonight, and discuss whatever you find."

They made plans to meet at seven thirty.

As Taryn drove back to the farm, she noticed a light-colored car behind her. She thought nothing of it, until it turned behind her. By the second turn, she became nervous.

She knew she was being paranoid, but her nerves were naked and raw. Instead of turning on the farm road, she kept straight. She finally turned into a roadside stand selling fresh strawberries, but she stayed in her car.

The other car sped up and away, leaving her there to tremble in peace.

CHAPTER 24

Taryn made certain the light-colored car was nowhere in sight before pulling out from the roadside stand. She regularly checked her rearview mirror, making certain no one followed her. The last thing she wanted to do was bring danger to the Zooks' doorstep.

And yet, where else would it go? Peter and Lillian lived next door to the King farm, the very place all of this had started, all those years ago. Lillian was already a part of this story. And she had read the journals, the same as Taryn.

It occurred to Taryn that she should warn her aunt of danger. But what, exactly, would she say? That a car was behind her from town? That her over-active imagination conjured up all sorts of wild scenarios?

If they did, indeed, investigate the past and find something viable, something concrete, she would tell her aunt then. But

until then, she thought it was best to keep this venture to herself. She would discuss it at dinner tonight with Bryce.

Taryn took the packet of letters out to the gazebo, where a
nice breeze blew across the water. It cooled her heated skin
and fevered senses, providing the balm she needed to continue
reading.

The third letter was almost lighthearted. If not for a few
random phrases, it could have been a letter from any sister
anywhere, written to a loved one at home. Rebecca described
their small apartment and the lap quilt she made, using a pattern Lillian had favored as a child. She talked about the meals
she prepared for her husband, and how cooking on an electric
stove had scorched more than one second-hand skillet. She
and Ahndray were not wealthy, but they were happy. She was
quickly adapting to the English way of life and found the television to be most entertaining. She was careful not to ask
direct questions, knowing the answers would never reach her.
This letter bore a postmark from Huntsville, Texas, in June of
1980.

The August letter, sent late in the month from California,
carried on the same happy theme, with the exception of the
closing lines.

My dearest, dearest Lillian,

*I have not mentioned this until now, because I wanted to be
certain. You, my dear sister, will soon be an aunt! Yes! It's true. I
will have a precious baby, somewhere around the first of the year.*

We are so happy. I wish with all my heart that you, and our sweet Mamm, could be with me when my time comes, but I am only being selfish. It is best this way.

Already my dresses do not fit, and my belly grows round and firm. It is a happy time. I love my husband so, and this baby we have made.

If I have not said this before, do this for me. Stay away from the barn. Stay indoors when the English come to buy our horses. They live in a wicked world you cannot understand.

Keep me and my sweet little family in your heart and prayers, as you are forever in mine. I keep our mother's old saying in mind:

Nothing lies beyond the reach of prayer, except that which lies outside the will of God.

Your adoring sister, Rebecca

By October, all that had changed. Tears gathered in Taryn's eyes as she read her mother's words.

Dearest Sister,

A most terrible thing has happened. Men with badges have come and taken my beloved Ahndray away! They say he has violated the rules of his work Visa, and he must return to his home country. Only now has he told me the truth about his life. His father is an American businessman, with a family here, while Ahndray and his beloved mother are left in France. His father is angry with him now and has reported him to the officials. His own father! How could he do that?

Promise me that you have destroyed my journals. That you avoid the English buyers. That you keep my secret from our father. For his own good, he cannot know what has happened. Promise.

I need your prayers more than ever, sweet Lillian. Pray for my baby and me, and that Ahndray can soon return to us. The baby will be here in the new year. I love this child already.

Forever sisters, Rebecca

Before Taryn could wipe the tears away and pull out the final letter, she heard Lillian call her name.

"Taryn! Taryn Clark, can you hear me?"

"Out here!" she called back, drying her face with the back of her hand. She hastily got to her feet and started toward the house.

"Would you care to help in the garden?"

"Absolutely! Let me change shoes."

She hurried up to her room, where she left the letters and exchanged her sandals for closed-toe shoes. She was back down by the time her aunt and young Emiline came from the big house, carrying baskets.

"I thought you might enjoy picking peas." Lillian smiled. "It's not hard work, but it's rewarding. I plan to cook them for dinner, if you care to join us."

Taryn's smile fell. "I wish I could, but I already have plans."

"Oh? I didn't realize you had made friends already. But that is good. Very good," she said, with a bob of her head and an encouraging smile.

Taryn didn't bother correcting her aunt. She hadn't mentioned hiring a private investigator before, even when it had been innocent enough. It would only stir the pot now.

"He seems nice," Taryn said with a shrug.

"A *he*, now is it?" Lillian asked playfully. "Tell me about him!"

Too late, Taryn saw that same matchmaking glint on her aunt's face, exactly like the one on Helen's. She groaned aloud. "Why does everyone think they have to set me up?"

Lillian looked slightly confused. "Set you up? As a trick?"

"No, as part of a pair! I'm perfectly happy being single."

"That's *gut*," her aunt said. "But you can be twice as happy as a couple, ain't so?"

"You're impossible!" Taryn proclaimed, but she laughed as she grabbed a basket and started down a row of ripened peas.

She soon discovered the best part of gardening. Aside from the satisfaction of gathering ripened vegetables and having nature's bounty all around, it provided ample time to think quietly, or, in this case, to visit. As the women and little Emiline moved down the rows, one across from the other, they tugged the plump pods from drooping stalks and chatted back and forth about inconsequential things. The conversation was light and varied, touching on everything from recipes and household chores, to culture differences and similarities. They talked of Lillian's children and Taryn's stalled career. The afternoon sun was warm, and Taryn soon broke a sweat.

One of the advantages to not wearing makeup, she noted, was how Amish women could mop the perspiration from their faces with their apron and be none the worse for wear. Taryn couldn't do it, for fear of smearing her mascara and giving little Emiline nightmares.

"How about a nice glass of lemonade before your date?" Lillian offered, their baskets overflowing and their backs only slightly crooked.

"It's not a date. But lemonade does sound divine."

"We'll have it on the swing yonder," Lillian said, nodding to the shaded glider under the big oak tree.

"I can help."

"*Ach*, you go rest. I don't want you all tuckered out before your big night out." She gave an impish grin, looking younger than her fifty-something years.

Taryn wandered out to the swing, considering something for the first time. Lillian must have been almost ten years older than Taryn was now when she gave birth to her last child. And here Taryn hadn't even had her first!

Would she ever have children, she wondered, taking her place among the cushions. Without even a boyfriend on the radar, she somehow doubted it.

Not that a boyfriend was required. These days, motherhood for a single, unattached woman was commonplace. Difficult, she was certain, by common enough, and socially accepted. But Taryn didn't much favor the idea of raising a child alone, and she wasn't in the market for a relationship. Worst of all was the fear that, as a single parent, something might happen to her and her children would be placed into foster care. She couldn't bear the thought of passing on such a curse.

Maybe she would just continue to enjoy Molly's children and her newly acquired cousins.

There were bound to be others, too, she knew. Her mother had often mentioned Rose and Abigail in her journals, and older brothers. It was tradition among the Amish to have large families, so Taryn knew there must be dozens of relatives she had yet to meet.

It was still a bit overwhelming, going from a family of one to an infinite number.

"That looks like a thoughtful smile," Lillian observed, as she handed her niece her frosty drink. The little girl wasn't with her this time.

Taryn's eyes darted to the adjacent farm. "I was just wondering how large my family really is. How many other cousins do I have, and where do they all live?"

"Oh, here, there, and yonder. Abigail married a man from Indiana and lives in an Amish community there. Rose and her brood live down near Gap. I believe she has at least a dozen children." She did a quick calculation in her head. "*Jah*, that's right. Two sets of twins. Gilbert lives at the back of the horse farm, his five sons now grown. Josiah lives in the house where your mother and I grew up. Both of his grown sons live there with their wives. He has three daughters, as well. I haven't been counting, but that's quite a number, ain't so?" Lillian chuckled.

"Too many to count!" Taryn agreed.

As their laughter dwindled, Taryn asked softly, "Did you never tell them about the letters? That my mother wrote to you?"

Lillian took her time in answering. "*Nee*," she said softly. "I told my father, but no one else, just as my sister had asked of me. I have many regrets, but that is one of my biggest." Wearing aprons and no makeup came in handy when wiping away tears, too. "I have carried the guilt with me, all these years. If I had told my mother, if she had known her daughter was safe, perhaps she would not have taken that last dose."

"Don't be so harsh on yourself, Aunt Lillian. It would have been just as difficult, knowing she was safe, and yet still wondering where she was, when she would write again. Worrying that each letter would be the last. That if something happened to her, you might never know."

She heard her aunt's heartbroken sob and realized how insensitive she had been.

"Oh! I'm so sorry! I didn't think. That's exactly what you must have gone through. I can't imagine how difficult that was for you."

Lillian's slow nod moved not only her head, but her whole body. "*Jah*, it was. And when we thought we might lose *Mamm*, when we did lose her in mind and spirit, there was no way to tell my sister. You want to know something else? We took her first to *Lancaster Memorial*, before the doctors told us there was nothing he could do. We left in November, before your mother came on New Year's Day." She turned to Taryn, revealing her pain. "How close we came to crossing paths! And to think Rebecca was here, so near, all that time, and we never knew!"

"I'm sorry." It was so little, but there was nothing else to say.

They drank their lemonade in silence, both absorbed in their own thoughts. Lillian was the first to speak.

"She was happy, don't you think, in her new life with Ahndray?" Her voice was a bit wistful.

"Yes, I think so, even though she missed her family. She obviously loved him very much."

"Have you... read the last letter?"

The way her words faltered filled Taryn with trepidation. What heartache would that last missive reveal? There had been so much already. "Not yet."

Lillian forced a smile as she laid her hand onto her niece's knee. "Don't worry over it now. Have a nice meal with your new friend and enjoy your evening. *Denki* for your help in the garden."

"It was fun," Taryn admitted, surprised to find the words were true.

"There will be more tomorrow. And tomatoes, and more squash. You may come have your fun in my garden whenever you wish!"

Taryn returned her aunt's playful smile.

"I may just take you up on that offer," she promised.

CHAPTER 25

Bryce fastened the last of the buttons on his forest-green, button-down shirt, giving his image a cursory glance in the mirror. Pressed shirt, starched khakis, brown leather belt, and loafers. At forty-four, his belly was still flat, his back straight, his body fit and toned. If judged solely by his physique and preferred hairstyle, he could have stepped from military life only yesterday.

He glanced at his watch, irritated with himself for taking longer than normal to dress. The pressed and starched white shirt had been too business-like. The silkier threads running through the dark-red version had been too date-like. Green, he finally determined, was neutral enough to make no preconceived promises.

This was hardly a date. He couldn't actually remember the last time he had been on one, but when and if he were to take a woman out romantically, she most definitely wouldn't be a client. If nothing else, Bryce Elliott was a true professional. He prided himself on having—and adhering to—a strict policy against business mixing with pleasure.

He had a similar policy on allowing personal feelings to interfere with business decisions, but even he had to acknowledge this was a gray area, and not so easily defined. Weren't gut instincts, for instance, best defined as personal feelings? It gave him a conscionable 'out,' a way he could reconcile his professional ethics with the occasional case that got under his skin.

This was one of those cases, in spades.

Like any investigator worth his license, Bryce did a background check on all clients before agreeing to take their case. Taryn Clark was no different. In his line of work, surprises were not a good thing, particularly when they pertained to an unstable client, or badly skewed information.

He found no mental instability in her past. No brushes with the law. No hint of ulterior motives, other than the ones she expressed. What he did find was a sad and solitary life, strung between foster care and group homes, from the time she was five until she became of age. Given her fractured childhood, it was surprising that her adulthood was so stable. She graduated magna cum laude from a major university and soon landed a coveted position with a top Philadelphia law firm.

On paper, Taryn Clark was the perfect client. Her career history was exemplary, her financials healthy, her personal life stable, if not stale. No surprises, no unnecessary drama, no theatrics.

The surprise was how quickly this woman, this case, had captured his attention and gotten under his skin. He normally avoided these type cases like the plague, but here he was, diving in headfirst to help her. He even cut his Florida trip short and came home early, just so he could get both feet wet.

If that wasn't letting his personal feelings get in the way of his better judgment, he didn't know what was.

Not that his feelings toward Taryn were romantic. Granted, they were complicated, but they were probably best described as 'protective.' And wasn't protection what he was all about? Wasn't that why he joined the Navy in the first place, to serve and protect his country? Born into a military family, he wasn't a warm and fuzzy kind of guy by nature, but, by God, he knew how to serve and protect.

Reading her background report, seeing her life story rationed out in black and white, he knew this was a woman who had seen little of either in her life. Normally, he preferred a facts-only report, uncluttered by personal biases and unnecessary details. But this was someone's childhood. It should have included some detail. Some sign of, well, childhood.

His own hadn't been the best, but it had been steady. The military base may have changed, but his parents' guidance and support were always a given. They may not have shown it with excessive displays of affection, but he had no doubt his parents loved him and his brothers.

Poor Taryn had nothing even close to that in her past. From the day she was born, she had been handed from one person to another, like a castaway doll. Before she even turned six, her adopted parents had divorced and the custodial parent, Teresa

Clark, was killed in a car accident. Paul Clark was unequipped to care for a child on his own, so she had gone into foster care.

The list was long and exhausting. Most of the host families declined renewing her time in their homes. It wasn't that she was difficult, they reported; she was simply unresponsive. Emotionally troubled. She didn't mingle well with her foster siblings, preferring to keep to herself.

It didn't bode well for her prospects. When given the choice, most host families preferred the 'easy' children. Overlooked and all but forgotten, Taryn was shuffled off to a handful of questionable homes.

Sadly, sometimes even the 'good' homes, the ones like the Michelins, didn't always prove to be good.

Bryce had to be honest with himself. From that first meeting, before he even read the report, he had known he would take her case. Something about it was intriguing. Instincts told him it was more than a simple 70's-era baby-out-of-wedlock story. Taryn Clark came into his office like a whirlwind—make that a thunderstorm—and caught his attention with her tale of a frightened but anonymous mother, identified only by her unique eyes.

She begged for his help, and help was what he was all about. She believed he could help her. She *trusted* him to help her. She trusted the fact he could find her birth mother and the roots she so badly craved.

Bryce knew it was unlikely. He knew the chances of a happy ending were slim. But he had hated to see that innocent belief and blind faith destroyed. They looked so hopeful, so refreshing, in her violet eyes. Even if he couldn't help her find the family she craved, perhaps he could be the one to let her down gently. He wanted to protect her from the ugly truth. The truth that finding one's past didn't always mean finding happiness.

It all came back to that protective nature of his.

Bryce clicked his tongue as he locked the stately old house behind him. That protective nature was as much a curse as it was a blessing. Look where it had gotten him in his ill-fated marriage.

⊗⊗⊗

Bryce was already seated when she arrived at the restaurant. He stood when she approached the table, ever the gentleman.

"I took the liberty of ordering a couple of appetizers and water for us both," he told her, helping her with her chair. "I hope that's all right."

"Absolutely."

Right on cue, the server arrived with one platter of warm bruschetta, one basket of crispy, curly calamari.

"I'm sorry I'm a couple of minutes late," Taryn apologized. "I got behind not one, but *three* buggies! I'm never sure if I'm supposed to follow behind or pass with care." She thought briefly of Rebecca's brush with an automobile, an accident that turned out to be no accident, at all.

"No problem. I've only been here a few minutes, myself."

Before leaving, the server asked if they would like something from the bar.

"Do you mind if I have a beer?" Bryce asked of his dinner companion.

"No, not at all. In fact, I think I'll have a martini."

That set the tone for the evening. Not quite business, not quite a date. It was simply two new friends, sharing a delicious meal.

They exchanged light conversation and general news topics of the day. Taryn spoke of her career as a legal assistant, not at all surprised when the private investigator was familiar with the law firm. They had handled a number of high-profile cases and were well known in the state, if not the nation. Bryce offered minimal details about his life in the Navy, and as a detective for the Harrisburg Police Department. Neither expanded on the topic of past marriages, or any subject construed as too personal.

"Dessert?" Bryce asked, as the server cleared away their plates.

Taryn waved away the very thought with one hand, touching her stomach with the other. "No room. None."

"You heard the lady." Bryce smiled at the server.

"Very well. How shall I make the check? Together, or separate?"

"Together and bring it to me."

"Bryce—"

He hushed Taryn's protest with a conspiratorial smile. "Don't worry about it. My newest client doesn't know it yet, but she's including a generous expense account. I'll turn this in with my bill."

Taryn laughed at the server's expression, but the young man left to do as requested.

"You may have just damaged your stellar reputation," she warned, "letting him think you pad your clients' bills."

"Just as long as you and I know the truth," he said dismissively.

Taryn sobered at his words. "Do you think we ever will?" she asked. She leaned forward to finger the rim of her empty cocktail glass, her voice pensive. "Do you think we'll ever really know what happened? Even with the journals, and the letters, there are so many holes in the story. Huge, gaping holes. I feel them gnawing at me, threatening to suck me into their abyss. I may know who my parents are, but I still don't know what happened to them."

Bryce leaned back in his chair and studied her with his dark, brooding eyes. He felt that protective urge kicking in again. He wanted to protect her, to spare her from the pain she felt. He could see it there in her face, and in her stunning violet eyes. He phrased his question as gently as possible.

"Have you considered the fact you may never know? That you may have to be satisfied simply knowing their names?"

"I have." She settled those violet eyes upon his. She took a deep breath and said matter-of-factly, "But that's not good enough."

"Taryn—"

"Hear me out. If it was just me, just for my own sake and my own curiosity, I might come to terms with it." She saw the pointed look he gave her and admitted with a sheepish smile, "I said I *might*, okay? I *might* be content, knowing their names and the fact I have extended family. Okay, medical backgrounds would be nice, because you just never know, but it's more than that."

The smile fell away, and she grew serious. "If this is what we think it is—and we both know it is—then a crime was committed. The toad man coerced Manuel King into doping his stock. No doubt, the Toad made thousands, if not millions, of dollars on the scheme. And it wasn't just the horses. He was doping Manuel's wife, supplying her with the cocaine he got her addicted to. It was all highly illegal and highly unethical. And if we're right about the other—"

She paused while the server brought the check and splashed a refill into their water glasses. Once he was gone, she leaned in closer and continued in a hiss, "If we're right about the rest of it, the Toad murdered Rebecca. We can't just let that go, Bryce. *I* can't just let that go."

"I don't have to remind you. We have no proof. No name. We don't even know if the Toad is still alive."

The fire that flashed in her violet eyes was a sight to behold. Bryce felt the heat sear him, all the way to his soul. His heart turned over in his chest, struck as surely by the blaze as if zapped by lightning. It settled a bit off-kilter, clumsy with its erratic pulse.

"You didn't bring the contract. Are you quitting, before you've ever begun?" she spat.

"I never said that. I just want you to have realistic expectations."

She remained stiff. "Understood."

"I don't want you getting hurt."

She softened at his comment, but her eyes still glowed with the dying embers of ire.

"I'm a big girl, Bryce. I've had plenty of experience in the getting-hurt department. I can handle it."

Two hours later, back in her room, she wasn't so sure.

CHAPTER 26

My dearest Lillian,

Do you remember that game we played as children? We would spend hours, spinning foolish dreams of what our future would be like. The farmers we would marry and the children we would have. How could we have known, all those years ago, in all our inno-cence, the life our Gott would choose for us? Such unschuld we had!

If I have a girl, I will name her that. In our Deutsch, it does not sound pretty. But I heard the name once, in Greek. So I shall name a girl-child Taryn, for her innocence. A boy-child will be called Andre. It is the name of his father, and it means courage. Courage is all I have left. Even my faith fails me now.

I beg your forgiveness, sweet sister, for what I must tell you. My landlord knows a young couple who will make excellent par-ents for my sweet child. Though it breaks my heart, I have signed the proper papers, giving my most precious possession to these

people. It is the hardest thing I have ever done, but it is the only
way. The toad made it clear. If my Ahndray comes for me, he will
find me in a grave. For myself, I do not worry. For our child, I am
terrified. The man cannot know of our bobbli. I must protect this
innocent life from the warts of such evil.

If I do not return, my landlord will mail this letter. If you are
reading it, please know I adored you, and our Plain life there on
the farm. I'm sorry I ever teased you, calling you my shadow. I
would give anything to turn now and see your precious face behind
me.

I know you do not understand. Why I left. Why I must give my
baby to strangers. Why I cannot return. Why we must say our
final goodbye in this way.

That secret, I shall take to my grave.

Please, remember me with fondness and think of me now and
again. Think of me when you see the violets in the field, waving in
the wind. That will be me, sending my love.

Forever sisters, Rebecca

"Hello?" His voice was coarse, frogged with a second drink
and the first stages of sleep.

Bryce had gone home and had a whiskey, straight up, before falling into bed. He had a full day planned for tomorrow,
dedicated to Taryn's quest for answers.

At this point, he wanted them almost as badly as she did.

"Bryce?"

"Taryn?" He sat up in bed, coming instantly awake. "Is everything okay?"

"Yes. No. I'm sorry. I woke you, didn't I?"

He could hear the quiver in her voice. "It's fine. What's wrong?"

"I read the last letter. Bryce, there's no doubt in my mind. The Toad had Rebecca killed. Whether to keep her quiet or to keep her father in line, I'm not sure. But this was a goodbye letter." Her voice broke. "She was murdered, Bryce."

He rubbed a hand over the buzz of dark hair. "Let's think this through, Taryn. If she was killed, how did she mail the letter?"

"She left it with her landlord, with instructions to mail it if she didn't return."

"That doesn't necessarily mean she was murdered. She may have left town in a hurry or been slow in returning."

"It was mailed in February. Plenty of time for her to come back, or to call and say not to mail it."

"Maybe she forgot." It was a lame excuse, but all he could think to say. Maybe he was still more asleep than he thought.

Her voice dropped to little more than a growl. "You haven't read the letter, Bryce."

"Then bring it over in the morning."

"I'm sitting outside your house."

"What?" he asked in surprise. He went to the window and peeked out the shade. Sure enough, there sat her car. His sigh was weary. "Come on in."

❧

Taryn hurried up to the door, watching over her shoulder. She didn't think anyone had followed, but it was hard to know. This was all new to her.

The door opened, and Bryce motioned her inside. He didn't look pleased to see her, but he led her past the kitchen, into what was his den. The wood was aged and the furniture masculine. The dim lighting made the close quarters feel that much more intimate, with him in a t-shirt crinkled from sleep, soft sweat pants, and absolutely no shoes on his feet. Taryn barely noticed.

"Can I get you anything?" he offered, vaguely indicating the bar opposite the fireplace. It was stocked better than his refrigerator.

"A shot of whiskey and a Valium."

He shot her an inquisitive look.

"Kidding." She drew a shaky breath, sank into a leather armchair, and muttered, "Marginally."

Bryce opened an under-counter cooler and pulled out two bottled waters, handing one of them to her. "Try this, instead."

She took a long draw of the cold refreshment, surprised to find that it helped.

"I think someone's following me," she blurted out.

"What! What are you talking about? When did this happen?"

She scrunched her face, trying to recall. Her days were running together.

"Was that just today?" She pressed the cold bottle against her temple. "Yes, when I came back from having coffee with you. I couldn't be certain, but I thought a white car followed me from town."

"Did you get a license number?" he asked sharply.

"No. But it was a white—or light—car. A Nissan, I think. Sporty model. I didn't go back to Lillian's. I drove past her road on purpose and pulled in at a roadside stand about a mile away. The car went on, but I think it came back tonight."

"I knew I should have driven you home!" He cursed mildly.

She shook her head. "Not then. When I left to come here. And someone called my cell."

His command was sharp. "Let me see your phone."

She pulled it from her back pocket and handed it over, knowing it would do no good. "Won't help. Unlisted number. I already checked."

"Did they say anything?"

"It was low, and garbled. Like they used an electronic filter. I think they said, 'go home.'"

Taryn stood and paced the floor. "I had just finished the letter, and I was crying so hard I could hardly answer. I may have misunderstood."

He looked at her questioningly.

"It's a hard letter to read. I—I was so upset. I couldn't just sit there in my room, and I didn't want to disturb the family. I decided to go for a drive, to clear my head." She turned and retraced her steps. "I admit, I wasn't paying a lot of attention. I think I saw a car down from the driveway, parked alongside the road. I didn't think much about it, since it's not all that late.

"I was almost to the stop sign, turning onto the adjacent farm road, when my phone rang. I was still crying, and trying to drive, and maybe I didn't hear correctly. But a car came up from behind, and it scared me. I turned toward town and sped up, and they kept coming. They were getting close to my bumper, so close I couldn't see their headlights anymore. We went around a curve and there was a truck coming in the other lane, and another behind it. The car behind me backed off."

"And then what happened?"

"Thank God, there must have been an accident somewhere." She realized what she had said and clamped her hands over her mouth. "I didn't mean that. Not the way it sounded. But I started seeing all these emergency vehicles. To be honest, I don't know what happened to the white car. I put the pedal to the floor and drove like a bat out of hell. The car didn't keep up."

She missed the smile playing on his face. She had turned again, to plop down into the chair.

"Here," she said, thrusting the letter at him. "See if this doesn't just break your heart."

She finished her bottle of water as he read, and then took to torturing her hair. It stuck up at odd angles, but neither cared.

Bryce looked up from the handwritten heartache, clearing the emotions that had gathered there in his throat.

"Heavy stuff," he agreed gruffly. "Tough to read."

Taryn stared into the fireplace, its hearth cold and empty on a summer night. Much like her heart.

"Did you know," she said, fighting to keep her voice steady, "that Lillian lost her first child? A little girl that she named Taren. With an 'e.'" Unshed tears swam in her eyes as she directed the bright shimmer toward Bryce. "Both sisters named their daughters after innocence. Or the loss, thereof."

"So your birth mother gave you your name," he noted softly. "She must have asked your adopted parents to keep it."

"This is all so confusing, Bryce. And so overwhelming. What do you make of the part about the Toad? He apparently knew Ahndray's father turned him in to immigration and warned him not to come back. Does that mean he found them after they left the farm? Was he watching them all along? But if so, he would know about the baby. About me." Her hands roamed through her hair again, mussing it unmercifully. "I'm so confused."

He perused the letter again, searching for clues.

"Maybe your mother called all bad men toads. I don't think it has a double meaning in Pennsylvania Deutsch, but you could ask. Maybe she really was afraid of frogs, like Helen said, and related all evil to toads and warts."

"Maybe," Taryn said, but her tone was dubious.

"I need to know more about the white car, Taryn," he said. His tone was stern.

"I can't think of anything else to tell you. I can't even be certain it was the same one tonight as this morning, but I think it was."

"I don't want you going back to the farm tonight. You can stay here."

Her eyes flew to his. "I can't do that!"

"I have four extra bedrooms in this house," he told her. "Two are set up for guests. You're staying."

"But—"

"Give me your keys, and I'll move your car around back, to my private parking."

"But Lillian will worry."

"She won't even know, until morning light. If you like, you can leave first thing in the morning. But I don't like the idea of you out on the roads tonight, and I don't need to drive. I had a stiff nightcap after I got home."

She should have known he was a stickler for drinking and driving, even in the smallest of amounts.

"If you insist," she said, but with obvious reluctance.

"I do."

She pulled her keys from her pocket and watched him leave the room. She idly wondered if he would put on shoes before going out.

He returned shortly, his feet still bare. "All done. Look. I know you're probably still all keyed up, but why don't we call it a night? I plan to start early in the morning. You can either stay here and help me scour the internet, or you can go back to the farm. Your choice, but let's get some sleep, shall we?"

Taryn lifted her head from where it rested against the chair's high back. "Believe it or not, now that I've sat here and relaxed, I think I'm ready to crash."

"Then let me show you upstairs to your room."

She trailed him through the stately old house, noting it was in varying stages of revival.

"You have a lovely home."

"Thanks. I'm doing most of the renovations myself, so it's a slow go. Do you prefer blue or beige?" Seeing her blank look, he expounded, "Decor. Do you prefer a room done in shades of blue or neutrals?"

"Doesn't matter, as long as they both have beds."

"They share the same connected bath, but the blue room has a queen-sized bed. It's right here." He turned a knob and pushed the door inward on a large, comfortably appointed room.

"Thank you, Bryce." She wasn't so tired that she forgot her manners. "I appreciate your hospitality."

He gave her a little wink. Tomorrow, it would occur to her that it was charmingly witty and rather attractive, but tonight she barely caught the reference. "Remember that expense account," he told her. "Just part of the services."

CHAPTER 27

The next morning, Taryn had no idea how to contact Lillian. There was a telephone shed erected between Zook Farms
and the King property next door, the Amish way of getting
around the restriction on use of the telephone. She knew they
had a cell phone—something about being untethered to land,
and strictly for business purposes, Susannah and Lillian had
both been quick to point out—but Taryn didn't know either
number. She decided she would explain her absence later. This
morning, she was determined to help Bryce get started on her
case.

"Where do we start?" she asked, joining him in the kitchen.
She had taken a shower and dressed again in her clothes from
last night. Sleeping in her underwear had spared the garments
a night beneath the rumple of bed covers, but they were still
dreadfully wrinkled.

He looked surprised when she came in. She mistook it for her sans makeup appearance.

"I thought I might as well borrow a couple of traditions from my Amish relatives," she joked, circling a finger in front of her face, "in case I ever want to convert. Sorry if the *au naturel* look frightens you."

"It's not that. I just didn't hear you come down." He continued to pull items from a paper bag, which did make a bit of racket. "I ran over to *Kaffi Korner* and bought breakfast. Take your pick. Your coffee's there on the bar."

She brightened at the sight of her favorite brew. "Wonderful. But you know it will only throw Helen and Katie's imaginations into overdrive." She selected a gooey bear claw, adding a banana-nut muffin for its marginal contribution of fruit, before she thought to add, "Unless, of course, you often buy breakfast for two. Which is totally none of my business, so don't even bother with an answer."

"You're right, none of your business. But the answer is still no. And believe me, they were dying to ask questions. Good thing I moved your car last night. I wouldn't put it past one of them to drive by this morning, just to satisfy their inquiring minds."

"I've heard about the small-town rumor mills. Guess it's true, huh?"

"Absolutely."

They took their selections to the banquette, where Taryn asked, "So, what's the plan for today? I want to help."

"I thought we could do a few generic internet searches. Nothing so deep it will set off any alarms. You can get started on that, while I call my Navy buddy."

"What am I looking for?"

"You can start with searching King Farms. They have a website, so it probably features past winners from their stock. Concentrate on the last part of the 70s. Take note of the races, the jockeys and trainers, and the owners. We can expand the search to the rest of the web, including old newspaper articles and archived magazines. We'll cross-reference them and see if we can establish a pattern. It's doubtful, but maybe toad man wasn't smart enough to cover his tracks, at least in the early years. Do you remember what year your mother first mentioned him?"

"I think it was in the second journal, so she would have been about twelve, I'm guessing. That would have been around 1975, I think. Her brother was already sick by then, and he was buried on her fourteenth birthday."

"So her brother was sick for quite a while. They must have racked up quite a medical bill, taking him to doctors and what not."

"I know he was in the hospital on more than one occasion. And one time, they took him to York, to see a specialist. It's clear to me that the Toad took advantage of a parent's desperation and forced my grandfather into doing his bidding."

"I agree. So concentrate on the years 75 through 80. If it comes down to it, I have a face-recognition program we can use to scan photographs. Maybe we'll find the Toad in some of the magazine covers and newspaper shots. Big wigs like him usually like to steal the show."

"You may as well get me a refill now; we have a long day in store." Taryn couldn't help but groan.

"Your second cup is in the microwave, waiting to be reheated."

⚜

They worked in tandem for most of the day. Breaking only for lunch and an occasional coffee, they spent the majority of the day in front of the computers. Bryce worked off his desktop, while Taryn pounded away on the borrowed laptop.

"I hate to tell you this, but I'm done." It was close to five o'clock, and Taryn's eyes threatened to cross. She had a kink in her back and her shoulders sagged. She stood to stretch, her knees almost giving way.

"You lasted an hour longer than I would have wagered," Bryce acknowledged. "Good job."

"Thanks."

"You're pretty good at research."

"What do you think a legal assistant does? We do all the legwork—and screen time—so that the lawyers can dazzle the juries and rake in the big bucks. All in a day's work."

He chuckled at her apt description and stood from behind his desk, resisting the urge to stretch his own aching muscles. To her surprise, he handed her a set of keys.

"What are these?"

"I'd like for you to take my car. Drive it back to the farm and leave your car here."

Her breath caught in her chest. "Do you really think that's necessary?"

Bryce shrugged, but his easy demeanor didn't fool her. "Call it an experiment. I'll follow behind at a distance, but I won't take the farm road. I'll make a point for your car to be seen out and about. If someone follows, I'll know."

"If you're sure..." She still looked uncertain, so he sweetened the pot.

"Did I mention it's a Corvette?"

She brightened immediately. "I see the brilliance in your plan."

"I thought you would," Bryce replied with a smug smile. He gave an exaggerated hand roll. "After you."

꧁꧂

"I thought you'd never get home!" Susannah chided, the moment she realized it was Taryn behind the wheel of the sports car. "Where have you been? And where did you get this car?"

"Is it yours?" her brother Carl wanted to know. He walked around the sleek model, admiring its curves and shiny chrome accents.

Taryn sighed. It seemed that even Amish men fell for the allure of a sports car.

"I'm sorry if I worried you," she told the exasperated young woman. "I had business to attend to, and I didn't know how to reach you. You'll have to give me your cell phone number." She turned to the man still circling the vehicle. "And no, it belongs to a friend. We swapped cars for the day."

"He came out on the short end of the stick!" Carl proclaimed.

"Probably in more ways than one." She only hoped Bryce was safe, acting as bait for the white car.

"Would you like to have dinner with us?" Susannah invited. "You can tell us all about your day."

Taryn readily accepted the invitation, for two reasons. One, she was famished. And two, she knew that with such an unruly and noisy brood, her inquisition would fall by the wayside. Dinner with the Zook clan was no time for complicated questions and answers.

It was another loud and delicious meal, but she declined offers to stay for coffee and pie. She really was exhausted.

She called Bryce as soon as she returned to her room.

"I saw your earlier texts," Taryn said. "Still nothing?"

"Yes, and no."

"What does that mean?" she demanded.

"No sign of the white car, but I did pick up a tail. It was a blue Toyota Camry."

"So what do you make of that?"

"You want my honest opinion, or do you want to sleep easy tonight?"

"Both. But tell me anyway."

"I don't think we're dealing with a novice. They knew to switch cars, to throw you off."

"Did they see you? Did they know it wasn't me driving?"

"That depends. Are you ever known to wear a big, floppy hat?"

Taryn burst out laughing at the image his words inspired. "I would have loved to have seen you!"

"Hang around. Same place, same time tomorrow."

She chose to focus on the positive, rather than the danger aspect. "So I get to keep the 'Vette? Because I have to tell you, I think my cousins may have left a little drool on the hood. And just to be clear, I may have left a bit on the gearshift. That is one sweet ride, my friend."

He didn't share her playful mood. "To be on the safe side, I think you should stay at the farm tomorrow. Continue your online search from there. If anyone's trolling the sites, the searches will come from a different IP address."

"I suppose it's just as well," Taryn sighed. "I think Susannah conned me into helping make pickles tomorrow. Or maybe it's jelly. To be honest, I'm so tired I didn't really pay attention. I just agreed."

"Well, you might need to know the difference," he pointed out. She could hear the humor in his voice this time.

"Good point, but it will have to wait until tomorrow. Good night, Bryce."

"Sleep well."

It was a nice thought, but it didn't pan out.

Her phone rang at twelve, two, and five. Each message was the same.

"Go home," the electronic voice warned. "Don't say you weren't warned."

Taryn tried to concentrate on the jelly-making process, but her nerves were frayed, and her mind was fuzzy with lack of sleep.

"Four cups of sugar, Taryn Clark," Lillian stressed for the second time. "Stir it in slowly, like *die Grossmammi* showed you."

"I'm sorry. I'm afraid I'll make a mess of it and ruin your whole batch."

"Nonsense. Simply pay more attention to your work."

"I'll try," she promised.

"Won't you be proud to take some jars back to your friends, and show them what you have learned?"

"Yes, of course. And it will make a nice thank-you gift for my neighbor. She's been watching my duplex while I'm away." She smiled, imagining Josie's face when she presented her with the jelly, made in part by Taryn's own hand. And Molly! She couldn't imagine what her friend's reaction might be. She suspected Molly was one of those people who just assumed food was produced at the grocery store.

The kitchen door swung open and Deborah came running in, her face flushed with excitement.

"Deborah!" Lillian rapped sharply. "What have I said about slamming the door?"

"I'm sorry, *Mamm*, but we just had another customer stop off the road. He bought one of *Grossdaadi's* carvings, and a jar of pickles. And he gave me this extra!" She held out her palm, showing a crumpled five-dollar bill.

"My, we are certainly getting *gut* business these last few days," Lillian said. She gave her niece a pleased smile as she washed the last of the strawberries. "You have brought us this good fortune, Taryn Clark."

Taryn faltered, dumping the sugar too quickly into the boiling water. It landed with a plop, sending a purl of liquid heat to splash up onto her hand. "Oh!" she cried in surprise.

"Whatever happened? Are you okay?"

"Please, can you take over?" Taryn quickly handed the long-handled wooden spoon over to her aunt.

"You should run cold water over that," the eldest of the Zook women advised. She set scalded jars onto the counter top, in anticipation of the sweet, tangy goodness soon to fill them.

"And wrap it in clean cloth," Caroline added.

"You know what? If you don't mind, I think I'll go up to my room and take care of this," Taryn said, already edging her way toward the door.

Let them think her hand truly pained her. They didn't need to know that it was her heart troubling her the most.

That, and her guilty conscious.

Before she even reached the deck, her phone rang. She looked down in dread, afraid she might see an unknown number. So far, the ominous messages had come from two such callers. She was relieved to see Molly's number on her screen, until she heard her friend's reason for calling.

After a brief chat, Molly got around to her message, "I was calling to tell you that a man dropped by the house yesterday. Said he was a former client of the firm and wanted to speak to you about a job offer. I gave him your number. I hope that was okay?"

"How did he know to come to your house? Who was he? What did he look like?"

"Uhm, older guy, I think with gray hair. Didn't catch the whole name. Smith, I think it was. He said he pulled up at your house, just as I was leaving. I noticed that your ivy looked a little droopy when I watered it Friday, so I dropped by with some plant food. Anyway, he followed me, thinking I might be you."

"That's all he said? That he knew me from the firm? How did he know to go to my house?"

"I don't know, Tar. I didn't ask a lot of questions. He seemed like a nice-enough guy, and it's not surprising that you would have job offers. You're an excellent legal assistant."

"Okay, Molly. Thanks for calling."

"Are you trying to rush me off the phone?"

"Sorry, but I burned my hand making jelly. I need to put something on it."

"Wait. *You* made jelly? Don't tell me you've turned Amish on me!" her friend hooted.

"You can't just *turn* Amish," Taryn fairly snapped. "Look, Mol, I need to go. I'll call you later, okay?"

"Sure. Take care of your hand. Oh, and bring me some of that jelly!"

Her friend's laughter still echoed on the line when Taryn punched *end.*

She immediately tried Bryce, but the call went to voicemail. She sent him a text, instead.

I'm getting worried. They know I'm here. Customer traffic off the road has picked up in the last few days. Yesterday, someone went to

my house in Philly. I suppose when they didn't see my car here, they
thought I went home. They don't know I won't give up so easily.

When he didn't readily reply, Taryn took care of her hand.
Tired from her restless night, she lay down across the bed and
dozed.

She heard her phone bing sometime later. She saw a text,
but it wasn't from Bryce.

Roses are red, violets are blue.

You can hide, but I'll find you.

CHAPTER 28

"*Mamm* says to tell you, you will have dinner with us again."

Young Deborah delivered the message to Taryn's door, on her way to help Pete herd chickens before nightfall.

Taryn's smile was wistful. "I'm not sure I'll be good company this evening, Deborah. But I appreciate the invitation."

"I don't think it was an invitation," the girl said, slowly shaking her head. "It was more like a summons. You didn't hear the sound of her voice."

"Oh." She had noticed that Lillian's mood had been rather sharp today. It was so unlike her normally cheerful and easy-going aunt. Taryn worried she had something to do with it. "In that case, I would love to come."

"Ooh, I think I hear another automobile! Maybe someone else will give me extra money!" The youth took off in excitement, before Taryn had an opportunity to warn her about talking to strangers.

Instinct told Taryn to stay out of sight, but curiosity drove her to the edge of the stairs. She peeked around the corner. Just as Deborah said, a maroon pickup eased up the driveway and came to rest behind Bryce's borrowed car.

Effectively blocking me in? The sinister thought whispered through her head, urging her to stay hidden there in the shadows.

She watched as a tall, broad-shouldered man gracefully exited the truck. Her knees sagged in relief when she recognized Bryce.

"Bryce!" she called, waving to get his attention. "I'll be right down!"

She ran back to the room to grab her phone and to pull a brush through her hair. She didn't bother to wonder about that last action. She hurried back across the deck and down the stairs, only to find Deborah finalizing a sale.

"This young lady is quite the salesman," Bryce informed her, but his dark eyes twinkled as he indicated the brown bag in his arms.

"So I see!" Taryn laughed. "Deborah, this is my friend, Bryce. Bryce, meet Deborah. She's the young artist I told you about, and the queen of the chicken coop."

The girl looked pleased, but like any good Amish, she was quick not to take credit for her talents. "It is God's gift, shared through my humble hands." She stashed the small assortment of jellies and jams, woodcarvings and handicrafts, into a large plastic tote, stowing them away for the evening. Tomorrow, they would come out again, in hopes of enticing more *Englisch* buyers.

Young Pete raced from the house, dashing past the gardens in the direction of the chicken coops. "Rooster's out!" he called over his shoulder.

"Sorry, I must help him." Deborah said hastily. In no time, she dashed across the yard and caught up with her younger brother.

"So. That's the family, huh?" Bryce asked in amusement.

"Only part. Just wait about twenty minutes, when Lillian rings the dinner bell. They'll come pouring out from the barns and the fields, like a mini army, dressed in aprons and suspenders."

He peered down at the bag he held. "Have any need for apple butter and fresh peach preserves?"

She shook her head. "'Fraid not. I helped put up strawberry jelly today. I have the battle scars to prove it." She held up the tiny pucker of red skin as proof.

"So it was jelly, not pickles."

"Right. Why don't you put that bag in the truck and we can sit on the gazebo? And whose truck is that, by the way?"

"Mine." He saw the confusion that crinkled her forehead. "What? You think I drive that flashy car around when I'm on a stakeout? That's for play. The truck is for work."

"And my car?"

"Parked out of sight."

She waited for him to stash the bag, tangible proof of young Deborah's sales prowess. They walked together to the gazebo, admiring the lush yard in the waning hours of daylight.

"Great yard," Bryce commented. "The Amish are known for their elaborate lawns and gardens. Makes you wonder where that 'pride is a sin' mantra comes into play." He dipped his head closer to hers and stage-whispered, "You know they try to outdo their neighbors."

"Lillian would no doubt say it is a tribute to God and the wonders of his grace."

He eyed her with a curious look. "You're really getting into this Amish lifestyle, aren't you?"

Taryn led him across the boardwalk, to the gazebo extending over the pond. The swing sagged as they took their seats. "Do I think they're good, honest, hard-working people? Yes. Do I think they would do anything to help a neighbor? Or a stranger, for that matter? Yes. Do I think I could ever live the way they do, working from dusk to dawn with few of the luxuries of modern-day life? Absolutely not. I admire them, but I don't envy them."

"Well said."

They were quiet for a long moment, watching the ducks splash in the water and the grasses sway in the gentle breeze. It was a peaceful time of day, heavy with the settling of overhead clouds and the sounds of cattle lowing during evening milking. Taryn detected the measured clip-clop-jingle of a horse-drawn wagon approaching. Peter, no doubt, or Samuel, coming in from the fields after toiling all afternoon in the hot summer sun. She could hear the squawk of the chickens and little Pete's exasperated cries as he tried to corral them. Taryn smiled, imaging the sight that must be.

When her eyes roamed over to the adjoining King Farms, the smile dimmed. She took a deep breath and turned to her companion. "Why are you here, Bryce?" she asked quietly.

There was nothing rude in her inquiry. Bryce understood her concern.

"I heard back from my old Navy buddy. As it turns out, he actually knows Ahndray Lamont. He's bought horses from him before."

"You're kidding! What a crazy coincidence!"

"Not according to my buddy. He says your father is well known for raising the best horses in the south of France."

"Does he know him personally? Does he know anything about his personal life? Does he have a wife?"

He answered in the order she asked. "Yes. Yes. No. Tabor— my friend—does know him. He's been in his home before and had dinner there, several years ago. He says there's no wife, or girlfriend. Apparently, your father is more the solitary type."

"So this is good news, right? We've established a solid connection. Why did I think you came bearing bad news?"

When he didn't answer, Taryn frowned. "Oh. I get it. That means Rebecca never made it out. She didn't make it across the ocean to find her true love and to live happily ever after." The news saddened her, but hardly surprised her.

"I learned a bit about his father."

It was the way he said it.

"And there it is," Taryn mumbled. "The bad news you came to deliver."

"It's news, at any rate."

"So give it to me."

"It seems that Ahndray's mother had a long-term affair with an American businessman. Even though the man has a wife and family here in the States, he had a second home there, with her. When Ahndray was old enough, his father arranged for a work visa to the United States and paid for him to come here. He didn't acknowledge him as his son, but he did take him on as an apprentice, of sorts."

"Sounds like a swell dad." Taryn's tone was sardonic. "Especially the part where he later has him deported."

"There doesn't seem to be any love lost between the two men. Among other things, Ahndray blames his father for his mother's premature death."

"So he took two women from Ahndray's life," she sympathized. "My mother, and his."

"So it seems."

Taryn thought for a moment. "Did you get his father's name?"

"Tabor wasn't sure he had ever heard it. Understandably, Ahndray doesn't like to talk about his father, but through the years, bits and pieces of his story have come out. But I did manage to track down the company that contracted Ahndray to work for them, here in the States."

"Was this before he worked for Manuel King?"

"Maybe. Or maybe he was contract labor, all along. Remember, Toad brought him here, that very first time."

"I should have known Toad worked into this somehow," she mumbled darkly.

"Ahndray worked for a company called *Ines International*."

Taryn was still for a moment, running the name through her mind. "*Ines International. Ines International.* Why does that name sound so familiar?"

"I don't think you would have found it so easily yesterday, but I did a little digging. *Ines International* has one quarter interest in *Roi Ecuries.*"

This surprised her. "So Ahndray still works for them?"

"I think it's more than that. I think his father owns *Ines.* I think his American father is still bankrolling his life there in France," Bryce surmised.

She thought over his words. "It makes sense, I guess. You mentioned something about an apprenticeship. If his father arranged for the work visa, it makes sense he could have been the employer. It probably made it easier to jerk his visa away, when he wanted to send his son back to France."

"There's more."

Taryn blew out a long breath. "Of course there is."

"According to their website, *Ines International* is a leader in cutting-edge genetics. They specialize in breeding horses for incredible speed and endurance, particularly for the racing industry."

Another frown marred her forehead. "Steroids?"

"They call it genetic enhancement."

Dread pooled in her belly. "Would some people call that *doping?*"

"I'm no expert in genetics or the molecular structure of drugs, but I can see where there could be a direct correlation between the two."

Taryn rubbed her fingers across her forehead. She suddenly had a nagging headache. "Okay, so walk me through this. Are we saying that Ahndray's father brought him here to the United States with the express purpose of having him promote his shady business practices? That he coerced my father into... what? Selling illegal steroids within the industry? Drugging the horses himself?" She gasped when she realized what she said. Her eyes rounded into perfect orbs. "King Farms! Are you saying Ahndray truly was doping my grandfather's horses?"

"It's a theory I'm tossing around," Bryce admitted. "Think about it. His father pays for their life in France and provides for Ahndray and his mother. He arranges for Ahndray to come here and work in the family business. Even if Ahndray is opposed to doping the horses, what can he do? His father pulls all the strings, including the purse strings. He controls his life."

"Do you suppose his father was in cahoots with the Toad? They sound like a matched pair. Both greedy and controlling, and completely unconscionable." Taryn's finger drummed against her lip in irritation, growing more agitated with every tap, as she contemplated her theory. "They both find people's Achilles heels and force them into doing their bidding. I bet they were partners, Ahndray's father and the Toad. Don't you?"

"No, Taryn, I don't think they were partners."

Something in his low, solemnly spoken words drew her gaze. Bryce's steady gaze made her nervous.

"Oh no," she said, shaking her head vehemently. "No, no, no. Absolutely not. You can't be suggesting what I think you're suggesting."

"It makes sense, Taryn. Think about the similarities. How easy it would have made everything. Think about your mother's final letter."

Taryn recalled the letter in her mind's eye. *"The toad made it clear,"* she whispered.

Bryce took her hand, pressing the relevance into her. "We wondered why that particular phrase was mixed in with talk of his father. You thought she might relate all evil men to toads and warts, remember?"

She still shook her head, reluctant to admit what she knew was true. "No. It can't be."

"I think it is, Taryn. I think the Toad was Ahndray's father."

"But he can't be. He just can't be," she cried, turning her stricken violet eyes to his. "That—That would mean... That makes the Toad my other grandfather!"

CHAPTER 29

Bryce pressed her head against his shoulder, strictly for means of comfort. He would do the same for a child, or an aging woman. His arm circled her for support.

To the girl coming up the walk, it appeared to be an intimate scene.

Her bare feet made no sound upon approach. "Sorry to disturb you but *die Mamm* says to invite your young man to dinner." Susannah's eyes danced with mischief as she sashayed up to the gazebo, her long skirts swishing.

"Oh!"

Taryn jerked in surprise, jarring Bryce's chin with the top of her head. He muttered a few choice words beneath his breath. He quickly released her and tended his bleeding tongue.

"I didn't hear you come up," Taryn said, hastily wiping her face, lest a stray tear linger.

"So I see." Susannah squirmed in delight, clearly misreading the situation. She eyed Bryce with interest. "You'll stay, won't you? The family would like to meet Taryn's new *friend*." She put emphasis on the word, her violet eyes twinkling.

Startled by the striking resemblance between the girl and Taryn, particularly in the unique color of their eyes, Bryce was clearly caught off guard. Like her younger sister, the Amish girl relied on her refreshing personality to sway him. Before she left to run back into the house, she had secured his acceptance to the dinner invitation. *"Kummit esse!"* she encouraged them.

"My young man!" Taryn complained when they were alone again. She rolled her eyes. "You're not even a full ten years younger than my aunt. She acts like we're teenagers or something."

"I think it's the something," Bryce said dryly.

"After the night before last, and now this, I'm never going to convince them we're not an item," Taryn complained.

"Should I have declined the invitation?"

"And insult my aunt? No way."

"If I can even eat," Bryce groused, holding his injured tongue.

She offered a grimace, if only in support. "Yeah. Sorry about that."

⁂

Dinner was every bit as delicious and noisy as Taryn had warned it would be. Bryce visited with the men, carrying his share of the conversation with ease. If she had briefly worried about him fitting in, she soon discovered it was for naught. Having lived in the area for so many years, he was more familiar with Amish customs than Taryn realized. He knew a surprising amount about farming, and deftly managed to work the conversation around to horses and the operation next door.

Lillian's son Jonah often helped his uncles and cousins when they took their animals to horse auction and spoke about the topic at length. Taryn remembered that Rebecca had mentioned the auctions in her journals. She couldn't listen in, as Susannah was in the middle of a lively tale about the conclusion of today's jelly making, but she made a mental note to ask Bryce about the conversation later.

Taryn noticed that her aunt continued to be withdrawn during the meal, but as they pushed back from the table, she spoke up.

"Taryn Clark, may I have a word with you and your young man? Susannah and Melanie will tend to the dishes."

Taryn felt like a schoolgirl, being called into the principal's office. She followed her aunt into *die Sitz Schtubb*, the sitting room reserved for visitors. Until now, Taryn had never been inside the room. The good parlor had a small settee, a straight-back chair, and the family's heirloom rocker, passed down from generation to generation. A large hooked rug adorned the floor, pretty china and knickknacks graced a corner cupboard, and a framed piece of artwork hung on the wall. The artwork was done on canvas and quoted the first lines of 'Amazing Grace.' Taryn was surprised to see the tiny speaker at the bottom.

*When would she remember that the Amish appreciated music
and beautiful things, just like everyone else, and most particularly
when they praised God?* Taryn chided herself for being surprised to find the piece there.

"Taryn Clark, I have become quite fond of you in this past
week," her aunt said without preamble.

Taryn chose to ignore the silent 'but.' Her voice was sincere as she replied, "I feel the same way about you and your
family, Aunt Lillian."

"I know you are a grown woman. I know the *Englisch* have
different ways. But I have young children in the house. They
are easily impressed upon, ain't so?"

"I agree, they are impressionable," Taryn said solemnly,
wondering where this was going.

"It pains me to point this out, but you spent the night out
recently." Lillian's eyes wandered to Bryce. They brimmed
with quiet accusation.

"Ma'am," he was quick to point out, "it isn't what you
think."

"It doesn't matter what I think. It's what my children think.
Susannah, in particular. She admires you, Taryn Clark. She
fancies she sees herself in you."

Taryn smiled at the compliment. She felt the same way
about the young girl, but now was not the time to be flattered.
She had to do damage control.

"I understand, and I will speak to her. But please understand, Lillian. Bryce is not my... That is to say, we're not..."

When she faltered with the words, Bryce stepped in to
clear matters up. In his strong, commanding voice, he made a

convincing argument. "The truth is, ma'am, your niece hired me to help her find her birth mother and the truth about her past. Allow me to formally introduce myself." He stood and offered his hand. "Bryce Elliott, *Keystone Secure Investigations.* I'm a private investigator, ma'am."

Lillian's hand wandered to her throat, and she paled by several shades. "Oh," she said. "Oh, I see."

Because he was an investigator, and a good one, Bryce noticed the unease in Lillian's response to his introduction. She smiled politely and asked the appropriate questions, marveling at her niece's wisdom to hire professional help. She claimed she would never have thought to do the same. She took part in the conversation, but she was clearly distracted. For whatever reason, he obviously made the woman nervous.

"I've shown Bryce the journals," Taryn told her aunt. "Or at least the pertinent excerpts. And he's read the final letter."

"Oh. I see," she repeated the words. This time, her voice was as pale as her colorless skin. She darted nervous eyes to the man still looming over them.

Realizing how menacing he must look, Bryce quickly took a seat. "I'd like to ask you a few questions, Lillian. Is it all right that I still call you Lillian?"

"Of course."

"It occurs to me that you would have known the man Rebecca referred to as The Toad. Is that correct?"

Her reply was stiff. "Yes, I have seen the man."

"Do you know his name?"

"*Nee.*"

The one-word denial was not particularly forthcoming. Bryce had to fish for more information.

"But you often saw him there on the farm? Is there anything you can tell us that could help us identify him?"

When she still hesitated, Taryn put her hand on her aunt's arm. "Please, Aunt Lillian. This is important. Bryce and I are both convinced it was this man, the man she called the Toad, who was responsible for my mother's death. He was an evil, evil man. He got your mother addicted to cocaine. He forced your father to dope the horses. And when Rebecca overheard them arguing, and found evidence of his crimes, he threatened her. She ran away to escape him, and to keep her family safe. But I think he caught up with her in the end. And killed her." Her voice was soft but filled with conviction. "The Toad killed your sister. My birth mother."

Lillian pulled her apron to her mouth, to capture the sob that tore from her throat.

"Please, Aunt Lillian, tell us anything you remember. This man has to pay for his crimes."

Even behind the lenses, her eyes revealed her terror. "I—I do not know his name. It's been many years since I saw him last."

"Would you recognize him, if you saw a picture of him?" Bryce asked.

Her answer was evasive, her gaze skittering off to hide in a corner.

"Perhaps. But it's been so long."

"Did he have any distinguishing characteristics? Did he have a scar, or a limp, or was he missing any fingers?"

Lillian shook her head. "I don't remember."

Bryce pressed for more details. Did she remember where he was from? Did his car have Pennsylvania plates?

"You must remember, I was but a child, too busy with childish games to notice my father's business dealings. Even that fateful year, I was only twelve, barely thirteen."

Bryce let out a frustrated sigh. He caught Taryn's eye over the top of Lillian's bent head, buried once again in her apron. He recognized the subtle warning he saw there. They weren't likely to get anything else from her tonight, and his formal interrogation wasn't helping.

"Thank you for your help, Lillian, and for that delicious meal," he said. "If you think of anything else, be sure to let Taryn know. Taryn, I'll walk you to your room before I go."

"I'll talk to Susannah," she promised her aunt. "Thank you, Aunt Lillian, for dinner."

After goodbyes, Bryce walked her up the exterior staircase and across the wide deck.

"Your aunt knows more than she's saying," Bryce said, keeping his voice low.

"I think so, too, but what? And why is she so frightened? Not that your questions were helping," she chided. "You sounded like a military sergeant, barking one question after another. This wasn't an official interrogation, you know."

He blew out a deep breath, not bothering to defend himself. "Old habits die hard, I guess."

She softened, but only marginally. "Would you like to have a seat?" It was a nice night out. The moon hung low in the sky, still making its trek across the darkened heavens.

He pulled a chair out for each of them, positioning them to overlook the barns and fields beyond.

"Now that my aunt knows about the investigation, should we warn her of the danger?" Taryn asked.

"Believe me, Taryn. Your aunt is fully aware of the dangers. Didn't you see how frightened she was?"

"Yes, but of what? We're the only ones who know she has the journals. Even with them, it's more speculation than proof. Her father's been dead for years now. Her mother is apparently comatose. Rebecca is gone. There's no one left who can prove any of our suspicions."

"You don't suppose your uncles were in on the doping, do you?" he speculated.

She shook her head. "I don't think so. Rebecca never hinted at that in her journals."

"I agree, but it was worth a thought."

"Should we go to the police, Bryce? No offense. It's not that I doubt your abilities," she was quick to say, "but should we tell them about the messages? About someone following me?"

"No offense taken. I'm friends with most of the guys on the sheriff's department and with the town police. They're a fine group of men and women, but they won't be of much help on this. They don't have the manpower, or the budget, or the experience to handle this. On a scale of one to five, this won't even move the meter."

His answer disturbed her, until he explained. "So far, they haven't done anything illegal. Followed you a time or two. Called you. Even the messages haven't been direct threats.

From a legal perspective, there's not a single thing the law can do."

"Someone is harassing me."

"But without knowing who that someone is, there's nothing to do for it."

"You're right, of course."

Bryce's dark eyes glittered in the moonlight. "That doesn't mean you and I can't do something about it."

"What do you mean?"

"Do you remember your analogy about the ice cream cone?" he asked quietly.

She frowned, uncertain where the conversation was going.

"You said you were so close to having everything you wanted, but not really. You said it was like someone handing you an ice cream cone, and then telling you not to lick it."

"Your point?"

"We find out who's harassing you."

Her frown only deepened. "What does that have to do with the ice cream cone?" she asked in confusion.

"We don't have to let the ice cream melt. You were only told not to *lick* it. No one said you couldn't bite right in and take out a chunk."

CHAPTER 30

Bryce returned her car early the next day and parked it in visible sight of the road.

"So, how do I look?" Taryn asked, twirling around for his inspection.

"I have to admit, if I didn't know it was you under that get-up, I'd never recognize you."

"You know," Taryn said with a bit of a giggle, "I've dressed up before. This is the first time I've ever dressed *down*."

Her face was free of makeup and her honey-colored hair parted in the middle and coiled into a bun at the back of her crown. The simple burgundy dress hanging from her shoulders boasted no remarkable characteristics, its fit intentionally loose. A black work apron wrapped around her waist and there were no shoes at all upon her feet.

Melanie shared a familiar saying among their People. "If you can't drop a Coke bottle down your waistline, your clothes are too tight."

Taryn had to admit, the Amish chose their clothes wisely, with thought to unrestricted movement, durability, and easy care. The fabrics were no-wrinkle polyester.

"You'll need to put on your shades," Bryce cautioned. "I know several others in the family have the same color eyes as you, but you don't want to call any attention to yourself. The idea is to blend in."

"Then this should do the trick." She made certain the black kerchief was secure on her head. "I think my aunt is secretly enjoying this. She has my day all planned. After working in the garden, I'm to sit out here and shell peas. If I finish with that, I get to hoe the flowerbeds. I'll have good visibility of any customers stopping by."

"I doubt these people will give up after just one day," Bryce warned.

"Don't worry," she all but groaned. "My aunt has plenty of work for me."

"Remember to keep your cell in your pocket. Call me if you need to. Try not to talk to the visitors more than you have to, in case you slip up and say something decidedly English but see if you recognize anyone."

"Deborah has a plan for that," she assured him. "I'm her 'simple-minded' cousin, visiting from Ohio. She says she can pretend to train me, so she'll be doing all the talking."

"Then I'll get out of here and let you enjoy your day playing Amish dress-up."

She saw the glint lingering in his eye. "I think *you're* enjoying this, too!" she accused.

"Amish is a good look on you."

In response, Taryn stuck out her tongue at him, in a very un-Amish way.

⸙

At least a half dozen cars stopped that day. The first was a group of four women, visiting from the Baltimore area. Deborah worked her charm, sending them each away with a brown paper bag. Two couples stopped by, one of them leaving with a pieced lap quilt and matching pillow. While Taryn stood aside and pretended to watch and learn, Deborah sold jelly to one man, and a dozen fresh eggs to another.

The egg buyer made Taryn nervous. He drove a light-colored car, possibly the same one that had followed her. He sat in his car for a moment before getting out, seemingly on his cell phone, but his eyes roamed curiously over the area.

That, in itself, wasn't unusual. Most people had an insatiable appetite for insight into the Amish way of life. Even when they knew of the Amish aversion to having their photographs taken, they snapped away on their cameras and made rude attempts to pry into their privacy.

But the egg buyer seemed particularly interested in Taryn's car, parked there in the driveway. While most of the other tourists marveled over the buggies in the three garage bays, this man seemed more intrigued with her ordinary automobile.

The last customer of the day came about thirty minutes after the egg buyer left. Taryn couldn't help but wonder if the two weren't using a tag-team system. This man drove a blue Camry.

"Say there, Missy, did you make this butter?" the man asked, deliberately directing his question to Taryn.

"I made it," Deborah said quickly. She tucked her head and looked at the man from beneath her prayer cap, appearing particularly humble. "Well, to be honest—and the *gut Gott* says we must be—*die Grossmammi* helped me, just this morning."

"Is this your die-ga-mammy?" the man asked, butchering the pronunciation as he all but leered at Taryn.

When Deborah broke out giggling, Taryn followed suit. "*Nee*, this is not my grandmother! My grandmother is old. *Ach*, but don't tell her I said so!" The girl hid her snicker behind her hand, pretending that the words had simply slipped out. "This is my cousin, from Ohio. Where are you from, Mister?"

"Huh? Oh, Harrisburg," he answered in a distracted manner.

"Is that in Pennsylvania, or in Ohio?" the girl asked.

"It's the capitol of Pennsylvania. Don't they teach that in those little one-room schoolhouses?"

"We're out for summer break," the child explained. "This butter is *wunnderbaar gut*. We just churned it this morning. Would you like some, sir, to take back with you to the capitol?"

The man was insistent about talking to Taryn. "Say, pretty lady. Tell me about churning butter."

"She didn't help with it," Deborah reminded him.

"But isn't the process the same?" He kept his eyes on the older of the two. "Do you use a churn, like they did in the old days?"

Taryn was at a loss for words, unsure of how to answer. She knew Lillian had a stainless-steel churn set inside a five-gallon plastic bucket, with a battery-operated drill attached through a hole in the lid. She had also seen a modern-day food processor on the counter in Lillian's kitchen, powered by another drill. Someone mentioned making smaller batches of butter in this fashion. She wondered if the man would know the difference, if she answered incorrectly.

Deborah came to her rescue. She moved slightly in front of her cousin and motioned for the man to lean closer. She dropped her voice and said in a conspiratorial manner, "Don't confuse her, Mister. She's a bit *schtupid*. Pretty as a flower, but *ferhoodled* in the head."

Playing along, Taryn giggled again. She twisted her hands shyly in her apron, managing to find her phone within her pocket. With any luck, she could snap a picture of the man and send it to Bryce.

The man studied her for a moment, but Taryn kept her expression blank, and her smile as guileless as possible. When a butterfly passed nearby, she pretended fascination. She chased after the colorful creature, laughing gaily as she pretended to have no other cares in the world. She heard the man grunt in disgust and conclude his deal with Deborah. He bought two sticks, never knowing when Taryn snapped his picture. Deborah had him engaged in deep conversation, trying to talk him into taking her last apple pie.

When he was gone, Taryn hugged her young cousin in glee. "You were brilliant! With those acting skills, you should be on Broadway!"

"Is that in Pennsylvania, or Ohio?" the child asked with an innocent smile.

☙❧

The rooster's craggy call bumped into Taryn's dreams, jostling her awake. Her first instinct was to bury her head beneath the pillows and go back to sleep. She was having a perfectly delightful dream about horses. The steed she rode was large and powerful, and she rode with abandon, racing across grassy fields and meadows covered in daisies. She could all but feel the wind in her hair, rendering it a tangled mess at her nape. The rooster was an intrusion, startling the horses in her dream world. Their graceful gait faltered, and Taryn fell from her mount, only to be trampled by the galloping mob behind her.

She pried one eyelid open at a time, fearful of the injuries she would find. Her bleary eyes settled on the white clouds, floating there on the horizon. She concentrated on focusing, until she could determine those weren't clouds, at all. They were the lacy curtains in her room, and that grassy horizon yonder was the standard green shade beneath them. There were no horses.

Taryn rolled onto her back and groaned aloud. Why, then, did she ache all over?

The memory of the day before came back quickly. This city girl wasn't accustomed to working in the gardens. Bending and

picking, hoeing and weeding, called upon seldom-used muscles. They all screamed at her now, as she reluctantly dragged
herself from the covers.

Her cousins came to dress her in a drab green dress on this
day, with a black apron completing the ensemble. Taryn
glanced down at her hands. She had taken off her nail color
yesterday morning, so as not to call attention to her pampered
hands and feet. Her manicure was truly ruined now. Telltale
traces of dirt lingered at her cuticles, hiding there in the crevices. She remembered ripping the edge of one nail, as she
struggled to pull a stubborn vine free from its hold in the
ground. She dared not look too closely at her feet. Perhaps ig-
norance, in this case, was bliss.

The day repeated itself, with Taryn working in the flowerbeds at the front of the house, nearest the sales stands.

The first car to pull in for the day was the blue Camry.
Taryn nudged Caroline, who knelt beside her in the damp soil.
"That's the same car as yesterday, but they're up to something.
That's a different man."

"I shall handle this. You stay here." Caroline deftly rose
from the flowerbed and brushed off her hands.

The man walked slowly toward the stand, his eyes darting
all about as he scanned the area. His eyes probed Caroline's
face before moving on to survey the other woman in the yard.
Taryn kept her head slightly averted as she tugged on the unwanted weeds and discarded them into a pile. She took great
care in her ministrations, seemingly absorbed in the tedious
chore. The man dismissed her, his gaze moving on to the

house and the vegetable gardens beyond. His attention lingered on the car, parked there in front of the triple garage.

"May I help you?" Caroline offered. "A jar of fresh strawberry jelly? Fresh eggs, or butter?"

The man picked up one of the jars, but his eyes kept roaming. "This fresh?"

"We just made it."

"Local berries?"

"Grown right here on the farm."

"I don't see the vines." It wasn't for lack of trying. The man still hadn't met her gaze, his eyes too busy prying into the landscape behind her.

"They're here," she assured him.

"I've never seen an Amish farm before," he said. He finally reined in his roving eyes and settled them upon hers. "You give tours?" he asked.

"I'm afraid not. We are much too busy working to offer such interruption."

He didn't take the subtle hint. "Sure would like to see those berry vines. Make a nice story, when I take this jelly home to the little wife."

"If you'll look closely on the way out, you'll see the vines growing wild all along the fence. Do you need a bag for that?"

"What? Oh, no." He glanced down, as if surprised to see the jelly in his hands. "I can carry it." He pulled a few bills from his pocket, his gaze once again roaming the perimeters. "Say, I thought you Amish didn't believe in cars."

Keeping her head tucked, Taryn moved in closer, to the flowerbed circling the tree nearest the stand. She knelt with her back to the man, but her ears tuned in to the conversation.

"We don't," Caroline said simply.

"Then why's there a car parked in your garage?"

"Can you believe it? The woman just up and left it! Right here in our way!" The indignation in Caroline's sharp words sounded so convincing, even Taryn was startled.

"What woman?" the man asked.

"The one who came to stay in the room. Left in the middle of the night, with only a note. Said to keep the car for payment. Now I ask you. What do we need with a car!" Caroline propped her hands onto her hips and put on such a convincing performance, Taryn had to bite back her laughter. She kept sneaking peeks from beneath her kerchief, thoroughly amused by the confusion on the man's face.

"You rent rooms?" he finally thought to ask.

"Not anymore!" Caroline threw up her hands in an act of outrage. "Not with *der Gascht* like that! You should see the filth of that room! Such a mess she left behind." She broke out into a tirade of angrily sputtered Pennsylvania Deutsch.

Looking more than perplexed, the man made a hasty retreat and left with his jar of jelly.

Deborah came running into the yard as the man backed away and left. "I missed one?" the girl asked in disappointment. Her eyes followed the car longingly down the drive.

"No concern. He was not a good buyer," her sister-in-law assured her.

"No," Taryn said, coming to join them with laughter in her voice, "but you are an excellent actress! The two of you make quite a team. You should take your show on the road!"

Neither of her Amish companions understood the reference. They looked down the lane toward the public thoroughfare in confusion, then back at Taryn. "We should move to the road?" Caroline asked.

"No, it's just an expression." She bumbled her way through an explanation but knew from the look on their faces that neither understood her ramblings. "You did a good job," she finished lamely.

"Oh, good. Good," Caroline said in relief. "I was nervous."

"It didn't show," Taryn assured her. "You did an excellent job. I think he believed you."

"I don't like telling an untruth," she admitted, "but I told myself it is like playing a *der Schabernack* on Samuel. Just a joke."

"That's a good way to think of it," Taryn agreed. She hated the thought of causing her family distress over their part in the charade.

"I told him I was only teasing, so my conscience is clear," she went on. "Is it my fault if the man does not speak *Deutsch* and hear my apology?"

Taryn was still laughing when she went back to her weeding.

❧

By mid-afternoon, the white car returned. Deborah flew out of the house and was there to greet the customer before he even crawled from the car. Taryn sat in the shade of the porch, shelling another mess of peas with Melanie and *die Gross-mammi* Zook.

"You were here only yesterday," the child remarked with candor. "Did you like the eggs that well?"

The man managed a sheepish look. "The truth is, I dropped them and broke them, before I could even take them home to my wife."

"Then you should buy two dozen today," the girl suggested innocently. "And some quilts to wrap them in."

"I don't need a quilt," the man said.

"A nice table runner, then? See? You can wrap it around the eggs, like this." She picked up a colorful runner quilted in blues and browns, stitched in the wedding ring pattern, and deftly wrapped up the egg cartons. "Buy the runner, and the eggs are free." Even at ten, she had long since mastered the art of marketing.

"Okay, sure," the man said. He was obviously distracted, his attention on the grounds he surveyed with his sharp gaze. He ignored Taryn, sitting there on the porch between an old woman and a teenager. He was looking for an 'English' woman, and all he saw were three Amish females of varying ages, shelling peas in their strange clothes and their strange language.

"That will be forty-five dollars," the child said proudly, slipping his purchase into a plastic grocery bag.

His eyes jerked back to the young shyster. "For a dozen eggs?"

"Two dozen, and a hand-stitched table runner. Your wife will love it!"

He didn't look pleased, but the man pulled a fifty-dollar bill from his wallet and tossed it at the child. "You may as well keep the change," he grumbled, "before you try to sell me something else."

"Would you like to buy a car?" she asked quickly, her eyes lighting with mischief.

That was one item he never expected to buy here, of all places. "A car?"

"I saw you eying that one there when you came by yesterday. I'll sell it to you, if you like."

"The woman who owns it might not be too happy about you selling her car," the man said, but he looked intrigued with her offer.

"Won't matter. She's long gone by now." The girl shrugged in a casual manner.

"What do you mean, gone?"

"Gone. Puff. Like smoke up a flue, *der Holsweg nausgagne.*" She used her hands to demonstrate. "Up and gone, with only the car and a big mess left behind."

"Where did she go?"

The girl scrunched up her face, pretending to search for an English word to translate. The man didn't need to know she was sending a silent prayer to God, asking for His forgiveness for such open deceit. "*Der Daedd* said to Good Riddance." She spread her hands wide again. "Wherever that is."

CHAPTER 31

Taryn relayed the day's events to Bryce over dinner. They ate at a busy family-owned smorgasbord, well known for its huge and varied offerings, and the uncompromising quality of their food. Many of the employees were of Mennonite or Amish faith, and all trained in excellent customer service and the preparation of authentic Pennsylvania Dutch cuisine.

"Why are you just now bringing me to this place?" Taryn playfully accused.

Bryce wiped the ham's honey glaze from his mouth. "If you think this is impressive, you should see their breakfasts. I can only afford to eat here on rare occasions, unless I want to buy myself a whole new wardrobe."

Taryn marveled at the swarm of activity around the huge dining room. "I can't believe this place is so busy. There's still a steady stream of people coming through the line."

"Makes it a good choice for meeting in public," Bryce agreed, slicing his fork through a generous hunk of meatloaf. "Hard to stand out in a place this big and populated. There's a gift shop in the basement, every bit as big."

"Maybe Deborah should get a job here. The girl is a natural salesman." Her voice held true affection.

"Sounds like she's quite the performer, as well."

"And Caroline, too. Both were very convincing." Taryn dipped her fork into a pile of hand-whipped potatoes.

"It sounds like your family has done a good job of covering for you. Any more messages on your phone?"

"Just my daily 'poem.'"

The last two had been variations of the first.

Roses are red, violets are blue.

Eyes so pure were always a clue.

And today's offering,

Roses are red, some violets are blue,

Forgetting the past, is best for you.

Bryce continued to quiz her. "And you haven't recognized any of the people who stopped by the farm stand?"

"No. But I'm fairly certain it's the same car that's been following me. Did the license plate number I sent you come back with any clues?"

"It's registered to a Wilford Downing in Philadelphia." He saw the way her eyes narrowed. "Do you know him?"

"No, but the name sounds familiar."

"Couldn't find much on him. No record, no outstanding warrants, no red flags. Works for a pharmaceutical company there in Center City."

Taryn shook her head in dismissal. "I'm not sure. It just sounded vaguely familiar." She popped a fresh asparagus spear into her mouth. "To convince these people I've left town, I can't be seen in my car. Can you drive me over to Lancaster tomorrow, so I can rent a vehicle for the next few days?"

"That won't be necessary. You can borrow the Corvette."

"I couldn't do that."

"Why not?"

"That's too much," she protested. "I could never ask that of you."

"You're not asking. I'm offering. Actually, I'm insisting. It offers the easiest solution."

Taryn was silent for a moment, staring down at the half-filled plate she had suddenly lost her appetite for. "Why, Bryce?" she asked softly. "Why are you doing all of this for me?"

His answer was simple. "You hired me."

"I hired you to find my birth mother. To fill in a few holes in my past. You never agreed to all the rest. The car chases. The danger. The loan of your expensive vehicle. This is far beyond the call of duty."

"When I commit to a cause, I give it my all," he told her.

"Is that what I am to you? A *cause*?" She dropped her eyes to her hands, which had slipped from the table to nestle in her lap. Her voice was small. "Am I really so pathetic?"

A nerve ticked along his clenched jawline. He shoved his own plate forward to settle his elbows upon the table, one fist resting in the palm of his other hand. Taryn couldn't help but notice the sculpted muscles along his forearms, a natural extension of his bulging biceps. Even in his civilian clothes, he looked every bit the military officer.

"You're hardly pathetic, Taryn."

"I just don't understand why you're so willing to do all this for me," she all but whispered. "It goes far beyond the norm."

His voice gentled somewhat. "You're not accustomed to people going the extra mile for you, are you?" he guessed.

She stared at a point beyond his shoulder. When she began to speak, her voice was low. "When my mother died, my father couldn't take me. He had a night job at the time, and there would be no one to watch me, essentially around the clock. His mother was older, and in no physical condition to tend to a rambunctious five-year-old. His brother didn't step up to offer, even though he was, supposedly, my godfather. None of them wanted me." Her voice was sad. Small.

"Your mother's family?"

"The same. Her parents had never approved of her adopting a child. They already had the perfect grandchildren, and they didn't need any more. Why take in someone else's unwanted child? My aunt—the sister my mother had never gotten along with since childhood—felt the same way. She had two little angels of her own. Taking on a little she-devil would have disrupted their perfectly ordered world."

When he would have broken in, she held up a warning hand.

"Her words, not mine. I overhead them talking, debating on what to do with me. They decided it was best—for *them*, anyway—to let me go back into the system. They claimed it was to give less fortunate souls a chance to have the family they always dreamed of." Her soft laughter, not really a laugh at all, was bitter. "I was only a child, but even I recognized it for what is was. A lie. A chance to wash their hands of me."

The words settled between them, heavy and ripe with heartache. Dishes rattled around them. Conversations drifted over from nearby tables. The sound of raucous laughter burst from a group of young men across the aisle. All around them, people enjoyed their meals with family and friends, oblivious to the pain and heartache served at their booth.

"I considered adoption, once." Bryce's voice was raw as he released his secret, unspoken until now.

Her eyes flew to his. Skittered away when she saw the pain in their dark depths.

"I was married for three years," he told her. Even as he said the words, he wondered why they poured from his mouth. He never talked about Maggie. Never.

"We met when I was home on leave. We married, and she came back to Italy with me. It was hard for her, being in a foreign country with no family, and no friends, and with a husband who was always on one mission or another. I tried to make it up to her, by giving her everything she could possibly need."

The nerve worked in his jaw again. He studied the tines of his idle fork as he spoke. "Turns out, the one thing she wanted was the one thing I couldn't give her. A child."

Rather than offer empty platitudes, Taryn offered something better. She offered a receptive ear.

"She wanted a baby more than anything. We went to countless doctors. Fertility specialists. There in Naples, here in the

States. I finally suggested adoption. Even when she resisted, I pressed the issue. I looked into it, and found there were hundreds of children, just waiting for the right parents to take them home."

"What—What happened?" she ventured to ask.

"We weren't the right parents." An edge moved into his voice, sharpening the tone, the overall feel of the story. Instinctively, Taryn knew she wouldn't like the outcome.

"Maggie didn't pass the background check. It seems there were... things... in her past that she failed to mention when we met. When we were planning our future, and when we were trying to have a child." His voice tightened, growing sharper still. "Things that a man should know about his wife, and definitely about the mother of his children."

The noisy group of boys stood from their table and moved along, still laughing and pushing one another in jest, as young men so often did. Bryce watched their retreat before he spoke again.

"Even though the military teaches its men to be officers and gentlemen, they're still men at their core. And men have a certain way of entertaining themselves, especially on long, lonely nights when they're stuck on a military base, hundreds of thousands of miles from home. And when those men find a particular type of movie, one that takes away some of that loneliness and reminds them of their sweethearts back home, the movie tends to circulate through base. And when the star of the movie bears a striking resemblance to the wife of one of the officers, word gets around. And when the officer hears such rumors about his wife, he protects her honor. Fights any man who dares to insult her, and him, even if that man is his own superior officer. And when such a fight ensues... well, all hell breaks loose."

His softly spoken words settled there between them, more heartache heaped onto the invisible platter already overflowing with such burdens.

Taryn's words came out hesitant, if not a bit squeaky. "I remind you of your wife?"

"Not in the least." He took a deep breath and slowly pushed it out. "You remind me of those children, waiting for the right parents. I always felt as if I had failed them."

His admission stunned her. "Whatever for? How could you have failed them?"

"If I had been wiser in choosing a wife, I could have made a difference for some of those children." The fork clattered to the table as he allowed it to fall. His words fell with it. "I could have been the right father."

"You don't have to carry the world on your shoulders, Bryce. You don't have to save it, all by yourself."

He pursed his mouth, considering her gentle input, even though his eyes didn't meet hers as he argued softly, "But I can do my part. It's what I was trained to do. To serve, honor, and protect."

He stood abruptly, muttering something about dessert.

Taryn knew he had revealed more about himself than he intended. His hasty departure was a way to save face, and to take the spotlight off him. She allowed him time to reach the dessert line on the right, before she wandered to the one on the left.

Maybe the delicious offerings would lift her spirits.

♋

Blood is red, violets are blue.
Don't try my patience, I thought you knew.

The text message woke Taryn early the next morning, rattling her phone before the rooster even crowed. The cryptic messages were growing more sinister by the day, each edging toward a definite threat.

With plans to help Bryce today from his office, Taryn dressed in her '*Englisch*' clothes today, long before Susannah arrived with breakfast. She had asked her aunt to add a bit extra this morning, so she could take the basket with her and share with Bryce.

She stopped by *Kaffi Korner* on her way.

"Good morning to you, Caryn," Helen greeted her with a smile. "You're becoming quite a regular, now aren't you?" Her eyes twinkled with mischief, insinuating another reason for Taryn's presence in town.

"Best coffee in town," came Taryn's easy reply.

"And close to Bryce's house, too. Quite convenient, wouldn't you say?"

"I imagine for him it is," she agreed.

"You wouldn't by chance be buying that second cup for our friend, now would you? It's his favorite."

Taryn refused to rise to the bait, even though the older woman all but begged for details into their relationship. "That's what I like about small shops like this," Taryn said, glancing around the shop affectionately. "You know your customers well enough to know just what they like. You don't always get that in bigger coffee shops." She handed over her credit card with a smile.

"I see how you avoided my question." Helen chuckled. She frowned when her machine beeped at her. "See now, you've gotten me all rattled, Carrie, dodging me that way. Can't even run a card correctly." She made a second attempt to slide the card through the reader.

Another beep. Seeing her frown, Taryn frowned. "Is there a problem?"

"I'm sure it's just this silly machine. Sometimes it runs a little slow." She tried the card twice more, before admitting defeat. "You don't by chance have another card on you, do you?"

Feeling uneasy—not to mention embarrassed—Taryn dug into her wallet and pulled out her debit card. She glanced at the expiration date on the declined card. Still good for two more years. Had she somehow missed a payment? She made a mental note to check with her card company.

"Now we're in business." The older woman smiled, as the reader happily spat out a receipt.

"Thanks, Helen."

Taryn collected her two steaming cups of coffee and headed to the door. She thought she was home free, until Helen's laughing voice called out, "Tell Bryce I said good morning!"

She resisted rolling her eyes, going with an elusive, "I will if I see him."

Thirty minutes later, Taryn crawled into the front seat of Bryce's pickup. Her tone was only mildly chastising. "You didn't tell me we were taking a field trip today."

"You object?" he asked in surprise.

"No. You just didn't mention it."

"Ever been to a racetrack before?"

"Collin used to like stock car racing, but I seldom went along."

"Collin?"

"The friend I was married to."

Bryce pulled onto the road and into the traffic flow before responding. "That's the strangest way I've ever heard someone describe her ex-husband."

"Calling him my ex-husband sounds so negative," Taryn admitted. "We're still close friends. Our marriage just didn't work out."

Her companion made no comment. Only after two more turns did he offer, "We're not going to the car races. We're going to the horse races."

"Oh." Obviously surprised, her voice brightened. "Now *that* I may like."

"As I said the other day, doing too many web searches could wave a red flag. A sudden increase in internet traffic to dormant sites could alert the wrong people that we're looking into things. So today, we'll give it a rest and do our research the old-fashioned way."

"In person?" she guessed.

"Best kind there is."

When her phone rang, Taryn looked down in dread. Her expression lightened when she saw the name scrawled across the screen. "Oh. Speaking of Collin... Hey, Collin. What's up?"

A few minutes into the conversation, a frown replaced her initial smile. By the time she said goodbye, a full-out scowl pulled at her features.

"Troubles?" Bryce asked.

"That was, obviously, Collin. He said he had a strange call a couple of days ago. Someone identified himself as a lawyer and said they wanted to speak to his wife, concerning an inheritance. He thought they were talking about Glynis, until they mentioned my birth date."

"Did he give them your number?"

"No. After just a few questions, he became suspicious."

"Isn't it a bit odd that they called your ex-husband? How long has it been since the two of you were married?"

"Seven years, but not so odd when you factor in the last name. Oddly enough, I married a man with the same last name as mine."

"You're kidding."

"Made it easy on me. Never had to change a single legal document, other than marital status."

"I suppose Clark is a fairly common name," he agreed, before turning his attention back to the case. "Did he say anything else?"

"They've had several hang-up calls on their home number. No caller ID, no message. And Glynis says one of her credit card accounts was hacked. Which reminds me. My card declined this morning."

He sent her a sharp look. "Does that happen very often?"

"First time ever."

"You might want to give them a call."

"Why the frown? What do you think is happening?"

"It sounds like they're taking the harassment to the next level. Someone is trying to put the squeeze on you."

Her phone rang again. "Oh, great. This is my next-door neighbor. Now what?" Even before she said hello, she knew it would be bad news.

Five minutes later, she relayed the conversation to Bryce.

"I think you're right. This is definitely the next level. That was my neighbor, who shares the other side of my duplex. Yesterday, two boxes were delivered to my doorstep. Josie brought them in for safekeeping, but she says today's delivery was too much."

"Dare I ask?"

"Apparently, I'm getting a new kitchen." Her tight smile was falsely bright. "A delivery van backed up to the driveway and deposited no less than five brand-new appliances, all top brands."

"That explains the maxed-out credit card," Bryce murmured.

Taryn dropped her face into her hands. "What am I going to do, Bryce? Now I have to go back to Philly and straighten this whole mess out."

"You aren't going anywhere."

"But I have to! There's several thousand dollars' worth of appliances sitting on my lawn!"

"That's exactly what they want you to do, Taryn. Someone is trying to flush you out, which means our little ploy worked. They believed you left the farm, and they're trying to draw you back home."

"It worked so well that now I have to go back and sort this all out." Her voice sounded defeated. "Turn around, Bryce."

"You're not going back. Let me make a couple of calls. In the meantime, contact your credit card company and dispute the charges. If your neighbor didn't say, ask them where the appliances came from. Report the order as fraud and demand they pick them up. The driver apparently left them without a proper signature, which puts them on the hook."

He pulled into the parking lot of the racetrack, but neither got out of the truck. They spent the next twenty-five minutes on their phones, making the necessary calls.

"Okay, the store agreed to pick everything back up," Taryn reported at last. "Stan is sitting outside on the sidewalk, keeping guard. The last thing I need is for someone to come along and steal everything before the van gets back. The card company will look into the dispute and refund my money in seven to ten days."

"Ouch. Hope that's not your only credit card."

"Fortunately, no. But if they hacked one account, I'm sure they can hack another."

"So maybe you should call the others and put a temporary freeze on your accounts. Same thing with your bank."

"That's all fine and good, but what am I supposed to do for the next few days? I have to eat. And I'm guessing the Corvette won't get nearly as good of fuel mileage as my car. I'll have to buy gas at some point."

"Remember that expense account I told you about? I'll share." He flashed a smile her way.

"I'm serious, Bryce. What am I supposed to do for money? I don't have all that much cash on me."

"Call your bank and explain the situation. Tell them you're out of town and will make an ATM withdrawal for X amount. All other transactions need your authorization. Freeze your card accounts with the same instructions. Only authorized transactions are allowed, and you'll call before each one."

"I can't believe this is happening," Taryn muttered, pulling out her wallet once again.

"Big bites, remember? Be proactive."

She all but growled at him, but forty minutes later, the deed was done. Bryce stood outside the truck and made a few calls of his own, until finally, they were ready to go inside.

"My legs have gone numb," she grumbled as he helped her from the truck.

"You'll be glad you took the time to take care of things. Here, put this on."

"Is this what you wore?" Her violet eyes danced with humor as she placed the floppy straw hat atop her head.

"Sure did. Would you like my scarf as well?"

She glanced at the atrocious item in question, stuffed there in the seat. If Bryce chose the pattern, he had terrible taste. "No thanks, I think I'll pass."

Seeing her curled-up nose, he seemed to read her mind. "In case you're wondering, a client left that behind. I thought I'd make good use of her carelessness."

"That was no accident, I can assure you. Your client left that hideous thing out of self-preservation, not out of carelessness."

He tried fighting the smile that tickled his lips. "Don't forget your shades."

As they crossed the parking lot and made their way to the horseshoe-shaped building, Taryn asked what they were looking for.

"The hallways are lined with pictures and paraphernalia from past winners. We're looking for names and faces. Anything that clicks with those we've already run across. Document anything interesting with your phone."

"Got it."

"Keep your face covered as much as possible. You never know who may be at the racetrack."

With that ominous thought, he ushered her inside.

CHAPTER 32

"I can't believe how many King horses there are on these walls," Taryn murmured as they strolled the curved hallway. The wall behind them was glass and overlooked the track.

"Like I told you before, your grandfather was well known for raising the finest horseflesh in the county, maybe even the state. His legacy continues, as you can see in recent pictures."

Though she had no right, Taryn felt a stirring of pride as she walked through the gallery. The horses sired at King Farms were superb, each one more magnificent than the last. Manuel King—her grandfather—truly knew how to breed and cultivate a fine animal. The majority of winners came from his stock.

The Amish breeder wasn't featured in any of the photographs. Even if he had been agreeable to facing a camera, breeders were seldom included in the fanfare of the win. That honor went to the owners, with the jockeys and trainers sometimes included. There was only one photograph, taken in the late 1970s, where a man in a plain black jacket and long beard stood off to one side. The broad brim of his flat-topped hat tilted down to shadow his face, but the caption identified him as Manuel King.

To Taryn's delight, several of the photographs from that period included her father. He was even more handsome and dashing as a young man. No wonder Rebecca fell for him so easily. Taryn snapped off several shots with her phone's camera, hoping the glass in the frames didn't leave too much of a glare.

"Finding something of interest?" Bryce asked, hearing her shutter click in repetition.

"My father." She kept her voice low for privacy sake. Sheer wonder softened it another notch.

She saw a few other familiar faces among the photos. Celebrities were always a welcomed addition to any photograph hoping for exposure. She recognized a rock star, a well-known athlete, one of her favorite authors, and a former senator, to name a few. Taryn even saw a few former clients of *Carver, Harris, and Harrison.*

She remembered that one of their clients had been a successful female jockey in a male-oriented field, and that another had owned numerous racetracks around the world. She wasn't surprised to see Thomas Baxter cozied up to the winner's circle, given the man's varied business dealings. She vaguely remembered horseracing as one of them.

"No luck, then?" Bryce asked as she turned away from the wall in dejection.

"No. Several of those photos are the same ones I found online. Only three or four faces repeatedly pop up in more than a handful of pictures. Not a single man stands there with a sign that says, '*It's me. I'm The Toad.*'"

He tried to frown at her dramatic proclamation, but a smile threatened. "No telltale warts or whiskers?"

"None that I could see. I even looked for someone who looked a bit like Ahndray Lamont, but that didn't work, either."

"Well, it was a good try, anyway."

She remained inconsolable. "The fact is, the Toad could be any one of those men in those pictures, or none of them. We're no closer to finding him now than we were before."

"It was worth a shot," Bryce insisted, defending their time there.

"So now what?"

When she would have taken the floppy hat off, he shook his head. "Keep it on until we're in the truck. And now I take you by the bank where I do business, so you can get some cash."

"There was an ATM back there. Why didn't I just use it?"

He hesitated before answering. He unlocked the door and helped her inside, then came around to get behind the wheel. Only after starting the motor did he say, "That was a reputable racetrack, but not all of them are. All the same, you probably didn't want your card being run through their systems."

"Oh," was her only reply.

※

"Aunt Lillian, I have a favor to ask."

Lillian was in the garden, collecting the day's bounty of fresh vegetables, when Taryn returned that afternoon.

"If it is within my power, I will grant it."

It struck Taryn that her aunt didn't offer an unconditional commitment. Most people would reply with 'sure' or 'anything,' and then backpedal when the request was too steep. Did Lillian's faith play into her reply? Was she so dedicated to keeping her word that she used caution, even when making a token promise? Or, Taryn wondered, was her evasive answer less noble? Did she suspect that what her niece asked of her might not be so simple to grant?

"I'd like to visit King Farms."

Lillian straightened from picking peas and turned her solemn gaze upon her niece. She remained silent for so long that Taryn began to squirm, caught there beneath her steady appraisal.

When she finally spoke, it was to ask a question, "Do you think that's wise?"

Taryn countered with one of her own, "Why wouldn't it be?"

"Because some things are best left be, Taryn Clark. Some things are best forgotten."

Yesterday's riddle flashed through her mind. *Forgetting the past, is best for you.*

Her aunt's reply stung. It felt like rejection.

"Is that what you think? That Rebecca should be forgotten?"

Lillian's head snapped back, and she sucked in a quick breath, as surely as if Taryn had slapped her. "Of course not!" she cried. "How can you say such a thing!"

"I want to see the farm where my mother grew up. The horses she loved so well. The place where she met my father. Is that so much to ask?"

Instead of answering, Lillian reminded her, "The farm belongs to Josiah now. It is not my wish to grant."

Knowing this answer could hurt as much as the last one, Taryn asked, nonetheless. Her voice was quiet. "Does he know about me?"

The shake of the other woman's head was slight, but it was enough to pierce Taryn's heart. Her aunt hadn't bothered telling her brother about their shared niece. That a part of their sister lived on, despite losing her all those years ago.

"I didn't mean to hurt you."

It was an empty sentiment and did little to ease the pain ripping its way through Taryn's heart. She struggled with tears burning hot beneath her lids, threatening to spill their trail of fire down her cheeks.

"There are things you don't understand." Lillian's tone was pleading.

Instead of answering, instead of demanding she *make* her understand, Taryn simply stared at her aunt with her clear, violet-colored eyes. Eyes that marked her as surely as any birthmark ever could.

Those eyes made it impossible for Lillian to deny her heritage, nor her indelible link to this family, and to the past that still haunted them. With a sigh of defeat, she dropped her head, unable to hold her niece's unwavering gaze.

"I will speak to him this evening," she promised. "If he agrees, I'll take you there tomorrow."

Not trusting her voice, Taryn only nodded.

She turned away, before her aunt could say more.

❧

Taryn went through the journals and letters again that evening, searching for clues she may have missed. She paid careful attention to each entry about the toad, but none of them offered a good description of the man. She only knew that he puffed out his chest, barked out orders, and expected others to do his bidding. He looked down upon them with his superior attitude and left warts of dissension wherever he went.

No matter how many times she went through her mother's writings, there simply wasn't enough to identify the man.

Her phone binged several times, alerting her to multiple messages. One was from Josie, telling her the appliances were gone. Another was the credit card company with confirmation of her instructions to freeze the account. A similar came in from her bank. One message was from Bryce, a brief update on research into horse racing and betting. One message was from an unknown number.

When blood spills red, violet eyes cry blue,

What's good for the mother, is good for the daughter, too.

A sob caught and hung in Taryn's throat.

Were these messages from The Toad, himself? Was this an admission that he had murdered her mother?

Or were they a warning that she was next?

CHAPTER 33

Susannah delivered her breakfast basket early the next day, along with another lesson on speaking Amish. On this morning, Taryn was not an attentive student. Her mind was groggy with worry and fatigue. She hadn't slept well the night before, and she was distracted.

The young woman finally admitted defeat. "I think we'll save this for another time."

"I'm sorry, Susannah. My mind must still be asleep."

She sighed as she collected the dirty dishes. "No matter. *Mamm* says be ready in two hours. She has somewhere to take you."

The news perked her right up. Taryn changed outfits and was ready long before Lillian called for her, just after ten. She hurried down and met her aunt at the foot of the exterior stairs.

"Today, I drive," Lillian informed her. She motioned to the buggy, hitched and ready to go.

"I've never ridden in a horse and buggy before," Taryn confided. She was more than a little excited. "I rode in a horse-drawn carriage once, around Independence Park." Collin had taken her on the romantic interlude for their first anniversary.

"A bit slower than your automobile, but much more energy efficient," her aunt assured her. She spoke to the horse, steadying her as she directed Taryn into the passenger's seat.

Taryn was surprised to see the fine burled woodgrain of the dash, all polished and shining. The intricate carvings were more graceful and more detailed than any automobile. There were several buttons and knobs, a built-in cup holder, and a speedometer. The front windshield opened on either side, and the buggy even boasted windshield wipers. The same gray-patterned, plush cloth upholstered both of the bench-style seats, the ceiling, and even the interior sidewalls. If not for the horse in front, Taryn might have thought she sat in a Model T or some such early version of the automobile.

Lillian crawled into the driver's seat—conspicuously minus the steering wheel—and instructed the horse to 'get up.' With a smooth jolt, the buggy rolled into motion.

"Why, Taryn Clark, you look like a child on her first pony ride!" her aunt teased.

"I feel like one, too," she admitted with a grin. "This is exciting."

"You'd think not, on a cold and windy day. Or in the scorching heat of the afternoon sun, come mid-August. Or when you forget to go to the restroom before you leave, and the horse is taking her own sweet time, hitting every bump and chug hole along the way."

They both laughed over Lillian's words and made light chatter as the horse clipped along down the gravel lane. As they turned left and pulled onto the public road, the chatter lessened. Both were nervous over the visit to come.

"My, those cars go by so fast!" Taryn cried in surprise, as a pickup truck came up from behind and whizzed past them. "And they're so close! How do your nerves stand it?"

Lillian only laughed. "*Ach*, you get used to it, same as you do in an automobile."

It took considerably longer by buggy than by car, but in no time at all, they turned onto the property adjacent to theirs. A dark wooden fence marked the perimeter of the property, and a fancily cut metal sign welcomed all to King Farms. Unlike the crops and cattle in the Zook fields, the pastures at King Farms waved with knee-high grasses, dotted with their signature Thoroughbreds.

"This is gorgeous," Taryn breathed. "Even prettier in person."

"The good Lord has blessed my King family and given them prime pasturelands to tend and fine horses to raise."

The women fell silent as the buggy traveled up the rocky road, so similar to the one next door.

"How did he take the news?" Taryn asked quietly. Her nerves jumped like spattered rain on hot tin.

"He was most surprised."

Taryn didn't dare ask if her uncle had been pleased. It was enough, she supposed, that he had agreed to meet her.

Or had he? As they pulled to a stop in front of a pair of large and modern barns, she noticed a distinct lack of activity. Unlike the bustling farm next door, where someone seemed to constantly be coming or going, Taryn saw no one stirring here.

"Is no one home?" she asked after a moment.

Lillian averted her eyes as she explained, "Much of the family is in town, doing the weekly shopping. Josiah should be here."

Some of Taryn's happiness seeped through the cracks of her aching heart. She could read between the lines. Josiah wasn't ready to welcome her into the family fold. Most likely, he had failed to mention her existence to the others, conveniently arranging for a vacated farm while she visited.

A tall, rawboned man ambled out from one of the barns. His long beard was more gray than brown. Taryn wasn't exactly sure, but she thought he must have been several years older than her mother, making him at least sixty by now. Hard work and experience lined his face.

After greeting his sister, the man turned his piercing violet eyes upon Taryn. Just for a moment, she saw his eyes cloud over with memories, but a few deliberate blinks cleared the mist away.

"You must be Taryn," he said. His greeting was neither warm nor cold, leaving her to wonder how he truly felt about her presence there.

"Yes, sir. And you must be Josiah." She extended her hand in a firm, confident manner.

At the contact, he seemed to soften. "So this is what our Rebecca would have looked like," he murmured. "She would have made a lovely woman."

Taryn's eyes flew to her aunt's. "I look like her?" she choked out. "I knew I had her eyes, but you never said... I didn't know..." She looked back at the man who still held her hand in both of his. "I had no idea," she murmured softly. "Thank you for telling me."

"So you'd like to see the horses, ain't so?" Josiah said, dropping her hand and taking a step backward.

"Yes, if I could. And the barns. Surely this one wasn't here when my mother was a girl?" She turned to the fully modernized structure behind them.

"No. The older barns are behind these. Come, I'll show you around. First, let's see the horses."

It struck Taryn odd that her uncle never questioned how she had come to be there, or how she had discovered her birth mother in the first place. She assumed that Lillian had filled him in, or that it didn't matter to him. She couldn't imagine the latter, given that Rebecca's fate remained a mystery to them, so she assumed her aunt had shared the story with him.

Unsure whether he knew about the journals, she kept their existence to herself. She would have denied it, even to herself, but there was the tiniest part of her that wondered if her uncle may have been in on the doping scheme, and if she could trust him with knowledge of the pages. It was hard to imagine he had worked with the horses, day in and day out, and not known something was amiss. She didn't think, not really, that he had been involved in her mother's disappearance, but an inner voice cautioned her to hold her tongue.

He showed her around the stables and the wood-fenced pastures closest to the homestead, introducing her to dozens of high-spirited but gentle horses. When he offered to let her ride one, she laughed and politely declined the invitation. Watching the magnificent animals from afar was one thing. Sitting upon their backs was quite another. Taryn didn't know the first thing about riding a horse, and she had no desire to do so now, no matter how lovely they were.

They were an hour into the informal tour when they heard the rumble of a large truck. Josiah looked up in surprise and saw the eighteen-wheeler stirring up a trail of dust as it navigated the long driveway. It pulled a shiny silver double-decker horse trailer.

"They're early," he said with displeasure. "I'm sorry, but I'm afraid we will have to cut our visit short. Business calls, ain't so?"

"Absolutely," Taryn was quick to say. "I understand completely. Will it be okay if Aunt Lillian shows me the older barns? I'd like to see the stables my mother walked through."

His hesitation was slight, but he soon agreed. "*Jah*, be careful where you step," he cautioned.

"Thank you. And thank you so much for having me here today and sharing this beautiful farm with me." Taryn's eyes had trouble focusing, suddenly blurred with emotion. "It means so much to me, seeing the same sights my mother saw, all those years ago."

Josiah made it to the edge of the driveway before he turned back to offer, "You may *kumme* anytime, young lady. Our door is always open."

He disappeared after that, following the big truck to the holding pens and loading chutes she saw in the distance. She soon discovered the farm wasn't as vacant as she first assumed; a half dozen or more men poured out from the outbuildings and lower fields, to assist in loading the horses.

Taryn was tempted to watch the process, but she was more interested in seeing the old barns. She turned to her aunt with hopeful, shining eyes.

"Can you show me the barns, Aunt Lillian? The ones where my mother spent so much of her time, brushing the horses' manes and giving the new foals their names? And later, where she fell in love with my father?"

With an awkward jerk of her head, Lillian led her to the ancient old barns standing behind the newer ones.

These were weathered and worn, their roofs not quite as solid, their white paint faded and dingy. Moss crawled up the side of one of the massive structures. A stack of hay peeked from the other.

"I've not been here in years," Lillian admitted. "Every time I came here, I saw Rebecca, laughing as she hugged the young colts and made pets of their stallion fathers. Soon, I quit coming. It hurt less that way."

"I appreciate you coming now, to bring me," Taryn acknowledged the sacrifice she was making, opening her heart up again to such heartache.

"Rebecca would be pleased, knowing her daughter traipsed the same aisles and stalls she once did. Come, I'll show you."

The interior was damp and dank, reluctant to give up the lingering odors from years past. The smell of moldy hay and ages-old manure permeated the air, bringing tears of a different kind to Taryn's sensitive eyes. She coughed and delicately covered her nose with her hand, breathing in through her mouth. This was the smell of nature, up close and personal. It was the smell of a thousand yesterdays, heaped one upon the other, and overwhelming in their intensity.

"Would you like to go out?" Lillian offered. "We can peek in through the openings."

"No, I'll acclimate soon enough," Taryn said. Her words held a confidence she did not feel.

"This is where we kept the birthing mares," Lillian told her. "If a mare was about to foal, your mother would spend the night in the stall with her, head set on being here when the time came. She sat with them, holding their heads in her laps, stroking their swollen bellies with her hands, speaking to them in soft words of English and Deutsch." Lillian laughed softly, her voice filled with the sound of fond memories.

She told story after story, recalling special times spent with her sister, and other members of her family. She even spoke fondly of her father, caught up in reliving early times *before* she felt he had betrayed them. All too soon, however, the years caught up and the memory invaded her, and hardened her voice again. Taryn feared, too, that it hardened her aunt's bruised heart.

"You never forgave him, did you?" she asked softly. They both knew of whom she spoke.

"How could I? He drove my sister away. He allowed this terrible thing to happen to our family. Because of him, I lost my mother, and my sister." Her voice was hard, even though her teary eyes glistened from behind her lenses.

Taryn changed the subject. "Where was my father's room?"

"Through here." Lillian led the way into the darkest corners of the barn. She moved with confidence, even when Taryn's feet faltered, and her eyes darted every which way, looking for hidden dangers and unknown creatures.

Used for storage now, the room wasn't large. Taryn tried to imagine it with a bed and a chest of drawers. Perhaps a small writing desk and chair. Had her father lain in bed at night, staring into the rafters and dreaming of a life with her mother? Did he hope for children one day? Miss his homeland? Did her mother ever sneak out to the barn to be with him, offering stolen kisses and tiny pieces of her soul, whispered in the moonlight?

As they turned from the small room, Taryn couldn't help but ask, "Do you know... Do you know where my mother found it? Where the satchel was hidden?"

Without a word, Lillian led the way down a small passageway, edged with roughhewn lumber and hung with old gears and belts, now rusted and rotted with age. Just before the passage spilled into another shed off the back of the barn, there was a set of built-in cupboards and shelves. Even now, Taryn could see how one of the boards didn't quite align with the others. Time had warped the ends of the wood, causing it to jut forward.

Or perhaps, she considered, it had always been that way, offering the perfect place to hide something within plain sight.

"There," Lillian whispered. "It was there." She pointed to the general area of the warped piece of wood, reluctant to reach out and touch the exact spot. In case it still held evil powers, she wanted no part in it, even after all these years.

"Thank you for bringing me here, Aunt Lillian," Taryn said, her own voice a reverent whisper. "I know it's painful for you, reliving the memories. But this means more to me than you'll ever know."

Not even the odor bothered her now. To Taryn, she imaged this was what roots must smell like. Dank, dirty, and slightly soured, but with the sweet hint of promise hanging in the air. The past and the future, all in one deep, powerful breath that stung the eyes and invaded the lungs and soaked into the very soul. Roots.

Caught up in the wonder of finding unexpected joy in such a rustic and primitive setting—particularly one that stank to high heaven—Taryn almost didn't feel the brush of her aunt's hand upon hers.

"Here," Lillian said, her voice low and hushed. "I have something for you. Don't let anyone see." She moved her hand from the folds of her apron and slipped a small package into Taryn's own pocket. When she would have pulled it out to see what it was, Lillian's hand stopped her.

"No. Not until you're in the safety of your room. And then only if you are absolutely certain you're alone."

Taryn kept her voice to a low murmur, to match her aunt's. Lilian's words were more of a breath, than a sound. "What is it?" Taryn breathed.

"Proof."

With that single word, just barely audible yet echoing volumes, Lillian turned and led the way from the dark, smelly, back corridor. The larger cavity offered more light and, as a result, more ventilation. Taryn pulled in a deep breath of air and immediately regretted it. Here, the smell of roots was identical to molded hay.

"The barns were Rebecca's playground," Lillian said, infusing her voice with happier thoughts. It was almost as if she feared someone listened in on them, but the great barn was empty, save for them. The vast space echoed with the sounds of their voices.

"I can imagine her here, playing with the horses she loved so well."

"We kept the calves and sheep in the other barn. Rose and I preferred to play with the baby lambs, but for your mother, it was always the horses."

Lillian led the way back into the sunshine and fresh air. The men were still out back at the truck.

"We should be getting home now," Lillian told her.

They climbed into the buggy and put the spindly wheels into motion. It wasn't until they were more than halfway down the lane, well and far away from another living soul, that Taryn asked her question.

"What did you put in my pocket, Lillian?"

Her aunt stared straight ahead, her full attention, it would seem, on guiding the horse down the lane. But as soon as the broken narrative began, Taryn knew the other woman had traveled back in time, to relive a day from the past.

"I went back to the barn," she spoke softly, "after that last letter. I had to know what it was that cost my dear sister her life. I knew of the hiding place. I had seen my father once, slipping something behind the warped board. It seemed insignificant at the time, but after reading the letters, I knew. She insisted I destroy the journals. It could only be because they would lead to the truth. I knew she had left her home, and all that was dear to her, to keep that same truth hidden."

Taryn heard the absolute heartache in her aunt's voice, and her own heart bled for her.

"I took a small package from the boards, and I hid it in my room. Just as I was turning, something shiny caught my eye, there on the floor amid the hay and the manure."

"A vial?" Taryn guessed.

"No. It was a button. I recognized it upon sight."

"The Amish don't use shiny buttons," Taryn recalled.

"*Nee*, but I knew someone who did."

Dread roiled in her stomach, turning it sour. Her words were barely a whisper, "The Toad?"

"Yes." She jerked her head in agreement. "I had seen the buttons often enough on his fancy overcoats. I once heard him boast that he had them custom made."

Taryn fingered the items in her pocket through the material, but as Lillian requested, she didn't look at them. "I have the button?"

"Yes. I know he often came to the farm and went into the barns. It didn't necessarily mean a thing. But finding it there, so close to the hiding spot... It seemed an omen. The proof I was looking for."

"But you've kept it, all these years."

"I've been afraid," her aunt admitted. "All these years, I never had the courage to tell anyone what I'd found." She turned to her niece. "I admire you, Taryn. You have shown me what true courage and conviction looks like. Because of you, it's time I come forward with my proof."

It was an odd time to notice, but she had finally omitted the surname. "You called me Taryn," she whispered, a small smile playing at her lips.

"You have become like a daughter to me. You will never take the place of my own sweet Taren, with an 'e,' but there no longer needs to be a distinction. You both hold a piece of my heart."

"And you have become the birth mother I never knew," Taryn whispered back. "I can't imagine loving her, any more than I already love you."

It was a long moment before either woman realized they sat at the end of the lane, at a dead stop. The horse stomped in impatience, her sides heaving a snort of disapproval.

Taking the slack reins in her trembling hands, Lillian instructed the horse to turn right. They inched down the road at a slow clip-clop, the horse's metal shoes tapping out a distinct melody upon the asphalt.

There was more to the tale. Lillian's voice grated low over the coals of heartache.

"The man came again, shortly after that. My mother was already gone, whisked away to one facility after another. None could help her. None could bring her mind back to us. I overhead the man and my father arguing. How could I not? They had a terrible shouting match, worse than any before that. Just before the man left, I heard what he said. He told my father to 'give it back.' He had something that was his, and he wanted it back. I knew he meant the package I had taken. I knew I had caused the fight between them."

When Taryn would have broken in with words of comfort, Lillian stopped her with a show of her hand.

"Before I could find a way to slip the package back behind the board, my father had an accident. A pin sheared on the horse-driven plow, something my father was always adamant about checking. There was no way to prove it, but the accident wasn't an accident at all, and I knew it." Even behind the darkened lenses, the guilt shone within Lillian's eyes. "He died of complications a week later. Because of me, because I hid the package that the toad man wanted back, my father lost his life."

"No, Aunt Lillian, that isn't so," Taryn argued softly. She caught her aunt's hand and held it steadfastly between her own, demanding she keep her eyes on hers. Unguided, the horse wandered up the lane on her own accord, knowing the way by heart. "You aren't responsible for your father's death. He died because he got involved with the toad man in the first place. Don't you see? It's the Toad's fault. One by one, he destroyed your family. *Our* family. And it's time he paid."

"It's too dangerous," Lillian whimpered. "I can't lose anyone else."

"You aren't going to lose me, Aunt Lillian. We're going to make that man pay for what he did. All I need is a name to go with the facts we both know, with this proof I have in my pocket. We can put this man away."

Taryn's phone buzzed at a most inopportune time. In deference to her Amish family's beliefs and their strong aversion to personal photography, she had chosen to leave her phone in the buggy while visiting King Farms. It lay now in Taryn's lap, in plain view of both women.

When the latest daily riddle flashed across the screen, it was all too easy to see.

Blood runs red, violet eyes so true.

The game is over. Now I kill you.

CHAPTER 34

"Lillian, wait!"

Taryn called after her aunt, but it was too late. She had seen the message and was running scared. Literally. She jumped from the buggy, before the horse even drew to a stop in the yard. Holding her hands to her ears and pleading for mercy from God, Lillian ran into the farmhouse, leaving Taryn there on the bench seat.

Just her and the threat.

And, she reminded herself as she crawled down unassisted, whatever proof was tucked into her pockets.

She went to the house, but Caroline met her at the door, a firm barrier between her and the woman she sought.

"Hello, Taryn." The young Amish woman pretended a polite smile, but the strain was obvious. "Did you have a nice visit next door?"

Taryn tried to peer beyond her, into the house where her aunt took refuge. "Please, Caroline. Let me in. I must speak to my aunt."

"I'm sorry, but she's not taking visitors."

"Visitors! I was just with her, not but two minutes ago! She ran into the house, before we could finish our conversation."

"I'm sorry, but she left distinct instructions not to be disturbed."

When Taryn tried to push the door inward, Caroline held firm, but her smile slipped a notch.

"Please, Caroline," Taryn begged. "It's important."

"I'm sorry, Taryn. I must do as she asks." Her eyes pleaded for the English woman to understand.

Knowing her arguments fell upon deaf ears, Taryn's shoulders slumped. She nodded her acceptance, not trusting her voice to speak as she slowly turned away.

Just before the door shut behind her, she thought to turn and say, "The buggy. I don't know what to do with it."

"I'll take care of it," Caroline promised quietly, before firmly closing the door between them.

With leaden steps, Taryn trudged up the stairs and across the deck. She closed herself inside her room and sank into the nearest chair, her shoulders already wracked with sobs.

She cried until there were no tears left to fall. She cried for herself, and for the sad, lonely childhood that left her craving a family to call her own, and this insatiable need for roots.

She cried for the mother she loved and lost, and for the birth mother she never knew. She cried for the choices Rebecca was forced to make, and the loneliness she must have

endured, driven away from her home by her father's dark secret. Taryn cried for the terror her mother must have known,
and for whatever terrible thing happened to her after that. She
cried for the fact she might never know her mother's final fate.

Taryn cried for the sweet nurse who stood by Rebecca's
side on that cold winter morning, and for the price she paid for
such dedication. Helen's loyalty cost her a beloved career and
a stellar reputation, and it robbed other patients of her tender
care. Taryn cried because the whole sordid mess was such a
shame, and because she really could use a cup of her specially
brewed coffee right now.

She cried for her grandmother, crushed beneath the misery
of losing a child and succumbing to addiction. She cried for
Manuel King, who was, by all accounts, a good and honest man
just trying to do the best for his family. Left with enormous
medical debt, one poor choice had led to the ultimate destruction of their Plain and innocent life. She cried for the choices
he made and the consequences he paid.

And Taryn cried for her aunt, caught within a maelstrom of
evil and greed she couldn't possibly understand. Lillian blamed
Manuel for her mother's condition and for her sister leaving,
and she blamed herself for Manuel's death. She had been only
thirteen at the time, trying to hold her fragmented family together and do what was right. Taryn cried for the sweet
woman who had carried the burden of deceit and fear all these
years, and the misguided guilt of her father's death.

Taryn cried for them all, and for the lives that could have
been so different, if not for a man whose name she didn't even
know. That man—The Toad—had truly been a wart upon her

family, a vile protuberance that destroyed not just their whole-someness, but their *wholeness*. One by one, he had driven them apart—first Rebecca, then her mother, her father, and then her newborn child. He was a blight upon their family, using them all to further his quest for money and power, and he still had his sights set upon Rebecca's daughter.

She cried now, not because she was afraid for her own life, but because she wanted, more than anything else, to see Toad punished for his evil deeds, and she didn't have the first clue of where to start.

It was quite some time later before Taryn thought to reach into her pocket and retrieve the pilfered items from the past.

With unsteady hands, Taryn pulled the package free. In her hands was a small, simple, cotton bag, hand-stitched from a piece of flowered material. It looked innocent enough, until she spilled its contents onto the table.

A tarnished button rattled out, spinning and clattering to a slow stop in the center of the table. But it was the zip-lock bag that drew a gasp from her lungs. That white powdery sub-stance may have looked like sugar, but Taryn knew there was nothing sweet about it. Though it was slightly yellowed from age and no doubt years of unstable temperatures, there was no doubt in her mind.

That was definitely cocaine.

Taryn ejected herself from the chair, popping upward as surely as if a spring had sprung. She paced the floor, unsure of what to do next.

She had never had a controlled substance in her possession before. Technically, she had never even seen the illegal drug in person, but that didn't mean she couldn't recognize it when she saw it. Taryn had no idea what its street value was, but she guessed in the thousands of dollars.

Its true worth, however, wasn't in its street value, but in its very existence. This was evidence.

Having a limited but intimate knowledge of the law and how it worked, her mind raced through the arguments of any decent defense lawyer. Anyone could have hidden the cocaine. There was no way to trace its origins, and perhaps not even its age. Lillian could have gotten the drug from anywhere, and from anyone. There was nothing tying this drug to the man they called the Toad.

Wheeling about to pace in the other direction, Taryn explored possible rebuttals. The molecular structure of the drug in 1980 may have been different from that of today's offerings, therefore establishing a timeline for its manufacture. The ziplock bag, and even the cloth pouch, might offer similar clues. Though doubtful, there could be a partial fingerprint left upon the bag, or a tiny smidgen of DNA. At the very least, it might offer circumstantial evidence that the story they told had substance.

Her thoughts came in starts and sputters, a disjointed tangle of nerves and worry.

"Bryce. I have to call Bryce," she muttered at one point.

The call went to voicemail, so she sent a text. When he still didn't answer, she paced some more.

After a while, she forced herself back into the chair, if only for the sake of the rug beneath her feet. Much more of her pacing, and it would be trampled bare. She forced her attention to the button, even when her eyes kept straying to the bag.

The button was made of brass and had tarnished through the years, but a bit of elbow grease might change that. She had watched enough television, however, to know to proceed with care. It was doubtful there was any evidence left to destroy, but just in case, she found a toothpick. She slid it beneath the shank and held the button up for inspection.

It slipped down the smooth sliver of wood twice, until she used a second toothpick for balance and held the button in place. She got her first good look at its face, noting the braided crisscross design and the fancily scrolled letters, most likely the brand's initials. It was hard to tell, but she thought the first letter was a 'T.' Tommy Hilfiger, perhaps? But no, that wasn't an 'H' on the button. It looked more like a 'P.'

"TP, TP. What designer was that, back in the day?" She ran the letters over in her mind, trying to image what they stood for. She tested several, before an amused smile lit her face. "I've got it! Toad Pond!"

She laughed as her own wit, recognizing the silly word play for what it was. She was a nervous wreck, fueled by anxiety and a touch of hysteria.

By the time Bryce returned her call, she was pacing again.

"Sorry, it's been quite a day," Bryce said.

"Has it ever! You will not *believe* what I have in my possession!" Her voice was shrill.

"What is it?"

"I can't tell you over the phone. It has to be in person."

She heard his sigh. "I haven't eaten all day. Meet me at *Shady Maple?*"

"Perfect. I don't think I've eaten, either."

"You don't *think* you've eaten?"

"I've been too busy walking the floor to stop to eat."

"Okay, then, I'll see you there in an hour."

She resisted the urge to tell him that was far too long away, but she still had to find a good hiding place for the bag. She agreed and hung up, immediately searching for just the right location.

It changed at least five times.

In the freezer was too obvious.

Under the mattress was too common.

Anywhere in the bathroom was too damp.

Beneath her pillow was too *close*.

After moving it time and again, she finally chose to slip the flowered pouch into the zippered cover of a couch pillow. She turned it against the cushions and piled two other pillows on top of it.

She made certain to lock the door as she left. It crossed her mind that poor Lillian had lived with the burden of the hidden pouch for almost forty years. The woman must have nerves of steel! It was the only explanation.

Taryn drove to the popular smorgasbord for the second time that week, but she kept one eye on the road behind her. She half-expected to see a patrolman on her tail. Didn't they have some sixth sense when it came to a stash of cocaine? Surely, her guilt was written across her face, and transmitted through the taillights of her borrowed car.

When the hostess seated them, Taryn requested privacy. The best the woman could do was a back-corner booth, but the tables on either side of them were empty. At least for the time being, they had a bit of privacy in the otherwise crowded restaurant.

"You're being rather mysterious," Bryce said. Instead of going straight to the buffet line, they settled in at the booth. "What's going on?"

She gave him a brief rundown of the day's events and the package buried in her couch cushions.

"I knew your aunt was hiding something!" he said, his dark eyes glittering with speculation.

"Apparently, she's held onto the items all these years, but she's been too frightened to come forward. And now, just as she's willing to give us the evidence and quite possibly a name, she saw this." Taryn pulled her phone out and showed Bryce her latest message, as if it were an afterthought.

Reading it, he was livid. "Someone threatened your life, and you're just now telling me about it!" It wasn't a question, but an outraged comment.

"Hush!" she hissed. "Keep your voice down!"

His face was set into hard lines. "Taryn, this has crossed the line. This is no longer harassment. This is an outright threat."

"Yeah, well, now Aunt Lillian is scared out of her wits. She ran into the house and barricaded herself in her room and refuses to speak to me. She had just told me how much she admired my courage and conviction. She was willing to share her evidence with me and give me a name. And then my phone buzzed, and she saw the message." Elbows on the table, Taryn plopped her chin into her hands and sulked.

"I don't think you understand the significance of this message," Bryce firmly chastised her. "This person just said they plan to kill you."

She gave him a withering look. "I know that. I also know they made similar threats before this, and so far, the worst they have done is hack my credit card account and follow me around." She held up a hand to stop his potential outburst.

"Not that those things weren't bad enough. But I don't think he actually means to kill me, at least not yet. He's trying to scare me."

"Is it working?" Bryce asked pointedly, his dark eyes glaring, daring her to deny it.

Her voice was small as she sat back against the booth. "Yes," she admitted. "Of course I'm scared. But I'm also mad, and right now, that overrules my fear. I am furious at this toad man, and the fact that so far, he's literally gotten away with murder. I refuse to sit by and let this happen any longer. One way or another, I'm going to find out who this man is and I'm going to make him pay."

"Great plan," Bryce agreed. His expression hardened. "Now, how are you going to make it happen?"

"Somehow, I have to convince my aunt to give me the man's name."

"And if she won't?"

That fire flashed in her eyes again, the one that turned her violet eyes into an electrical current, alive with energy and passion. The surge jolted Bryce all the way to his toes.

"My uncle invited me to come back, anytime I wanted. If I have to, I'll snoop around until I find their old records, and I'll go through them, one by one," she vowed. "If I have to comb through every customer they ever had, I will find that man's name, and I will make him pay."

Seeing her determination and the set of her jaw, coupled with the fierce glow within her eyes, Bryce had no doubt she would do just that.

"Then Lord have mercy on his soul," he murmured.

"Toads don't have a soul," she tossed back. She stood and stalked off toward the buffet line.

She ate with a coming appetite, realizing just how hungry she truly was. Apparently, she had worked up quite the appetite while pacing the confines of her room. The delicious comfort food worked to soothe her nerves and by the time she was ready for dessert, she was almost relaxed.

Bryce's calming voice and assured manner may have been partly to credit for the change of attitude. He spoke confidently of how the investigation was going and detailed his plans for the upcoming week. He even offered to take the flowered pouch for safekeeping, and for her peace of mind.

By the time she went in search of sweets, she felt the first wave of calm for the day. Even this morning, she had worried over meeting her uncle, and how he might greet her.

Taryn scooped a small portion of warm bread pudding onto her plate, adding a dollop of ice cream and a thin sliver of chocolate cake. On impulse, she added a small lemon cookie. She helped herself to coffee and started back to the dining room.

"Well, fancy meeting you here," a voice said in front of her. Taryn looked up in surprise.

She wasn't sure if her heart sank down to her stomach, or if her stomach rose up to bump into her heart. Either way, the two seemed to collide, and the result was not pleasant. Taryn felt slightly nauseous as her heart started to clamor.

"M—Mr. Baxter. What—What are you doing here?" she stammered, hoping her profound dismay didn't reflect upon her face.

"The same as you, I'm sure. Having a delicious meal at one of the area's finest restaurants." The businessman smiled down at her, but the smile never quite reached his eyes. As always, his attitude managed to be both condescending and magnanimously indulgent, all at the same time.

"Yes, it's a very impressive place," she agreed, wondering how she would gracefully go around him. He stood directly in her path.

"Do you come here often?"

"I've only recently discovered it. Still a newbie," she said, shrugging a bit and indicating her sampler of desserts. She attempted a step forward, but he didn't back away.

"What about the area? Do you come to Lancaster County often?"

"No. And you?"

"I have business in the area, from time to time. Actually, Taryn, I've wanted to talk with you. I may have a business proposition you'd be interested in, now that the firm has closed."

"Thank you, but I'm not looking for a job just yet."

"Whenever you're ready, then. May I get your number?" he inquired smoothly. "Or your card, perhaps?"

"Sorry, full hands," she said, again indicating the plate of dessert and the cup of coffee. She rushed on to say, "But I know your number is in the phone book, and I'll give you a call when I'm back home and in the market. Thanks, anyway, for thinking of me." This time, she moved deliberately to the side and made her escape.

She was still visibly upset when she joined Bryce back at the table. Her eyes darted over her shoulder, half-afraid Thomas Baxter had followed her there.

Out of habit, Bryce stood when she approached. His focus sharpened when he saw how upset she was.

"Taryn? Is something wrong?" He immediately put his large body between her and the perceived threat of danger. Always the protector. "Did you see one of the men who came to the farm? Did someone send you another message?"

"What? Oh no, nothing like that." She waved him back into his seat as she took her own. "I just ran into someone I know. One of our clients from the firm. I—the man always rattled my nerves," she admitted. "He wanted to offer me a business proposition. He's easily old enough to be my father, but the way he looks at me..." Her voice trailed off and a ripple moved through her shoulders. "I get the impression the proposition didn't have much to do with business, at all. The man just gives me the creeps."

Bryce nodded to the bread pudding on her plate. "Take a bite of that," he said, choosing to steer the conversation to higher ground. "Guaranteed to lift your spirits. There's not much that warm bread pudding can't cure."

She surprised herself by actually laughing. "Now you sound like Molly!"

CHAPTER 35

It was an amazing sight, watching the entire Zook family fold their black-clad bodies into the confines of two covered buggies and a two-wheeled cart. With minimal fuss and effort, they piled into their unique mode of transportation and were gone from the farm in little time, leaving a distinct emptiness in their wake. Without the murmur of a dozen voices, punctuated by laughter and movement, the farm was unusually quiet. Just like her aunt.

Lillian still hadn't spoken to Taryn since yesterday's incident.

The farm normally brought peace and tranquility to Taryn's soul, but after yesterday's text, she had to admit that she was a bit on edge. Bryce would be here any moment, but the stillness in the interim only enhanced her nervousness.

They would visit another racetrack today, this one in nearby Bucks County. Bryce raised the point that, with a reputation for producing excellent horseflesh, it stood to reason that Manuel King's client base would reach far beyond the immediate area. He felt it prudent to expand their search. Not only did this track feature a gallery of past winners, but he had also arranged an informal meeting with a board member from The State Horse Racing Commission. The man was willing to talk with them about the ever-present threat of doping and to share the names of known participants. Currently, there was a growing controversy over the common practice of giving horses *Lasix* before a race, so their timing for an inquiry was quite relevant.

After dressing for the day, Taryn made certain the flowered bag was still secure in its hiding spot. She considered relocating it but knew doing so would entail another thirty-minute dilemma. With any luck, Bryce would be here in five.

She heard the chickens putting up quite a squawk and thought it must be him. She hadn't heard his truck pull up, but the walls were well insulated and created an excellent sound barrier.

Taryn slipped her purse over her shoulder and locked the door securely behind her. Hearing the chickens cackle with such fervor brought to mind the sight Pete and Deborah made each evening as they herded the flock into its coop. She chuckled now, thinking of her newly discovered family and how quickly they endeared themselves to her heart.

It was really no wonder. A parched desert swelled in response to the most limited amounts of rain, and if there ever was a heart dehydrated and begging for dew, it was hers. It took little effort on their part to saturate her arid heart with affection.

The commotion from the chicken pen grew louder, pulling Taryn back to the deck railing. From there, she had a clear view of the garden and the coop beyond that.

"Dang it!" she exclaimed softly. "How did Kellogg get himself so tangled up?" Seeing the rooster—named after the iconic image on the cereal box—caught in the fabric of the chicken-wire fence, she knew she had to help.

Using care where she stepped in her open-toed sandals, Taryn skirted the garden and picked her way through the muddy path out to the chicken coop. An early morning shower had washed the dust from the grass and trees but left it to gather into muddy puddles scattered here and there.

Taryn approached with trepidation, afraid the fowl might not recognize her efforts as an offer of help. His foot caught on the way up and over, so now the feathered creature faced her. Most importantly, his sharp beak was within striking distance of her hand, and Taryn had no desire to be pecked, particularly when doing a good deed.

She let herself inside the pen, sandals and all, and approached from the rooster's backside. Dangling there the way he was, the mighty bird couldn't curl his large body backwards and retaliate for any temporary pain she might inflict.

Apologizing profusely to the feathered fowl, Taryn worked the scaly yellow toes from the prickly wire. In truth, the long digits looked more like human fingers, with their joints and pointed nails. An image of the infamous Grinch came to mind, taking her mind off the slightly disgusting task of touching the rooster's foot. A few moments later, Kellogg let out an undignified screech and flapped his wings, as he awkwardly took flight and landed just a few feet away. Free of the fence and only slightly worse for wear, he reestablished his importance and grandeur in the farmyard by warming up and unfurling a distinguished—and very loud—cock-a-doodle-do.

Taryn laughed aloud. "Okay, buddy, I hear you. And I'm going to take that as a thank you." She knocked her hands together to clean them and started for the gate. If she wasn't mistaken, Bryce just pulled up.

She was mistaken.

From where she stood behind the garden, she had a clear view of the driveway and of the large black car now sitting at the neck of the lane, and effectively blocking the drive. That definitely was not Bryce.

Her heart ticked up a notch as unease settled into her shoulders. It could be a customer off the road, but it was Sunday morning. Surely even the most clueless of tourists would know the Amish didn't do business on Sundays. Taryn remembered a time when that was the norm for people everywhere, not just the Plain communities.

Unusually cautious, Taryn stood back, allowing the tallest of the staked tomato plants to camouflage her presence. She crouched down a bit as the driver opened the door and stood.

She was glad a healthy distance separated them, or else he might have heard the gasp that escaped her. Did the man ever give up? Was Thomas Baxter really so presumptuous that he thought she would welcome further attempts to contact her?

And how had the man found her, in the first place? The nerve of him!

She was tempted to march out there and give him a piece of her mind. She had never liked him from the beginning, or the way he watched her with those cold, calculating eyes. For years, professional duties and loyalty to the firm kept her in line. All those times she was forced to work with him, she had swallowed her sharp retorts and hid her revulsion.

When she had drawn up the papers making his connections to a Pittsburgh strip club seem innocent enough, her skin crawled at the thought of those eyes, leering at the nearly naked bodies of the women dancing. When he publicly touted a firm stand against marijuana use, and opened no less than three dispensaries in Colorado, Taryn bit her tongue. When she created the layers of shell corporations to hide the man's close ties to legalized gambling—and knew, somehow, that he had connections to the illegal varieties as well—Taryn remained silent. Bound by the same rules of client confidentiality as the attorneys she worked for, Taryn couldn't go to the press as she yearned to do. But what would voters think, if they knew he held majority interest in the state's most highly protested casino?

All those years, she did her job and never said a word.

But that was then, and this was now. There was nothing holding her back now. She could tell the man exactly what she thought of him and his bloated, arrogant ways. Why, he was nothing but an old, puffed-out toad!

It started in her stomach. That odd, unsettled feeling, like someone had tilted her tummy and left it slightly askew. The sensation quickly escalated, seeping into her gut until it felt soured and twisted. Her heartbeat quickened. Her breath came in small, quick pants. She swallowed hard.

It couldn't be. It just couldn't be.

Still, she kept hidden there behind the tomato plants. She wouldn't go forward and share her low opinion of the man to his face. Not just now. Not until this funny feeling worked its way out of her stomach and she had shaken the silly notion of fear from her head. The man was pompous, conceited, and full of his own self-worth, but he wasn't dangerous, not unless you stood within range of all that hot air as it escaped. Despicable, but not dangerous.

Was he?

It was that little wiggle of worry that kept her firmly in place. She crouched lower, watching as he surveyed his surroundings. Even from there, Taryn could see the smirk of distaste upon his face. His lip curled as he looked at the three-bay garage, empty now except for the utility wagon. Her sensible sedan sat off to the side, unused and already collecting grass beneath its frame. Deborah, ever the saleswoman (and even if it were only make-believe), had propped a hand-made *For Sale* sign in its back window. He dismissed the drab scene, more interested in the flashy Corvette. She thought she saw a cunning smile replace the smirk.

His attention zeroed in on the apartment over the garage. As he started up the steps, Taryn knew this was her chance to escape, but where would she go? He had the driveway blocked. If she stayed there, he could easily see her from the deck.

Taryn kept low, inching her way into the thick rows of to-matoes and corn. She silently apologized to her aunt for any plants she might crush, but she rooted her way amid them the best she could.

She could see Thomas Baxter as he stepped onto the landing, and as he peered into the windows of the long, multi-purpose room. She shrank back as he stepped to the rail and overlooked the farm below. She was certain he could hear the thud of her heart from there, or the blood surging through her body at record speed. Huge chunks of ice bumped their way through her veins, clanging and clamoring, and making her cold in the warm morning sun.

Taryn saw him move toward the door at the end of the deck. She had locked the door behind her, but there was no guarantee he wouldn't force his way inside.

And the flowered bag was inside...

CHAPTER 36

Taryn scolded herself. She was being ridiculous.

Thomas Baxter was a well-known businessman and was on the fast track to running for the highest office in the state. He wasn't the first person to have his fingers in a variety of business ventures, even those that were questionable. She had absolutely no reason to think the man would break into her room and snoop around.

And even if he did, it was doubtful he would find the bag.

Why, then, was she still hiding? A plump ear of corn tickled her ear, its silky husk practically begging her to pluck it from the stalk.

Taryn knew she had limited choices. She could stay cowered there in the garden until he left or come out in the open. Neither option appealed to her.

The third choice was to make her way forward from the garden, around the rambling farmhouse, and out to the road.

His attention focused on the window beside her door, but sooner or later, he was certain to see her open run for the road. Plus, it was beginning to mist again. A glance at the spongy overhead clouds told her they could spill their contents at any moment.

Or, she could go backwards. Into the barns.

Taryn couldn't say exactly why, but at the moment, that seemed like her surest bet.

With Baxter still at the window, Taryn slipped from the leafy cover of the gardens and hurried toward the chicken coop. The chickens protested her unwelcome presence, but their clucks weren't boisterous enough to draw his attention. She paused behind the safety of the hen house and looked back at the deck.

Her heart skipped a beat when she saw no sign of Baxter. That meant either he let himself into her room, or he headed back down the stairs.

At any rate, it meant she had to move. The space between the chicken yard and the barn was wide open. An implement or two sat to the side of the graveled dirt drive, but the highly visible road was the straightest path, leading directly into the barn. She could only hope Baxter had his back turned, and she could run fast enough to escape his attention.

With a deep breath of courage and a quickly muttered prayer, Taryn shot out across the yard and ran straight for the drive. She stopped several feet into the barn, hoping she was far enough into its depths not to be seen. It took a few moments to replenish her lungs with air, as she looked around to find the best place for cover.

She was inside the dairy barn, where at least two dozen cows were contently lazing in their stalls. Some were lying down, chewing their cuds and wiling away the hours until the next milking. Others stood, nibbling on the hay and grain scattered before them. Taryn had no time to marvel at their massive udders, or to wonder how securely they were tethered to the metal railings. She ignored the large, docile eyes that turned to her in mild curiosity.

A few of the bovines called to her in greeting, their low, mellow sounds more of a murmur than a bawl. Taryn tuned out the ovation, her ears keyed to noises from outside. Was Baxter bumping around in her room? Had his long car purred to life yet? Was that the swish of fabric she heard, as he made his way out to the barn?

She had to know. She knew better than to stay here in the central corridor, which meant she had to find a window. Some way to track his whereabouts and know whether the man left or came looking for her. Spotting an empty horse stall along the front outer wall, Taryn hurried its way. She shoved on the gate, but it wouldn't budge.

With hardly a thought to her khaki capris and sandals, she crawled over the panel. She refused to think of what that spongy feeling was beneath her shoes, or what might be oozing over the soles and onto her toes. She concentrated on the closed shutter, and the thin slant of light beneath it. If she bent her knees and held her head exactly right, she could see the vegetable garden from here. Taryn squeezed between a stack of old buckets and an assortment of shovels, so she could get a better view.

She could only see the edge of its bumper, but the car still sat in the driveway, meaning Baxter had not given up yet. And judging from the way the chickens were beginning to scuttle and squawk... Yep. There he was. He glanced over his shoulder every now and then, and gave the chicken coop a thorough eye exam, but he continued on his path toward the barn.

In her hasty retreat, Taryn knocked over the buckets. They clattered noisily off one another, but layers of old muck and hay muffled their landing. She didn't bother to see if Baxter had heard the racket from outside. She was already on the move, crawling back over the gate.

For the most part, the cement floors of the barn were swept clean. The corridors were lined with assorted farm-related paraphernalia, but there was ample room to navigate, even at a hurried pace.

She heard him before she saw him. Just before she turned onto the nearest cross aisle, she heard his voice. She glanced back to see his shadow fall across the opening.

"Taryn? Taryn, I just want to talk. I have an offer to discuss with you."

She knew better than to be fooled. No offer of a job would send the almighty Thomas Baxter into a lowly barn. If he came looking for her, he had more on his mind than business. Legitimate business, at any rate.

Taryn paused only long enough to make a choice.

She had been inside the barn once before, and knew it was a like a maze. Rows of stalls and pens, with alleys and crosswalks that led to more stalls and pens. Nooks and crannies stuffed into every available inch.

The skeleton of the old barn was a hodgepodge of wood and masonry. Cement walls integrated with patches of stone and mortar, and boards so ancient they were practically petrified. A network of timber beams, iron pipe, and sturdy wooden planks braced the structure and held it all together. If there were time, she would have stared in awe at the history-laced complex, marveling at the size and age of the beams, and wondered how a mere mortal could have manhandled them, perhaps as much as a hundred years ago.

But there was no time. She had to head deeper into the bowels of the great barn, and she had to do it without alerting him to her whereabouts.

"It's no use, Taryn." From the faint echo of his words, she knew he had fully moved into the barn now. "You know how determined I can be. I won't give up so easily. Come on out, and we can have a nice conversation."

Taryn kept going, hoping to get further away from the man. The stalls on her right were empty, but cows randomly filled those on her left, their back ends facing her. She left a wide berth between her and their hind legs, just in case one decided to kick.

"I hear you're looking for your mother," Baxter said. As usual, his voice held a condescending note. She wondered if he practiced the method. No doubt, he used it to make underlings feel foolish, as if having an original thought of their own was somehow laughable. Mildly entertaining, but useless. She had heard the patronizing manner often enough at the office, but there was no place for it here, at her family's homestead. Or for the man's inflated opinion of himself.

"I knew her, you know."

The words stopped her in her tracks, just as he had known they would.

Her feet ground to a stop, but her mind churned. Thomas Baxter knew she had come here on a quest to find her roots. Thomas Baxter knew her mother. Thomas Baxter was here on the farm, actively seeking her out.

She thought of the unsettled feeling she had earlier, when she first saw him there on the deck. The turmoil in her gut. The suspicions whispered in her head. The absolute dread she had felt. The panic.

The horror.

It came over her in waves now, threatening to drown her. It washed against her in surges, each swell hitting her with staggering force.

Thomas Baxter taking a keen and unusual interest in her, from the first moment she started at the law firm.

More than once, the businessman commenting about her unusual eye color, asking if it was a family trait.

His business holdings in France.

His interest in horses, and in gambling. He owned world-renown race horses, stables, and now a casino.

She suddenly remembered how she knew the name Wilford Downing. He was one of Baxter's employees, a manager for an offshoot distributor, part of the *Ines International* umbrella.

And *Ines*. The name had sounded so familiar before, even though Bryce pronounced it wrong. He said it in one syllable, like the word *tines* without the *t*. Thomas Baxter used the

French pronunciation, rolling the name into two distinct syllables. *Ee-nes.*

The facts rained down upon her.

Wilford Downing was one of the men following her. Downing worked for Baxter.

Baxter kept popping up in Lancaster County. Not just now,
but all those years ago.

Ahndray Lamont worked for *Ines International*, a Baxter
holding.

Ahndray Lamont was her father. Did that make Thomas
Baxter...

The Toad.

It was the only way Taryn could think of him. Her mind
would not allow her to make the other logical conclusion, that
Baxter was her father's father, and therefore her grandfather.
She couldn't deal with that just now. It was bad enough that he
was the Toad.

Thomas Baxter was the Toad.

As the words sank in, Taryn felt her knees weaken and
threaten to buckle.

Her stunned revelation gave Thomas Baxter the advantage.
When her feet forgot how to move, his not only remembered,
but made quick work of it. She was still rooted to the spot
when he unknowingly kicked something—most likely a dried
cow chip—on the adjacent aisle. A few more seconds, and she
would have been standing in sight when he turned the corner.

She ducked into the first opening she saw.

Taryn swallowed her fears and sidled up between the two
large bovines. One turned her large, deep-brown eyes upon

the unexpected guest, while the other swished her tail. When the black and white hide swayed toward her, Taryn bumped into the other cow. It was all she could do to bite back a scream as a long, nubby tongue with the texture of sandpaper slid across her arm.

Taryn bit her tongue and endured the Holstein's gentle abuse. It was better than the alternative.

"I know you're in here, Taryn. I know you're hiding, but it won't do any good. Come out, and let's discuss this like adults." Baxter's voice waned momentarily, as he turned his head to look in the opposite direction. All too soon, it grew stronger. She knew he had turned her way and was making his way down the alley. Ever closer to her Holstein sandwich.

"It was the eyes," Baxter said, his voice almost conversational. "The moment I saw your eyes, I knew you had to be Rebecca's child."

Taryn swallowed her gasp.

"Eyes so violet are unique, everywhere but in this one corner of Lancaster County. Did you ever wonder about that, Taryn? How an impossible eye color could be so common? It's a defect, you know. An abnormality. A mutation of the genes." His chuckle lacked any measure of humor. "But what more could you expect, with all the inbreeding? These Amish bloodlines are so muddled, after generation upon generation of recreating in such limited social circles. Be glad your eyes are the only thing that came out deformed."

Taryn shrank deeper into the stall, bonding with the beast that seemed so taken with her. Her skin no longer crawled from the stroke of the cow's rough tongue. It crawled now with the chill of Baxter's words, and the way he made her most unique feature seem vile and disgraceful. Taryn pressed closer against the cow's warm body, finding an odd sense of comfort in the contact. She absently rubbed her hand back and forth across the coarse hair.

Baxter's voice, getting closer still, turned bitter. "And then my son comes along—my own flesh and blood! —and offers his DNA into the gene pool. Tainted our dignified bloodline, traceable back to Scottish royalty, with the blood of these Plain people! He married your mother behind my back. Bred her and impregnated her with a child." He all but spat the words, as if they left a foul taste in his mouth.

Taryn gave her bovine friend a final pat and bid her a silent adieu. Swallowing hard, she ducked beneath the second cow's head and slipped through a tiny gap in the iron railing.

The freedom on the other side of the stall was short lived. A crude cement wall forced her to make a decision, and she made the wrong one. She wound up in a small equipment room, effectively trapped.

Coming ever closer, Thomas Baxter continued his one-sided conversation.

"I took care of your father. Sent him packing back to France, where he should have stayed in the first place. It was his mother's doing that he even came to this country," he grumbled. "Ines made me swear to bring him here when he was old enough, to find a place for him in the family business. But he didn't have the stomach for the job that needed to be done. He's too much of an animal lover."

Taryn heard the tirade, but she was busy trying to find her way out of a dead-end situation. A large steel tank sat in the middle of the room, with hoses and tubing attached to it. A few smaller steel jugs were scattered around it, all with identical, strange-looking apparatuses. The tubes on the smaller vats branched off into four cylindrical cups, each edged in rubber, with a smaller set of hoses dangling nearby. A five-gallon bucket claimed to hold powdered soap.

None were suitable weapons of defense, but Taryn grabbed a jug and held it like a shield before her.

"I got rid of your mother, too," he said. The off-handed manner in which he said it made her blood boil.

He stepped into the doorway, that familiar smirk upon his face.

"Ah, at last." Satisfaction gleamed in his eyes, along with something much more sinister. It was in the leer he gave her, seeing her trapped there, and at his mercy.

"I remember a similar incident," he recalled softly, his eyes bright with the glow of evil, "almost forty years ago. Another woman. Another pair of violet eyes. Another room with no way out."

"How did you do it?"

The sound of her own voice surprised her, in itself so cold and matter-of-fact. It revealed nothing of the rage burning just beneath the surface, or of the pure hatred she felt for this man. Self-preservation still would not allow her to think of him as her grandfather.

"How did you kill Rebecca?" she asked, just as calmly.

He looked down at his hands, flexing his long fingers. Despite his advance in years, there was no denying he was still a strong and virile man. His fingers moved easily, unencumbered with arthritis or crippling joint disease. He spoke not a word, but Taryn knew he had killed her mother with those very hands, no doubt snuffing the air from her lungs.

Her own fingers fidgeted with the attachments at the end of the hoses. She bided her time, until she had at least a few answers to her many questions.

"Where?" she asked. This time, there was a croak to her voice. She refused to think of the connotation, connecting her in any way to this horrible toad.

"Where did you kill her? And when?"

"What makes you think I killed your mother?" he asked. His lips curled into a hideous smirk. In his arrogance, he leaned casually against the doorframe. It was his way of show-ing that he was in charge. He was relaxed and enjoying himself. And he had her pathway blocked.

Taryn's eyes flicked over him, taking in the tailor-made clothes and slick persona. Her eyes drew to the buttons on his casual but oh-so-chic blazer. She wasn't stepping closer to con-firm her suspicions, but she was certain the buttons matched the one upstairs in her room. That hadn't been an inscribed TP. It was TB, for Thomas Baxter.

"It makes sense," Taryn said, her fingers still busy. "She was never heard from again, after she left the hospital. You just said you got rid of her. I doubt you sent her to France to be with my father, so it makes sense that you killed her. Before you do the same to me, I just want to know how you did it. When you did it."

"You ask a lot of questions. Just like your mother."

"But you silenced her in the end. Aren't you going to tell me how?" Taryn appealed to his larger-than-life ego, knowing he couldn't resist talking about himself, and the things his sick mind considered accomplishments.

"You'll know soon enough. Like the old saying goes, like mother, like daughter."

"At least tell me why. Why you killed her, and why you're planning to kill me."

"There's one thing I've always admired about Amish women. They know their place in the world. They belong in the kitchen and in the bedroom, not in business matters." His eyes glittered dangerously. "Your mother didn't understand that part. She was too nosy, and she thought she had a say in her father's business dealings. I proved to her how wrong she was."

"And me?" Again, her voice warbled, croaking on her abhorrence for this man and the things he was capable of doing.

"You're as nosy as your mother," he accused. "I knew she gave birth, but it took years to track the child down. Imagine my surprise when you showed up at the very law firm that handled all my business. One look at your eyes, and I knew. You have your mother's eyes and your father's nose."

"So why wait? For years, you've known who I was."

"Because you've suddenly decided to poke your Lamont nose into matters that don't concern you. You've stirred up just enough interest to cause trouble for some of my more...

sensitive business matters. I plan to announce my candidacy for governor soon, and I can't afford any negative publicity. You understand. It's a matter of bad timing."

"Oh, good." Taryn's voice dripped with sarcasm. "I'd hate to think you wanted to kill me for anything I might have done on my own. But if it's just a matter of bad timing..." Despite her casual shrug, the look she gave him with her flashing violet eyes was enough to wilt a lesser man.

Not so, Thomas Baxter. He beamed back at her, almost as a proud grandfather might do. "I admire your spunk. Always have. And you're highly intelligent, too. Too intelligent not to put the pieces together and create quite the problem for me. So you see, you really leave me no choice."

"I do understand it could be a problem," she agreed. "And you're right. It could put a real kink in your bid for office. You don't want anyone finding out that you used *Ines International*—and your illegitimate son, brought to America through your own personal influence—to dope Manuel King's horses with genetic enhancements and illegal drugs. And you certainly don't want anyone to know how you kept Manuel in line by getting his wife addicted to cocaine. Even without the details of how you murdered my mother, voters wouldn't take kindly to hearing about your past."

Baxter's eyes narrowed thoughtfully, and his smile, if possible, turned colder. "As I said, you're too intelligent for your own good. Definitely for mine."

"It makes sense now," Taryn realized. "You came forward and donated that second scholarship, all those years ago. You weren't a concerned philanthropist. You were trying to flush out Rebecca's baby."

"It would have been so much simpler, if I had just found you then. Infant mortality is seldom questioned."

"Did you bury her body?"

The question, asked completely out of the blue, took him by surprise. "I felt as if I owed her that much," he admitted. "There's a modest grave in the Gordonville cemetery, with the name Violet Cheval. I thought the moniker was fitting, given it was the horses that cost your mother her life. The French translation was in deference to your father."

"It wasn't the horses that killed her." Taryn's voice was as cold as his heart. "It was your greed."

"Put the milk jug down, Taryn," he said, using the same indulgent tone he might use with a child. He left his stance from the doorway and came into the room, crowding her with his menacing presence. "Don't make this harder than it needs to be."

"This is a milk jug?" She pretended new interest in the stainless-steel canister. "Then what are all these hoses and attachments for?" She stepped closer, just enough to be within reach.

Taryn swung the canister with all her might. The hoses flung outward and curled around his face like octopus tendrils, taking him completely by surprise. The steel jug hit him alongside his jaw and caused him to stagger backwards.

Taryn knew he wouldn't be down for long, if at all. She didn't hang around to find out. With wings on her feet, she flew out the door.

The backside of the cement wall led to more stalls and sectioned-off areas, but less natural light meant the space was dim. Taryn focused on the crude ladder jutting out from between a giant wood beam and another stone wall. Without second-guessing herself, she scrambled up the ladder.

Taryn stepped softly, hoping the boards didn't creak and give away her location. She crept further into the loft, careful of the piles of equipment and stacks of hay. Battery-operated lanterns hung at intervals but were unlit, leaving the space murky and shadowed.

She had little choice but to follow the trail left between hay bales. The windy path snaked around beams and braces, opened unexpectedly into hay holes for easy dropping, and left her completely disoriented. Even when she passed an actual set of steps, crude though they were, and peered down, she had no clue to her whereabouts in the barn.

And where was Bryce, she wondered, not for the first time. What was taking him so long? He should have been here by now.

There were no suitable hiding spaces amid the tightly packed hay, forcing her to keep going. As she passed another opening with a ladder, movement from below caught her eye. Taryn shrank back as Baxter passed, his back to her.

Eyes wide, she bit back a gasp. He now carried a long pitchfork.

The sound of an incoming call was a shrill giveaway in the stillness of the barn. She answered before the second ring, noting Bryce's name on the screen.

"Bryce!" she hissed in a whisper. "He's here. Thomas Baxter is the Toad, and he's here in the barn. He's trying to kill me. Call 911."

"Taryn! Are you all right? Do you mean Thomas Baxter, the multi—"

She cut him off before he could finish. "Yes, that one. Hurry."

She stuffed the phone into her pocket and went back the way she had come. With any luck, she could reach the set of steps before he could maneuver the ladder behind her.

Either he didn't trust the ladder, or he anticipated her next move. Regardless of the reason, Thomas Baxter chose to take the same crude set of steps, and they reached them at the same time. Taryn managed to duck out of sight, just as she saw him put his foot on the first stile.

There was no time to hide, but she rooted betwixt and behind the hay bales anyway. She held her breath as his tall form cleared the stairs and stepped onto the landing. If she had been closer, and braver, she might have pushed him, toppling him back down the passage. But she was neither close nor brave, huddled there in a quivering mass.

"You may as well come out," he said into the small opening. Suspecting she hid within one of the bales, he stabbed them at random. "I heard you moving this way, and saw straw falling through the cracks. I know you're here somewhere." A dozen more jabs, and his breath grew labored. "You're making me angry, Taryn!" he raged.

The long tines of the pitchfork came dangerously close to where she hid. The slightest noise on her part, and his aim would be more accurate.

"I know the police are on their way," he said. "I'll convince them it was the other way around. You knew the details of my business. You were trying to blackmail me. You lured me here, so you could press me for money." He jabbed at a bale across the way, moving to the opposite side of the opening. Taryn dared to peek between the straw. "When I refused to pay you, you came at me with this pitchfork. You left me with no choice but to defend myself."

He moved further along, poking and thrusting the fork as he went. He paused once or twice to mop his face with his embroidered handkerchief and to catch his breath.

He did so now, the fork buried deep into the hay. It was now or never. Taryn jumped from behind the bales and dashed toward the steps.

"No you don't!" he cried, flinging forward to grab her with a long, outstretched arm.

With momentum of the grab behind him, Baxter was unable to stop his forward thrust. When Taryn whirled and dipped, twisting out of the way, there was nothing there to catch him. Nothing to stop his fall. Thomas Baxter fell headlong down the crudely constructed steps. The pitchfork he had pulled from the hay was of no use to him now. He stabbed it frantically into thin air, striking at nothingness.

He landed on the top of his head, one step from the bottom.

The sound of his neck snapping was like that of a breaking tree limb. It echoed in the open cavity of the space and made Taryn sick to her stomach.

Swallowing the bile that gathered in her mouth, Taryn inched to the edge of the opening and peered down. The dignified Thomas Baxter lay sprawled upon the steps, his head at an odd angle from the rest of his body. An arm folded beneath his prone body. His legs were askew, his once-neat blazer now dusty and wrinkled. One shoe was missing. A fine trickle of blood already seeped from his lax mouth.

There was no doubt the man was dead.

Taryn trembled, chilled from the ice that flowed through her veins. She hugged her arms to her, but the shaking wouldn't stop. Not even when she heard Bryce burst into the barn and call her name.

She wanted to call to him, but her voice wouldn't work. Like the rest of her, her vocal chords were frozen and useless. She didn't think her legs could support her any longer, but her knees locked in place. So she stood rooted to the spot, staring down at the Toad, the man who killed her birth mother and who was responsible for so much ruin and destruction.

She felt nothing. No remorse. Not even relief. Her emotions were as numb as her body.

She heard the wail of sirens approaching, and the quiet rustle of Bryce, moving cautiously through the barn below. The cows called to him in greeting, shuffling their feet as he moved through the cavernous space, until at last, he reached the backside of the barn and the gruesome scene on the stairs.

"Taryn! Taryn, where are you? Come out. You're safe now." He called her name repeatedly, until he saw her there, barely visible from the stairwell.

"Taryn! Are you hurt? Say something!"

She managed to shake her head.

"Hang on, Taryn. I'm coming up. Just stay there. I'll come to you." He knew better than to contaminate the crime scene, going instead to search for another way up. "Hang on," he called over his shoulder as he ran. "I'm coming."

Taryn had no choice but to wait. Her body was as rigid and fragile as a sheet of ice.

One wrong move might shatter her forever.

CHAPTER 37

By the time evening shadows crept in, Zook Farm was blessedly quiet.

The crime scene crew had gone, taking the intrusive lights and sirens with them, along with the barrage of people, personnel, and reporters who inevitably accompanied such a spectacle. In the wake of so much commotion and frenzy, the quiet calm of dusk was never so welcome.

"You should eat," Lillian scolded, noting the untouched food on Taryn's plate.

As tradition mandated, the stove was idle on Sunday. Lunch was cold fried chicken and pickled beets, even though no one had much of an appetite. Lillian reran the offering at supper, adding sliced ham, bread, an assortment of jams and butters, and several bags of chips. Allowing Taryn special privileges, she didn't insist her niece join them at the table but brought her sandwich to the couch.

"I can't," Taryn protested.

Seeing the shiver that still ran through her shoulders, Lillian tucked the crochet throw more snugly around the younger woman. "There, now. That's better, ain't so?"

Taryn managed a wan smile. "Thank you."

Lillian took a seat beside her on the couch. The no-nonsense polyester rustled but remained wrinkle-free.

"I can't say it too often, Taryn. *Es dutt mer leed.* I'm sorry for today, and for not speaking up, all those years ago. I beg you *vergewwe.*"

Taryn noticed that when her aunt was especially upset, she tended to use her native language. With a bit of a smile, she put her hand upon her aunt's and said, "If that means what I think, there's nothing to forgive. None of this is your fault, Aunt Lillian."

Still, she fretted, "I should have told what I knew. Even if the ministers forbade it, I should have come forward." Taryn felt her aunt's worry, winding through her and leaving her fraught with tension.

"You would never have disobeyed their instructions," she pointed out. "And you were only thirteen. There wasn't much you could do."

They sat silently for a moment, listening to the rest of the family gathered at the table. Even after the solemn tragedy of the day, laughter floated from the dining room and lightened the air. It worked like a magical thread, weaving into the fractured pieces of Taryn's soul. Stitch by stitch, sounds of the family gathered at the table—laughing, talking, even arguing—mended the ripped fabric of her heart, pulling it together in a semblance of order. For the first time since those awful moments in the barn, Taryn knew she would eventually heal.

"*Denki*," Lillian said after a moment.

"For what?"

"For not telling the police the full story."

Taryn's smile was small. Sad. "What was the point? The doping happened almost forty years ago and stopped with your father's death. Why tarnish his good name, and the integrity of his horses? People still think highly of his legacy, and they think fondly of your mother, assuming grief took her mind. I couldn't tell one truth without the other, so I chose to say nothing at all."

"Many *Englisch* would set out to ruin his name, even in death."

"But not Amish?"

"We believe in forgiveness. Even when someone does us harm, we pray for them. We know hardness in our hearts is a sin."

"I can't say I'll ever forgive Thomas Baxter for what he did," Taryn confided, her admission filled with truth.

"*Nee*, but you didn't smear his name, either. You showed compassion for his wife and family, when revenge could have been so much sweeter."

"The smear will probably come," she predicted with a heavy exhale. "The media can't let things go. They'll want a reason for what happened. A headline to go with the story. A reason why the mighty Thomas Baxter was here at the farm. They know I worked for the law firm. It won't take long for someone to connect the dots, assuming I knew something I shouldn't. Which I did," she admitted.

"*Ach*, but if they dig in the mud, it will be on their hands, not yours."

A sad smile touched Taryn's lips. "When I came looking for my roots, I jokingly said I may have to dig in the mud to find them. I had no idea how true that statement would be."

"Families aren't perfect. They can be messy and unruly, and downright worrisome. But the *gut Gott* gives us to them, so that we may bring love and forgiveness, and a chance of redemption. You've brought that to our family, sweet Taryn. Because of you, I've finally forgiven my father. After all these years of resentment, the hardness in my heart has softened." She grabbed her niece's hand within her own. "*Denki*, for that."

"Thank *you*. You've given me the family I always wanted. You welcomed me into your family, and into your home. You have no idea what being here has meant to me. Knowing I have family—*meeting* my family—is more than I ever hoped for. I finally have roots."

"You sound as if you're leaving. If you think you can escape us that easily, you have another think coming, young lady." Lillian's mouth lifted with a smile, but she tapped her niece's arm with a firm pat.

"Believe me. I'm not trying to escape. Never that."

"*Gut*, because I've been thinking. Why go back to the city? You have no job there, no family."

In truth, the thought had occurred to her, but Taryn hadn't yet voiced it, thinking the notion too foolish. She felt certain she could find a suitable job nearby, but where would she live? She wasn't a country girl.

And yet, Taryn knew she had never felt at home in the city, either. Philadelphia always struck her as too loud, and too crowded. Too busy. She felt uncomfortable in the city, like a turtle wearing another tortoise's shell. Lancaster County was the first place she had ever felt at ease. She recalled the feeling that seeped into her soul the first time she set eyes on the Zook farmhouse, the whisper in her heart that welcomed her home. Perhaps this was where she belonged. If not here on the farm, at least nearby.

Perhaps she should try a small town on for size. New Holland, perhaps?

"And you can't go," Lillian continued, "before you've met the rest of your family."

Taryn eyed her aunt curiously. "I've never had the opportunity," she pointed out.

"It's time that changed, ain't so? I'm hosting a *Meet Our Taryn* dinner Sunday after next," she announced.

"When did this come about?" Taryn asked, half-laughing, half-frowning.

"Peter and I discussed it this afternoon. I'll send Susannah and Melanie round with the invitations tomorrow. There's much to do, so don't be thinking you'll get out of helping." She pretended to sound stern, even though Taryn saw the teasing sparkle in her violet eyes.

Guessing what a huge undertaking it must be to host the extensive King clan, Taryn was overwhelmed with her aunt's offer. No one had ever gone to such lengths for her. Such generosity and love were almost foreign to her.

"I wouldn't dream of it." Her voice, sticky with tears and emotion, had trouble pushing out a whisper.

"You'll bring your young man, of course."

Taryn brushed away a tear and gave her aunt an exasperated sigh. "You know he's not my *young man*, Aunt Lillian. First of all, he's in his early forties. And second, we're not romantically involved. You know this already, so why do you insist otherwise?"

"Because I have two eyes in my head, and I know a thing or two about matters of the heart. You two have feelings for one another."

Knowing a blush crept across her face, Taryn felt like a schoolgirl. "We *have* become friends," she acknowledged.

"Some men are like porch swings, you know," her aunt told her. With a show of her hand, she elaborated, "Sometimes they need a little push."

This time, Taryn's laughter floated in the air.

⚜

If Taryn thought working in the garden was strenuous, it was nothing compared to working in Lillian's kitchen. After a full week of cooking, baking, and prepping for the party yet to come, Taryn was exhausted. She understood why the Amish didn't work on Sundays. Religious reasons aside, their bodies needed the day to recuperate from the week's labors.

On this Lord's Day, she treated the family to pizza for supper. She ordered it from the nearest pizzeria—still several miles away from the farm—and Bryce delivered it in hot bags. They ate while it was still marginally hot, another noisy, boisterous affair that never failed to lift Taryn's spirits.

Taryn knew her family liked to spend their Sunday evenings in quiet reflection. They caught up on correspondence, settled in to read circle letters and the latest issue of *The Diary* (a grand-scale circle letter written and circulated each month among Amish communities nationwide), entertained themselves with puzzles or reading, and rested for the week to come.

"I don't know if I'll ever get used to that," she admitted to Bryce, as Peter bade them good night and closed the door behind them.

"What? All the noise at the dinner table?"

"No, I love that! I mean the fact they're getting ready for bed, and it's still light outside."

"It's the best time of day, in my opinion," Bryce agreed. "Shall we enjoy it in the gazebo?"

"Absolutely."

He lightly touched her back, guiding her over the earthen walkway toward the pond. It was a gesture of politeness, though unnecessary. The path was flat and clear, trodden smooth by a thousand footsteps.

When her eyes fell upon the swing inside the gazebo, Taryn couldn't help but smile, recalling her aunt's recent words.

"You know," she ventured to say, "everything is cleared up now with my accounts. If you'll give me a final bill, I'll write you a check."

"I'll tell my secretary to get on that, first thing in the morning." A smile hovered around his mouth.

"Remind her about that expense account."

"Of course. That's the majority of the bill." This time, the smile broke through. It struck Taryn, once again, what an attractive man Bryce Elliott was, particularly when he smiled.

They walked along in silence, until both spoke at the same time. Laughing, they broke their words off and waited for the other to speak.

"Ladies first," he insisted.

"As you know, I no longer have a job in the city. And it looks like I'm not getting that new kitchen, either. With nothing tying me to Philadelphia, now seems like a good time to relocate, and I've grown rather fond of Lancaster County. The first thing I'll need, of course, is a job. You've mentioned how over-worked your secretary is. I'm wondering... would you consider hiring me at *Keystone Secure Investigations?*"

When an uncomfortable silence stretched between them, Taryn chided herself for being so impetuous. Here she went again, spinning dreams. Plotting out an entire forest, when all she had so far was a single root. Would she ever learn? Whether she was four or almost forty, her hopes kept getting tangled up with ribbons and roots!

"Forget it," she said, waving her hand in dismissal. "It was presumptuous of me to ask. Whether you hire someone is your business. I shouldn't have—"

"Don't apologize," he interrupted. He allowed her to step into the gazebo first, giving her the much-needed time to compose her crushed dreams. As he took a seat beside her, the swing dipped beneath his weight. A cautious note carried in his voice as he elaborated, "It's true. Business is so good I'm overwhelmed, just trying to keep up. I've considered hiring an actual assistant."

Her voice was small. "But not me."

His was low. "Not for the reasons you may assume."

Her violet gaze lifted to his. "If you're going to give me some song and dance about being over-qualified, I'm probably willing to work for a lot less than you think."

"It's not a matter of salary."

She cocked her head a bit to the side. "I thought we worked well together. I thought—"

"We did. We do. You're excellent at research, and very intuitive. You'd definitely be an asset to the firm, given your skills and experience."

The first bubbles of happiness floated up from her heart. Maybe she still had a chance.

"But there's something we need to address first. We need to clear the air."

The bubbles wavered, now uncertain in her chest. "I'm listening."

"You have to know, I'm a stickler for the rules. I'm a firm believer in policy and procedure. And one of my biggest policies is that I never get involved with a client. Personally." His voice took on a new tone she had never heard before. For the first time since she had met him, Bryce sounded unsure of himself. "Romantically, that is."

Pop! One by one, the bubbles deflated.

"I understand." Her voice was tight, her eyes straight ahead on the pond. Could this be any more embarrassing? Why had she ever listened to her aunt's foolish notions? He knew of the fanciful, foolish thoughts bouncing around in her head. In her newly acquired collection of Amish words, he knew how *fer-hoodled* she was! Now that foolishness cost her not only her pride, but a potential job, as well.

"Do you? Because I'm not sure I do," he admitted. He ran his hand over his closely clipped hair. "What I'm trying to say is..." He broke off mid-sentence. "Would you please look at me?" he blurted, slightly exasperated with her aloof demeanor.

Taryn reluctantly turned to face him, wanting to look anywhere but into his eyes. She finally ventured a glance and was stunned to see the expressions playing upon his face. Uncertainty. Vulnerability.

"I broke all my own rules with you," he admitted. He sounded anything but pleased. "And if I hired you... I don't know how that would work, Taryn. I'm not sure what the rules are. Or if I'll be able to follow them."

"I guess I don't understand," she said, clearly at a loss to where this led.

"You don't make it easy on a guy," he grumbled below his breath.

She looked more closely and saw something in his dark eyes that rejuvenated the bubbles. *Interest.*

The bubbles percolated again, burbling up to tickle the corners of her mouth.

Taking the smile as encouragement, Bryce reached out to push a honey-colored tendril from her cheek, tossed there randomly by the breeze. Time sputtered and came to a stop, in rhythm with her breath. It caught in her lungs.

A gentle breeze wasn't the only thing that stirred between them.

"Starting a relationship with a client is bad enough," he said, his tone bordering on a miserable note. The lines etching his face were tight. "But starting one with an employee... There are rules about that sort of thing."

The corners of her mouth lifted. "Remember the analogy about the ice cream cone? You advised me to be proactive."

"Your point?"

Just like Lillian's porch swing, the man needed a gentle push. Taryn placed her hand atop his and gazed directly into his eyes. "Start the relationship *before* you hire me."

The tightness fell away from his face, and from his heart. A smile moved across both. His arm slid along the back of the porch swing. "That's actually not a bad idea," Bryce murmured.

"I've been known to have one, a time or two," she agreed. If not for the smile in her words, they might have sounded smug.

As he tugged her closer, Taryn documented this moment in her heart, lest she ever forget. The light of day was quickly fading, swirling soft patterns of shadow and light into the evening sky. Long streaks of clouds and color played on the horizon, blending hues of the sunset into a magnificent shade of violet. It made a *wunnderbaar gut* backdrop for the horses silhouetted in the distance.

To Taryn, the streaks in the sky looked just like roots.

Bryce's kiss tasted much the same. Whisper soft, it was the promise of things yet to come.

Taryn savored them all. This kiss. This wonderful sunset. This Plain but loving family she had discovered. This feeling of contentment in her soul.

This *belonging*.

This, she knew, was the sweet promise of new and tender roots.

Acknowledgments

I've often called the Amish countryside of Lancaster County my 'happy place,' for it brings to mind a simpler, gentler time. I love seeing the horse-drawn implements in the field and hearing the clip-clop-jingle of a passing buggy. Even though I live in the country myself, theirs seems to be extra-special.

While I don't pretend to understand all the customs and ways of the Plain community, I've tried to be as accurate as possible. With the help of local input, a few borrowed phrases quoted by Priscilla Stoltzfus in *Positive Thinking*, and bits and pieces of information I've gathered over the years, I hope I have portrayed the area and its People in a positive and realistic manner. I also relied upon *Speaking Amish* by Lillian Stoltzfus, the online Pennsylvania-Dutch Dictionary, and *A Housewife's Handy Reference* by Salinda Lapp for reference.

Thank you so much for spending this time with me and reading my story. I hope you've enjoyed it and will encourage others to discover it for themselves.

ABOUT THE AUTHOR

Becki Willis, best known for her popular The Sisters, Texas Mystery Series and Forgotten Boxes, always dreamed of being an author. In November of '13, that dream became a reality. Since that time, she has published fifteen books, won numerous awards including a RONE, and has introduced her imaginary friends to readers around the world.

An avid history buff, Becki likes to poke around in old places and learn about the past. Other addictions include reading, writing, junking, unraveling a good mystery, and coffee. She loves to travel, but believes coming home to her family and her Texas ranch is the best part of any trip. Becki is a member of the Association of Texas Authors, The Writers League of

Texas, the National Association of Professional Women, Sisters in Crime, and the Brazos Writers organization. She attended Texas A&M University and majored in Journalism.

Connect with Becki at http://www.beckiwillis.com/ and http://www.facebook.com/beckiwillis.ccp?ref=hl. Better yet, email her at beckiwillis.ccp@gmail.com. She loves to hear from readers and encourages feedback!

CPSIA information can be obtained
at www.ICGtesting.com
Printed in the USA
FSHW012310011118
53461FS